THE MILLENNIUM JOB

Also by Rob Gerrand

Transmutations (editor)

Fortress

The Best Australian Science Fiction Writing: A Fifty Year Collection (editor)

Rewrite Your Life! (with Eve Ash)

Rewrite Your Relationships! (with Eve Ash)

Forthcoming

The Green Job

Everyday Poems

THE MILLENNIUM JOB

ROB GERRAND

NORSTRILIA PRESS

NORSTRILIA PRESS

norstriliapress.com

Norstrilia Press

11 Robe Street, St Kilda, Victoria 3182, Australia

Cover design by Peter Ball
Book design by David Grigg
Typeset in Adobe Garamond Pro and Crimson Pro

ISBN
978 0 6453696 1 8 (paperback)
978 0 6453696 0 1 (eBook)

Everything happens for a reason.

—***Devs***, by Alex Garland

Sunday

1

Deirdre Makepeace stirred and, half-awake, felt a body next to her. She opened her eyes, and saw the back of a man's head, shortish dark hair—a strange man beside her in her bed, his back to her. She felt cold, and hung over. The room smelt musty. She groaned. What had she got herself into last night? Someone else in her bed. God. How could that be? She moved her hand a little and touched his back. It was cold, too. It felt wet.

Grey half-light filled the room. She looked at her hand. There was blood on it.

Her throat issued a muffled sound, a kind of yelp. She jumped out of bed and ran into the adjoining bathroom, washed her hand under the tap, scrubbing it with soap, rinsing and rinsing. She took a gulp of the running cold water, her pulse racing. Her headache thumped.

She tiptoed back to her bed, to the other side, and inspected the face. Eyes shut, dark eyebrows, thin nose. She groaned. She had never seen him before. He was a complete stranger.

Feeling faint, Deirdre reached for the phone and dialed Fran. Fran Callas would know what to do.

The phone rang, and rang. After at least a dozen times, she heard a sleepy voice, "Hello...?"

"Fran—" She didn't know quite what to say.

"Deirdre?" A note of irritation crept into Fran's voice. "Do you know what time it is?"

"Something terrible's happened."

"I didn't get to bed till after one."

"Fran. Can you come over? Please?" Deirdre found she was crying. She stopped, got control of herself. "There's a strange man in my bed."

"What the fuck? So, you ring me on a Sunday morning? To tell me there's a man in your bed?"

"I've never seen him before in my life."

"So tell me something new," Fran said. "What's the big deal." She seemed awake now.

"I think he's dead."

"So where did you meet him?"

"I just told you, I've never seen him before in my life." Even saying it sounded unreasonable.

"Come on, was it a, you know..." Fran's voice drifted off. She could imagine her mouthing "One night stand".

"Didn't you hear me? He's dead. Can you just get over here. Please?"

"Dead?"

"Yes. Please come down."

"Okay, okay, okay." Fran hung up.

2

THE NIGHT BEFORE—what had happened? What time was it now? She looked at her clock. 8:43am. No wonder Fran was pissed. So, what had she been doing?

A buzz, a knock on the door. Deirdre opened it, and Fran stood there, a mixture of excitement and irritation on her face. She raised a questioning eyebrow, and swept in. The air in the apartment was stale, and Fran grimaced. "Where is he?"

Deirdre gestured towards the bedroom. Fran looked back at Deirdre, moved towards the door, glanced in. She walked quickly around the bed to the side where Deirdre had been sleeping, so she could see what she imagined Deirdre had seen when she woke up. Deirdre followed. A man's head lay sideways on the pillow, with dark hair, some blood crusted on it, neck and shoulders revealed, the sheet and doona drawn up covering his back. Pale, dank skin. She moved around to get a look at the face. Fleshy cheeks, eyes shut, heavy eyebrows, high forehead, long narrow nose. In his forties.

"You don't know him?"

Deirdre looked at the body again and shuddered. "Ugh," she said, and hurried out of the bedroom, and leant against the wall of the living room. "No. I've never seen him before."

"Well, how did he get in here? Into your bed? How much did you drink last night?"

Last night Deirdre had been at the Pink Mustard Christmas Party. She had drunk a bit—in fact she'd drunk several oyster shots, mixed with vodka and lemon juice. She remembered they'd been delicious. And then switched to red. "I did have a few, I suppose." She stumbled into the closest chair, and groaned, holding her head in her hands. Fran followed and sat on the couch opposite her.

She looked up at Fran, and giggled, and was shocked at herself. God. There was a dead man. How could that be? It was awful. She felt drained. She tried to think. "I don't really remember getting home."

"Have you called the police?"

"Do you think I should?" Seeing Fran's face, she added, "How can I explain it? How could it have happened? What did I do?"

Fran just looked at her. She felt panicked, scared. Her stomach roiled and she felt she was about to throw up. She groaned again, rubbed her head. She had to do something.

"Couldn't we just, sort of, move him out into the lobby?"

Fran kept looking at her, shook her head. "Do you think that's wise?" she said.

Deirdre shivered, her face white.

"I'd love a coffee."

Deirdre stood up and walked to the island bench, which separated the living room from the kitchen, and switched on her espresso machine. She got two aspirin and fizzed them in water, drinking it down. Her head throbbed, there was pain at the back of her neck.

"Look, just call the police," said Fran, "Let them worry about it all."

"But I can't remember anything. I'm frightened. Maybe I did meet him at the party. But how did this happen? It's so embarrassing. Can't we just move him? Then call the police?"

Four apartments fronted the level 17 lobby of Deirdre's apartment block. It was possible.

"We could put him in the lift!"

She brought the coffees around together with a couple of nectarines. They both sipped at them for a time, eating the sweet fruit.

"Come on Fran. It's Sunday morning. No one's around."

"What about the blood? It's a dead man, for Christ's sake."

"It's just on the pillow case—I'll … wash it." Deirdre watched Fran as she sipped her coffee. She shook her head again, as if clearing it. She finished her cup. "Okay. Let's do it."

"Do it?"

It seemed different, Fran agreeing. But it would make things so much less embarrassing.

DEIRDRE PULLED THE SHEET BACK, and the two women inspected the body. There was no shirt, in fact no clothing at all above the waist, but he had his pants on, dark gray suit pants with a belt. She pulled the sheet completely off and saw he still wore his socks and shoes. Deirdre tentatively touched a shoulder, and recoiled. It was cold and clammy. "Just grab him under the arms," Fran said, irritated. "I'll get the feet."

Deirdre tried lifting. The body was heavy. "Let's get a shoulder each. That's the heaviest part. We can drag his legs. We don't want to get blood on anything."

This approach worked, and the two women succeeded in dragging the corpse to the apartment door.

While Deirdre held the body slumped half against her, Fran opened the door a fraction, peered out. She darted out, pushed the lift button, then trotted back inside.

They waited, a good minute, then there was a gentle "ping". The lift doors slid open. "Quick," said Fran.

They dragged the body into the lift, pushed it inside, so it slumped against the rear wall. Fran pushed the button to 23, the top floor, and both women returned to the apartment.

Deirdre sat down, her face white, breathing in short shallow pants. Fran went into the bedroom and took off the pillowcase the man's head had rested on. The pillow itself seemed clean. She checked the bed; there seemed to be no further signs of blood. She looked at the carpet: all clear there too. Looking back at the bed, she suddenly stripped off the sheets and the other pillowcase, and took them all out of the bedroom.

"I'm going to strip the bed and wash the sheets and pillow cases right now. Okay? Can I use your laundry?" she asked.

Deirdre nodded, her eyes glazed.

3

Detective Inspector John "Winner" Nguyen took the call at 9:33 on Sunday morning. "A body in the lift, you say? And where are you? In the lift? I see. And where's the lift?"

"The Belvedere Apartments. In South Melbourne. You know, in Clarendon Street."

"The Belvedere, Clarendon Street." Nguyen wrote it down. "What's your name, sir?"

"Gerald Kraeje." He spelt it out.

"And which apartment do you live in, Mr. Kraeje?"

"It's number 43, officer, on the 4th floor. And let me tell you, it's a nasty shock getting into the lift and finding a deceased person, I must say. I mean, at first I thought he was just a drunk. Ghastly sight—he didn't have a shirt on. And there was a bit of blood. He must have been assaulted. I was cross, started to get mad—we don't have that type here. I went to shake his shoulder. Cold as ice. Not nice at all. So I am calling you from this lift phone. With a dead body next to me."

"Well, why don't you go to your apartment—number 43 is it? We'll see you shortly. Please don't touch anything in the lift. We'll note that you've touched the buttons and the phone, but don't touch anything else. What's your phone number by the way?"

Nguyen wrote it down, turned to Sergeant Graham Brothers. "This could be a nutter. Stiff in a lift—in South Melbourne, The Belvedere."

"Not your usual, for that sort of thing, The Belvedere," Brothers said. "Up market joint, isn't it? How did he sound?"

Nguyen thought. "Querulous. A bit annoyed. Not frightened. I suppose we'd better check it out."

4

FRAN PUT THE BLOODIED PILLOWCASE into the laundry trough and turned on the cold tap, rinsing out the blood. For a time, the blotches didn't seem to want to move but, slowly at first, it started to fade leaving a vague outline on the white cotton. This too then became faint. She rubbed the outline with soap and threw it into the washing machine with the sheets and the other pillowcase, adding some detergent powder from a packet on the shelf in front of her. She switched on the machine.

Returning to the living room, she sank into a chair opposite Deirdre and stared at her for a time. Deirdre seemed to be shivering.

"Put a blanket round you. Got to keep you warm. It's probably shock. Wouldn't be surprised."

Deirdre just sat there, pale-faced. Fran jumped up, grabbed the blanket from the bottom of Deirdre's bed, put it round her shoulders.

"Thanks."

They sat for a while, a faint smile now flickering on Fran's lips. She burst out laughing—couldn't help herself. "The things you get yourself into," she spluttered.

Deirdre slowly started to smile, then slumped back in her chair, closed her eyes.

"Shall we call the police?" Fran asked after a time. "I mean, what we did, moving it. It was stupid."

"I suppose," Deirdre murmured. "But who is he? How did he get here?"

"You sure you don't know him? Never saw him before?"

She shook her head.

"Tell me again. What was it you did last night? There must be a clue there, somehow."

"I went to that Christmas party. I drank—I remember there were some delicious vodka shots … I think I did have a bit too much."

"Too much? How do you mean? You still getting pissed?"

"Well, as I said, I don't remember getting home." Deirdre groaned and rubbed her temples. Her headache, despite the aspirin, pounded.

"Did you go anywhere after the party?"

"I don't know. I just don't know."

"Well, who did you talk to, who did you drink with?"

"Oh, God." Deirdre shut her mouth. "I flirted with a guy, really cute." Her voice trailed away. She started again. "He was in marketing—at a football club. Really tall. I remember, we sort of got into a corner. We may have kissed."

"Kissed." Fran shook her head. Her friend was never slow. "And…?"

"And I don't remember. I think I went to the ladies. When I got back he was gone."

"Who was he? Did you meet him there?"

"I think his name was …" Deirdre shook her head. "Sam, Stan, Steven." She brightened. "I think it was Steve."

"So you flirted with 'Steve', you kissed him—or did he kiss you? You went to the loo and when you got back 'Steve' was gone."

Deirdre nodded. "I suppose."

"You suppose. And then?"

"And then … and then nothing. I don't remember. I woke up in bed. I rang you."

Fran had known Deirdre since university. They had studied arts together, become good friends, and now both lived in The Belvedere Apartments. Fran worked at a software company, Dreams.com, in communications, and Deirdre worked in IT at the Bank of Ballarat, at their head office in Melbourne.

Deirdre was basically single. A long relationship for Deirdre was a week. She picked up guys when she felt like it, but her real relationship was with her work. Fran felt she should disapprove, but couldn't bring herself to do so. Their friendship was too strong, and they were similar in many ways. Except she didn't go in for all those one-night stands.

"Something else must have happened."

"Well, all I know is what I said. I had some drinks, talked to this guy Steve …and that's it. And then woke up here. I don't remember how I got home. The only thing I can think of is someone got me a cab."

"But did you, you know, fuck?"

"Fran! Who? Steve at the party, or the dead guy? Oh God."

"I mean, you'd know this morning, wouldn't you…?"

Deirdre squirmed. "I don't think so. At least I'm pretty sure I didn't. Not with Steve. And I know it didn't happen this morning because that's when I saw the dead guy. And he still had his pants on."

"So you don't think so!"

"Well, no, I didn't."

Fran thought some more. "Before we call the cops—before *you* call them—you'd better check everything's okay."

Deirdre nodded, but then her eyes shone. "I've got an idea—we don't have to call the police."

Fran was puzzled. "What do you mean, we don't have to call the cops?"

"Someone else will."

"How do you mean, someone else will?"

"Well, we left him in the lift. Someone's bound to use it. They'll find him. They'll call the cops."

Fran thought about it. "It might work. Yes. Okay. And if the police knock on your door—as they're bound to—you don't know anything. Okay? I'm going back to my place."

Deirdre smiled with relief. Fran had agreed with her. "Thank you, Fran. Thank you." And now she was going to forget about the whole thing. Not her problem any more. She hoped.

"Give me a call if you need anything," Fran said.

Fran lived three levels below Deirdre, on level 14. She went to the door, opened it, turned and waved a kiss at Deirdre, who still slouched in her chair. Then she went across to the lifts and pressed the down button. There was the usual muffled clanking in the lift shafts.

Fran thought, we put the body in the middle lift. If that one comes, I'll just send it back to the bottom, and wait for the next. I'm not getting in with that body.

There was a ping and the indicator for the middle lift lit up. A couple of seconds later its doors slid open. Fran leaned in to push its 1 button. Her jaw dropped. The lift was empty.

5

IT WAS LESS THAN fifteen minutes to The Belvedere from the St Kilda Road station; traffic that morning was light and they arrived at 10 to 10. Brothers parked in a No Standing spot in the street. Nguyen got out and looked up. The Belvedere was only six or seven years old. It had single, two- and three-bedroom apartments. It looked well built, though these days you could never tell what they were like inside. As far as Nguyen knew, it was clean and mostly owned or rented by professionals.

It was cool, a southerly breeze blew and some early morning drizzle had freshened the streets. "Great weather," Nguyen said. They'd had a week of searing heat in the 30s, and the cool change was welcome.

Brothers shrugged, didn't say anything.

The two could see into the entry foyer through the high glass panes. It was well lit and empty. Checking the number on the notepad that Brothers held out, Nguyen pressed 43. After a time they heard, "Yes?" through the tiny loud speaker.

"Detective John Nguyen here, Victoria Police. We spoke this morning," Nguyen said.

The door buzzed and let them in. The lobby was plain, with high ceilings, the walls finished in a light cream, the floor tiled in grey. There were three lifts and Nguyen pushed the call button. He noticed a security camera—the lobby was covered. Within 30 seconds the lift on the left appeared, empty. Brothers pushed the button again, holding the door. The middle lift arrived. It too was empty.

"Third time lucky?" Brothers muttered, sending the first two lifts to the top floor, 23, and pushing the button again. The third lift appeared after another small wait. It too was empty.

"What the hell?" Brothers said.

"Let's get this Kraeje bastard down here," Nguyen said, furious. "He's got some explaining to do."

Brothers went outside and buzzed apartment 43 again.

"Yes? Is that you Detective?"

"Can you come down, Mr. Kraeje? We're in the lobby."

Presently a lift door opened, the left one, and a man emerged.

"Mr. Kraeje?" The man was about 175 cm tall, overweight with a pudgy, shiny face, dressed in lycra. He looked to be in his 30s. "I'm Detective John Nguyen. This is Sergeant Graham Brothers."

"Yes," Kraeje said.

"Suppose you tell us about this body you say you found in the lift."

"What do you mean, say I found. It's in the middle lift." He turned and pointed at it. "That one."

"Not that we saw."

Kraeje looked dumbfounded.

"Slumped against the back corner."

"Show us."

Brothers pressed the lift button. The middle lift opened straight away. All three peered in; the lift was still empty. Brothers looked at the floor, the walls. "No sign of a body," he said.

The two policemen turned to Kraeje. "Well?"

"It was there. It must have moved."

"Moved?"

"It must have." He shook his head. "I don't know. That's your business. I did my duty—I called you, didn't I? If you used your brains you would realize that someone must have moved it."

"And who would that someone be?" Nguyen asked.

"That's no concern of mine—isn't it your job to find out? Bodies shouldn't appear and then disappear from lifts. This is a respectable building."

"Okay, Mr. Kraeje, can we go up to your apartment?" Nguyen gestured towards the open lift.

"Why do you want to go to my apartment? All I did was what any citizen should do. Called you, because I saw the body. It's nothing to do with me that it's gone."

"So you're certain there was a body?"

"Of course I'm certain. Why do you think I called you?"

"Okay, okay. Keep your hair on. I thought you might be more comfortable talking to us in your apartment. We can keep talking here, if you prefer."

Kraeje thought for a while, then nodded. "Okay, I suppose we'd better go up."

They entered the left-hand lift and rose up to level 4, and Kraeje let them into his apartment. It had a living area with a dining table and four chairs and a kitchen at the side, then a couch and two armchairs and a large TV. Through an open door to the right of the kitchen Nguyen could see a small bathroom.

"Just you live here?"

"Just me. Why?"

"Just asking. Is that the bedroom?" He indicated a door at the side of the living room.

"Yes. I suppose you want to see inside?" Kraeje spoke angrily.

Brothers opened the door and glanced in, then shut it.

"Sorry Mr. Kraeje, You'd appreciate we have to be thorough. Could I ask where you were coming from this morning, before you found the body in the lift? Were you coming back, or going out?" Nguyen asked.

Kraeje hesitated. "I was just going out. I cycle every week. My bike's in the basement garage."

Nguyen glanced at Brothers. "Then why didn't you call from your home, instead of riding with a dead person?"

Kraeje looked sheepish. "I was in the lift. I'd pressed the button. I didn't realize he was dead. I told you. I saw this man slumped in the corner. Without a shirt. I thought at first he must have been drunk. Then I poked him. I was going to tell him to get the hell out. But he didn't respond. And he was cold. Figured he was dead. It was a real shock. So I called you. The lift had gone down, then, to the basement. So, I did as you asked and went back here and waited for you. No bike ride," He shuddered.

"You don't plan on traveling …?"

"Traveling? No. No. Not at all. Well, I still want my bike ride. Is that okay?"

"Sure. No problem. Look, thanks for calling us. We'll check on a few things. Perhaps he was just drunk, and woke up and went. However, we may need to speak to you again. And please call us if you remember anything else."

Brothers gave him a business card and took down Kraeje's phone number again.

"By the way, is there a manager for these apartments? A sort of concierge?"

"That's Bert Smallways. He's the building manager. If any of us has a problem, he arranges to get it fixed."

"Which apartment is he in? Do you have his phone number?"

"I do." Kraeje checked his phone. "He's in 205." He gave them the phone number.

"Thank you, Mr. Kraeje. You've been a great help. And don't forget, call us if you remember anything else." Kraeje nodded and opened the door to his apartment to let them out.

Nguyen and Brothers returned to the ground floor lobby, and Brothers rang the number of the building manager, introduced himself and asked him to come down to meet them.

Shortly a thin tall man with a stoop emerged from the lift, looked around and approached them. "Yes? You wanted to see me?" He had a querulous tone in his voice.

"Mr. Smallways?"

"Yes."

Nguyen introduced himself. "And this is Sergeant Brothers, who rang you. We're here because an incident has been reported."

"Incident? What sort of incident? We try not to have incidents here."

"Well, until we know more, it's just an incident. A man was reported in the lift, probably drunk. It may come to nothing, but it's possible we may need to speak to some of the residents. We'll need your help if we do."

The man peered at Nguyen and Brothers, then nodded.

"A drunk?" he said.

"Seems so."

"Okay—but where is he now? I presume it was a man?"

"Well, he's gone. That's why we may not need to bother you. But he may have been assaulted. So if we hear more and need to take it further, we'll give you a call."

"Okay. In all my years here, we've never had an assault. We haven't even had a drunk in the lift, or if we've had one no one has ever told me about it."

"Thank you, Mr. Smallways. We appreciate your help, and we'll be in touch if we need to."

6

LATE THAT MORNING DEIRDRE rang Fran and asked her to come back up to her apartment. As she rode up in the lift, Fran was thinking about Deirdre and her ridiculous one-night stands. She couldn't get her head around it. Since Alan, she'd seen no one. Hadn't wanted to see anyone. And Alan had been eight months ago. No not eight months, it was, God, over a year ago. She knocked and Deirdre opened the door, threw her arms around her and hugged her.

"Fran. Thanks for coming up again."

Fran shrugged, looked at Deirdre in the eyes.

"I'm just worried," Deirdre said. "I can't stop thinking about it. I reckon we should talk to the police, anyhow."

"But we've tampered with everything. Shit, we got rid of the evidence."

"I don't care. We have to call them. Otherwise, who knows what might happen?" She started to cry, her body shaking. "How would you like to wake up beside a dead body, and not even know who he was?"

Fran watched, leaned over and gave her another hug. Deirdre clung to her. "You silly. It's just shock. You'll get over it."

"But someone must have killed him," she wailed, between sobs. "Someone must have put him in my bed. How did they do it? Did they drug me? How did they get in? The door wasn't forced." Deirdre paused, took a breath, calmed herself. "The whole thing is driving me crazy. I want to pretend it never happened, but I just can't stop thinking about it. So, I'm trying to think about it logically. I remember coming back from the loo at the party, after I was talking to whatsisname— Steve. And then I woke up in bed, here."

"So?"

"So, I either got really pissed—" Deirdre grimaced, facing a truth she usually ignored—"or I was drugged, my drink spiked or something."

"But if your drink was spiked, how did you get home?"

"I don't know! That's the whole point." And then she drew a slow breath, and then breathed it out just as slowly. "What I'm trying to say is, whatever happened, someone else must have put the body here. Must have killed him and put him here. Put him in bed next to me."

"Calm down, Dee."

"I am calm."

"Then stop shouting."

"I'm not shouting." Deirdre closed her mouth, smiled shamefaced through her tears. She was shouting. "Sorry."

She took another slow breath, walked to the kitchen bench and poured herself a glass of water from the filter jug. "What I mean, what I'm scared of, is that whoever did this is still around somewhere. He must have some reason for what he did—"

"You say 'he'?"

"Whoever. He or she could do it again. That's why I need to call the police. What if it happens again? So I've decided I have to call them." Deirdre sat down; however, she made no move to pick up the phone.

"You're right," Fran said. "It might be embarrassing, but you have to call them."

Deirdre got up, walked across to the phone and dialed.

7

BACK AT THE STATION BROTHERS LOOKED AT HIS WATCH and called across the desk to Nguyen, who was in his office with the door open as usual. "Want some lunch?"

"Sure—but just a quick bite, okay?"

"Okay, how about a sandwich? I'll go out and grab a couple. What do you want?"

At that moment the phone rang and Brothers picked it up. "Sergeant Graham Brothers." He listened, put his hand over the mouthpiece and said to Nguyen, "Would you believe it? We've got another one."

Nguyen looked up. "Another what?"

"Another Belvedere. Another stiff."

Nguyen shook his head. "You've got to be joking. Here, let me take it."

Brothers put the phone on hold, and transferred it to Nguyen.

"Hello? This is Detective John Nguyen."

A woman's voice came on, faint, girlish. "I found a dead body in my apartment. Can someone please come?"

"Who's speaking, please?"

"Deirdre, um, Deirdre Makepeace."

"Okay, Ms Makepeace. You say you found a body. What sort of body?"

"It was a man. He was in my bed, for God's sake," the last coming from her in a high-pitched squeak.

"And you're at The Belvedere apartments?"

"Apartment 1703."

"And you found him in your bed?"

"Yes. Can you please come."

Nguyen took down the details, hung up and said to Brothers, "Here we go again."

As they were leaving the office, Nguyen said, "Hey, Graham, I've just had a thought—can you grab the fingerprint kit? And the DNA swabs? We'll take them with us."

NGUYEN AND BROTHERS BUZZED Apartment 1703 from the lobby and waited.

"Yes?"

"Police, here," Brothers said. "Sergeant Brothers. You rang us."

"Oh, yes. Thank you. I'll come down and let you up. The lifts are keyed."

After a time, a lift door opened and a face peered out, saw the police and waved at them. They entered the lift.

"Hi. I'm Deirdre Makepeace."

Nguyen watched her as the lift rose to level 17, and saw a tall darkhaired woman, maybe late twenties, early thirties, who seemed downcast not meeting their eyes. She seemed deflated, thought Nguyen, beaten down.

She let them into her apartment. It was similar in layout to Kraeje's, but seemed larger. "Please take a seat," she said in a low voice.

"The body?" Brothers asked, gesturing.

"It's not here. Didn't I say that?"

"You rang to say there was a body in your bed, and now it's not here?" Brothers voice rose.

"I moved it."

"You moved it? Well, where is it?"

"I moved it out. Out of the apartment. I didn't know who he was. I don't know how he came to be there. So I … panicked. I moved him out."

"So where is the body now?"

"I don't know."

"Well, where did you move it to?"

"Into a lift."

"And…?"

"And it's not there now."

"Which lift?"

"I'm not sure. Whichever came first. I think the middle one."

"The middle lift. Let's get this clear. This body. Can you describe it?"

"He was old—in his forties, I'd say. Dark hair, black. Solid. He had his pants and shoes on, but no coat or shirt."

"Was he a big guy?"

"I suppose. I'm not sure."

"Was he bigger than you?"

"I suppose. Yes, I think so."

"Heavy?"

"I'll say. And really clammy."

"So, how did you manage to drag him to the lift."

Deirdre looked up; she'd been looking down at her hands. "I had some help."

Seeing the expressions on the two officers' faces, she said, "A friend, lives downstairs."

Nguyen and Brothers looked at each other.

"This friend…?" Nguyen said.

"Fran. Fran Callas."

Again the two police swapped glances.

"Please call her and ask her to join us."

Deirdre took out her mobile phone.

8

The door buzzed, and Deirdre opened it to Fran.

"Fran—this is—" Deirdre realized she couldn't remember the policemen's names.

"Detective John Nguyen." He shook her hand. "And this is Sergeant Graham Brothers."

Fran stood there, looking at them.

"Come and sit down, Fran. Don't just stand there." Deirdre pointed to the sofa. Fran sat on the two seater couch, and the two police sat back in the chairs facing it.

"So, could you tell us," Nyguen said, "what happened?"

"Uh, Deirdre called me—"

"What time was that?"

"About two hours—" she checked her watch— "three maybe four hours ago. Before 9."

"And ...?"

"And there was a body, a dead man, in Deirdre's bed."

Nguyen glanced at Brothers.

"And ...?"

"And we put it in the lift." Fran shrugged, smiled weakly.

"And why was that, Ms Callas?"

Fran's face paled. "I don't know. It seemed a good idea at the time?"

"And why was that? A good idea?"

Deirdre broke in. "I panicked. I didn't know who it was. I just wanted to get rid of it ... the man."

"Can we see where you found him?"

Fran sighed as Deirdre led them into her bedroom.

"He was there—in my bed."

Brothers looked at the bed, then at Deirdre.

"And the sheets?"

"I washed them," said Fran.

"You washed them?" Brothers couldn't hide his incredulity.

"In the washing machine."

"Jesus fucking Christ!" Brothers muttered under his breath. "And just why did you do that?"

"To get rid of the blood." Deirdre sobbed. "I thought it would all go away."

Nguyen signaled and they all went back to the living room.

"Would you like a cup of tea?" Fran asked, raising questioning eyes at Deirdre, who nodded.

Brothers glanced at Nguyen, and they both nodded, in unison.

Deirdre sat down on the two-seater couch, where Fran had sat earlier, and Brothers on the same chair he had sat in before. Nguyen stood against the wall next to the kitchen so he could watch Fran while she made the tea.

"Ms Callas. Could you fill me in, please?" Fran could have sworn that there was a note of frustration in Detective John Nguyen's voice.

"I live a couple of floors downstairs. Deirdre called me. I came. I tried to help."

"But this body. You didn't know who it was?"

"I'd never seen him, it, before."

"And where was the blood?"

"Just on the back of his head. And on the pillow."

Fran brought in four mugs of tea and a carton of milk.

"Does anyone take sugar?"

Nguyen and Brothers shook their heads.

"Milk?"

They nodded, and she poured a little in each mug, handed them out.

"Now, Ms Makepeace. You didn't know this, er, man?" Nguyen asked.

"No. I woke up and there he was, next to me." She grimaced. "I drank a bit last night. I don't know how he got into my bed."

"Where were you drinking? Here?"

"No. At a work party. A Christmas do."

"Do you know a Graeme Kraeje?"

"Graeme who?"

"Graeme Kraeje."

"No, I can't say I do. Who is he?" She paused. "Oh sorry—is he the dead man?"

"No, not at all." Nguyen looked exasperated. "He lives in this building."

She shook her head. "No, I don't know him. What was his name again?"

"Graeme Kraeje." He rubbed his forehead. He was exasperated. "So, tell me, where were you last night? You said you were out at a party. Where was this?"

"A city bar, Glimmers. You know it?"

Nguyen shook his head. "And how did you get home. With this man?"

"No. I already told you. I never saw him before in my life. I … don't really remember how I got home."

Nguyen stared at her. "You don't remember?"

"Well I must have had a few drinks. I'm sorry. Maybe I was drugged. All I remember is waking up. And finding the man next to me."

She told them the details of how she'd been invited to a work Christmas party, what she could remember.

"We need to get your prints. Both of you. Is that okay? And a DNA swab." Nguyen said.

Deirdre looked at Fran, who shrugged.

Brothers took their fingerprints using the kit he had in his coat pocket. He took out two small glass test tubes with cotton buds in them, and got them both to swab the inside of their cheeks.

As they left, Nguyen handed Deirdre his card. "Our forensics people will come to take a look, probably later today. And we will need to take a formal statement from each of you. Sergeant Brothers will arrange that. We'll get going now. Thanks for the tea. If you remember anything else, please give me a call. Any time." He handed both women his card.

9

AFTER THE POLICE LEFT, Fran turned to Deirdre. "You know, something's weird here."

"Weird? Weird? Of course it's weird."

"I mean, we have to think about this."

Deirdre looked blank.

"You wake up next to a dead man. Someone you have never seen before, and somehow a dead man was put in your bed. How?"

Deirdre began to say something then stopped. "Go on," she said.

"You got home somehow. Either drunk or drugged, but you got home. How? And the man got into your apartment, too. But how? If we can think about that we might get somewhere."

"Surely that's the job of the police."

"Of course it is, but do you reckon they'll get anywhere? I mean, they don't seem to believe there even was a body. But we know there's someone out there who put it in your bed. And that someone may do it again."

"Put another body in my bed?"

"No. Not that. Or at least, I hope not. I mean he or she may kill someone else. So, why was he killed? If we can figure that out, we'll know how to stop it happening again." Fran smiled in triumph.

"But we don't even know who the dead man was. Let alone who put him in my bed."

"Yes, well." Fran paused, frowned, then smiled. "But we have to start somewhere. Who else was at the party last night? Let's talk to them. Maybe that will jog some memories."

Deirdre pondered. "Thanks, Fran. I really appreciate it. You're always there for me. You think clearly. You know," she smiled, "you're not just a pretty face."

The party had been at Glimmers, a city bar in Russell Street.

"Who invited you," Fran asked, as if reading her mind.

"Adam Mendoza—he's Pink Mustard's IT guy."

"Pink Mustard?"

"I helped them with an encryption problem with their payments system, and we've kept in touch. Friends. Kind of. At least friends enough that he invited me to the Christmas party."

"Friends? He doesn't get work from you, from your Bank I mean?"

"Yeah, well, both. Friends and work."

Who else was at the party? A blur of faces. Steve the footballer. Maybe she should start with him. But who was he? She had no idea about footy. Maybe Adam would know.

"I think I should call Adam and ask him how I can get I touch with Steve. He would know. He invited him, too. But I can't call him on a Sunday. I guess I'll call him first thing tomorrow morning. He can tell me how to reach Steve."

IN THE CAR BACK to the station, Nguyen said to Brothers, "That's a weird one."

"Do you reckon they're telling the truth? I mean…" Brothers paused. "Did they know the guy? In fact, was there a guy?"

"We'll get forensics to do the lift over, as well as Makepeace's place." God, thought Nguyen, what a morning. How will the boss react to this?

10

Superintendent Forell frowned, then pursed her lips.

"So you haven't seen the body?"

"No," Nguyen said.

"And there are no signs of the body? Not even in the bedroom?"

"No—but forensics will report soon."

"Are you sure there is a body?" The calmness of Robin Forell's voice was famous for being more effective than the shout or roar from most other supers.

Nguyen hesitated. "Well, you see … We think there's a body. But it could be there is no body."

Superintendent Forell stared at the two of them. She did not look amused. Nguyen held her stare, and seeing her uncompromising steely look he felt a sudden need to laugh, which he suppressed with some difficulty.

"Well, I suppose we'll just have to wait for the report, won't we?" she said.

"Sup. Let's assume there is a body, okay?"

Forell nodded.

"Then someone has removed it."

"We know someone removed it—they told you so. What are their names? Makepeace and Callas."

"No. I mean, from the lift. Someone got it out of the lift."

"After that little queen rang us," Brothers said.

"What little queen?" Forell's mouth tightened. "Is there something else you're not telling me?"

"Kraeje. The guy who found the body in the lift. If there was a body."

"And what precisely has Mr. Kraeje's sexuality got to do with the price of fish?"

"He just got up my nose." Brothers suddenly remembered who he was talking to. "Sorry, that's not the point."

"Someone moved the body—if there was a body—out of the lift," Nguyen said. "Brothers will check the security cameras. I noticed them in the lobby. There might be some in the basement garage too."

"And," said Brothers, "the body might be down there too."

"You didn't check the car park?" This time Forell's voice did rise. Brothers went red.

"We're just about to do that, boss. Come on. Brothers." The two detectives left the office, closing the door behind them.

"Jesus. Let's get back there pronto. We need to check the lobby, get the tapes. And check the basement."

NGUYEN AND BROTHERS MET the forensics team who were leaving the lobby as they were entering it.

"G'day, Winner, Bro," Sue Gossiter said. "How are they hanging?" She was petite and wiry like a terrier. And friendly, but Brothers knew that could quickly turn if you pushed the wrong button. He grunted, non-committal.

"Find anything?" Nguyen asked.

"Some traces of smears in the lift. Probably blood. And enough to process. We'll check out some dirt from the carpet on the girl's floor. There could be traces in it of something left by the man's shoes. Nothing obvious in the bedroom. We'll run the prints, as per usual."

"Did you check the basement garage?" Nguyen asked.

"You didn't ask us to. Do you still reckon there was a body?" Seeing their faces, Gossiter grinned. "It didn't just wake up and piss off?"

Nguyen winced. "The witnesses seem pretty sure he'd bought the plot. We'll have a look down below. Can you come down, too?"

"What, and miss lunch?"

"Come on Sue, we're all missing lunch."

Sue paused, looking thoughtful. "And in return?"

"I'll make it up to you."

"Hmm." There was a gleam in her eye. "I'll keep you to that."

Nguyen nodded wearily. "Sure, Sue. Maybe I'll take you to lunch."
She smiled.

"But come on down with us now. Get your guys to look around.
You know … if you see something suspicious, check it out. No need
to do the whole garage at the moment. Just do the suspicious stuff."

The lift arrived and Nguyen entered and held it open for Sue, her
crew and Brothers, Sue grinning at him as he pressed the Basement
button.

The basement was well lit and had three levels, with enough space for
about thirty cars on each. The floor was concrete, with the odd drop of
oil and grease and tire marks, but nothing obvious near the lots.
Gossiter and her crew checked all levels, stopping here and there to
examine the floor and taking some samples. Nguyen and Brothers
looked around the lower two levels between the cars and in the stair
well.

"At least there's no sign of a body down here," Brothers said.

"Hmm—maybe it would have been better if there was one." Nguyen
rubbed his jaw.

"Come again?"

"Then we'd have the whole thing wrapped up."

"I see what you mean."

"Unfortunately, now it does look like someone took the body—or
that it did wake up and walk. Best get Sue to take a look, just in case,"
Nguyen said.

Brothers nodded. "Yes—and also I suppose she'll have to look at each
lift lobby as well."

"And we'll need to check who Makepeace saw on Saturday night."
Nguyen groaned. This was turning into a nightmare. Where had the
quiet Sunday gone?

Sue came up to him. "We're done, Winner."

"How soon can you let me know if you've found anything?"

"When we've processed everything."

"How soon?"

"As soon as we can. And remember, you owe me, and believe me, I will collect." Smiling with satisfaction, she led her crew to the lift.

Monday

11

FIRST THING MONDAY MORNING, Deirdre rang her boss, Vanessa Bigelow. Vanessa was highly regarded as an IT guru, and had assembled a diverse team. She was a good boss, and as long as you got results, she left you alone, although she did check regularly that what had been agreed upon was being delivered. She had a great analytical brain and a low tolerance for what she termed sentimentality.

Deirdre still felt as if she had been kicked in the guts and, not wanting to go into details, thought about the best way to approach the conversation. How would she put it to her? It was so embarrassing. She couldn't mention the dead man. In her bed. Sighing heavily, she dialed. She would just say there had been a death, letting Vanessa assume it was family.

"Oh, Deirdre. I'm sorry to hear that. A death can be pretty traumatic," Vanessa said. "Was it someone close?"

"I don't want to talk about it at the moment. Is that okay?"

"Sure—sorry." Vanessa was silent for a few moments. "I certainly don't want to press you. It must be terribly upsetting. Why don't you take some time off? Don't worry about work for a few days."

"Thanks so much, Vanessa. I really appreciate it. It means a lot."

"In fact, don't come in till next Monday. If we need anything, we can always phone or email."

She knew Vanessa hadn't got the picture of what had happened. She sensed she thought it was a boyfriend who had died. She certainly didn't want to explain it.

Next, she thought about Adam, who'd hosted the party. She was angry with herself. How could she have wiped herself out, at a work function? It was so completely unprofessional. She didn't recall drinking all that much. Well, she'd had a few shots. Had she gone on to somewhere else? Or, it suddenly occurred to her, had her drink been spiked? She'd try to avoid all that with Adam, talk about the party, who was there, get Steve's number from him, as if she wanted to see him again. Which was true. She did want to see him again.

She rang Adam.

"Deirdre!" Adam's voice was friendly. "How are you? Great party, wasn't it. I didn't see you leave."

"Hi. It's ..." How could she put it? Suddenly all her prepared ideas flew out the window. Adam was always a good listener, and trustworthy. "Adam, I think my drink must have been spiked. I don't remember leaving. Or getting home. In fact, that's why I'm ringing."

"Your drink? At Glimmers?"

"Well, someone could have put something in it."

"At Glimmers? What a terrible idea. I can't see how that could have happened. We knew everyone there."

She thought for a moment, decided to go for broke. "Anyway. Can you keep this to yourself? Completely confidential?"

"Of course, Deirdre. Mum's the word. You know me. What on earth is it?"

"The thing is, when I woke up there was a man in my bed."

"A man? Well, these things happen. I know it's not pc, but I wouldn't have minded waking up with a woman in my bed—or even a man," he added with a touch of wistfulness.

There was a pause.

"Deirdre? Sorry."

"It was dead. A dead man."

"What? Dead? A dead man? Who was he? Someone from the party?"

"That's the thing. The police have been, but—" She took a deep breath. "I don't know who he was. Never saw him before. Unless he was at the party. But how did he get in my bed? How did I get home? I was hoping you saw me leave. You didn't notice?"

"Geez, Deirdre. Are you okay? Must have been a hell of a shock. A dead man. God. Sorry. No, I didn't see you leave."

"Did you see me talking to a footballer? Steve, I think his name was."

"Steve? Steve Dalmatico? Were you talking to him? What a legend."

"I think I was. Do you have his number, so I can call him?"

"Oh, Deirdre. You had me going there. You want Steve's phone number. You didn't need to go into — a dead man. Dead drunk, eh?"

"Adam. Adam."

"Yes?"

"There was a man, a dead man. He wasn't drunk. He was dead. D E A D. I'm not joking."

"My God. Sorry. I thought. No. Okay. Okay. I'll get Steve's number. Will the police want to talk to us, too?"

"I don't know. Probably. The number?"

She could hear Adam clicking. He gave her Steve's mobile number. "You must feel terrible. Can I do anything?"

Deirdre shivered. "No, thanks, Adam. Just keep it to yourself for the time being. Look, I'll call you in a couple of days when I've got my head around this." She entered the number in her phone.

"Sure. Take care." Adam hung up.

Now, for Steve. She googled Steve Dalmatico. Yes, he worked in marketing for the St Kilda football club. There didn't seem to be much there about him apart from footy matters. No wife or girlfriend mentioned on the first few entries she glanced at. She took a breath and dialed. The call rang a few times, then went to voicemail.

She decided to leave a message. "Steve," she said. "This is Deirdre from Saturday night. We talked at Glimmers. The Pink Mustard party. Can we meet for a coffee?" She gave her number.

Within seconds her phone rang.

"Deirdre?" The voice was warm and a bit hesitant.

"Yes. Hi, Steve."

"Sorry, for not answering straight away. I get so many cold calls I usually don't answer them." His voice lost its hesitance. "It was great at Glimmers, wasn't it? A coffee would be good."

"What's a good time? Do you have time today? This afternoon?"

"Hang on a sec." Another pause. "Yep. Yep. Yep. That works. How about three-ish? Whereabouts?"

"Do you know Sixpence?"

"In South Melbourne? In Clarendon Street? Yep."

"See you there at three. And, thanks."

12

DEIRDRE ENTERED SIXPENCE JUST before 3:00pm. It was brightly lit, quiet, with a handful of people seated at three of the small tables. Steve wasn't one of them. She sat down so she faced the door. A waitress with glossy straight black hair came over. It was stunning.

"Would you like a menu?"

"I'm just waiting for a friend. I think we'll just have coffee." The waitress walked back to her station behind the counter. Deirdre watched her, touching her own hair. That could have been me ten years ago.

The girl returned with two glasses and a water bottle.

Deirdre filled her glass and took a sip, drumming her fingers on the table. No sign of Steve. Calm down, she told herself. I've barely been here two minutes.

"Hi there!"

Deirdre started. She hadn't even noticed him come in.

"Hi, Steve."

She scrambled up, and after hesitating shook his hand. He was tall, a good 20cm taller than her, and she was not short.

"Nice to see you again." She noticed again his warm voice, and how he actually seemed interested in her.

"Yes, good to see you, too—to be honest, I don't really remember what we talked about. But I do remember talking to you." She laughed, then reddened as she thought how that must have come across.

"Well, we can talk here, can't we?" Again he smiled. He wasn't an oaf at all.

The waitress returned to take their order.

"What can I get you?" she had a warm low voice.

Steve looked at Deirdre, raising his eyebrows.

"A latte, please," she said.

"I'll have the same."

He had hardly looked at the waitress. His attention was on her. She waited till the waitress had gone, then said, "Steve -" she liked saying his name. Pull yourself together. "Steve, something terrible happened after I met you."

His smile turned questioning, but he said nothing.

"I woke up the next morning with a stranger in bed with me."

"And ...?" He stopped smiling. "Why call me then?"

"Because he was dead. A corpse. In my bed."

"A corpse? Who was he?" Steve seemed unfazed by the news.

"I don't know. Have no idea. I called the police. They can't find him."

"So where do I come in?" He sounded a bit testy.

"Well, you're the last person I can remember talking to before I woke up the next morning. I figured someone must have spiked my drink -"

"Now hang on -"

"No. Not you. Not you."

Deirdre started crying. "Oh, God. I don't understand what's happening. I thought you might have seen something, or noticed where I went."

Steve had relaxed again, and watched her as she wiped her eyes.

"Sorry about that," she said. "It's just so bizarre."

He put his hand on hers where it lay on the table.

The waitress returned and placed their coffees down on the table.

"Anything else?"

"No thanks," Deirdre said.

"Well, let me think," Steve said, after she left. "It was very noisy; we couldn't talk properly. In fact, we were going to get in touch later. We were going to swap numbers, but you disappeared—I think into the Ladies."

"So we got on?" She groaned inwardly.

"Yes, we got on." He smiled again. "Hey—let's think about this. We'll work it out."

Deirdre told him the whole story, including calling Fran, washing the bed linen, heaving the body into the lift, the body's disappearance, and the fact the police didn't seem to quite believe her. Talking about it matter-of-factly calmed her down, and yet it seemed even more absurd as she told him.

Steve checked his watch.

"Do you have to go?" she asked.

"Not for a while. I've got about another 30 minutes. Let's see. How did you get home? We don't know." He smiled at her. "Let's assume you got a cab or an uber. That can be checked. Let's assume you got up to your apartment by yourself, but you left your door open. Is that likely?"

Deirdre thought. "It's possible. I must've been pretty out of it." She liked the way Steve was calm and methodical.

He continued. "And then this guy comes in—he's been bashed but he's still conscious. He goes into your bedroom and flops on your bed. He dies. You're out to it all. You don't notice till you wake up."

"But —"

"But?"

"He didn't have a shirt on."

"So, maybe he was in a fight."

"That's one possibility. Or what if someone saw me getting into the lift, plastered, and took this guy up and whacked him into my bed?"

"Whacked him?" Steve grinned. "Also possible."

"If that was the case, why would anyone do that?"

"Let's worry about the why's a bit later. What else might have happened?"

He thought.

"I reckon your first idea is most likely," Deirdre said. "He was hit, saw my door open, collapsed on my bed."

"Why is that?"

"Because say he had been assaulted and he jumped in the lift—maybe with me! Say he was trying to escape someone, then he went into my apartment with me. Or followed me. That way he escaped whoever had hurt him."

Steve nodded. "It seems a better idea than someone just putting him into your bed. Why would they do that?"

"So—" Deirdre paused. "So maybe he was bashed in my building."

"Therefore, maybe whoever did it doesn't know he's dead."

"Or where he went."

"But how did he disappear? Why couldn't the police find him?"

"Two things. Either he wasn't dead—just dead to it all." Steve smiled. "And woke up in the lift. Went on his merry way."

"Two things?"

"Or, someone got rid of him. Probably whoever hurt him first."

"Where does that leave us?"

"That's the police's problem."

Deirdre smiled at Steve. "Thank you."

He looked at her quizzically.

"You've made it much clearer."

"Clear as mud."

"Yes. But at least it sort of makes sense—even though it doesn't make sense at all." They both laughed. She gazed at him. He kept smiling.

"I've got to go—team meeting," he said.

She thought, he's listened to me. Really sweet. I haven't asked him anything. "Can we meet again?"

"Of course," he said. "Are you free tomorrow evening?"

"Yes. Hey, would you like to, um, come around to my place?"

Seeing his look, she said, "So you can see the scene of the crime."

"Of course."

She gave him her address. "And you could have a bite, if you like."

He nodded, smiled. "That would be good. If it's not too much trouble."

"I'll whip something up."

They agreed he'd come at seven.

13

Nguyen's mobile rang.

"John Nguyen. Hello? Oh, hi Sue."

"G'day, Winner. Got some news for you."

"Good or bad?"

"Yes." She waited for his groan. "We've found fingerprints, from the lift. And some DNA."

"That's great. Are you putting it through the database?"

"Is the Pope a Catholic? It's in the queue."

"And?"

"You're meant to ask, is it in the near queue or the far queue."

"Okay, okay. I get it. But how long will the *far queue* take?"

"Could be tomorrow—if there's a match."

"Thanks very, very much, Sue. Great work!"

"No wuz."

He hung up, turned to see Brothers looking at him expectantly.

"That was Sue Gossiter. We've struck it lucky. A print in the lift. DNA, too. Should get a match, if there is one, sometime tomorrow."

The next day a report came back from forensics. There were no matches from the DNA but Deirdre and Fran's prints were on the horizontal stainless-steel rail inside the lift. Plus a host of others, with Kraeje's on the lift buttons and phone. None of the prints matched anything in the database. They had been able to identify DNA from the tiny smears on the walls of the lift, which had been confirmed to be blood. They were still waiting on the national print database results.

Nguyen took the report into Superintendent Forell.

"But no body, eh?" Forell frowned. "It can't have vanished into thin air. Therefore, someone took it." She glanced at Nguyen. "I suppose you don't think the women took it?"

Nguyen pondered. "No. I doubt that. Nor Kraeje. I think he's clean, too. So someone took the body."

"Well, what have we here, then? This Makepeace finds the body. Ergo someone stuck it in her flat. In her bed. She puts it in the lift with the help of her pal. Kraeje sees it and rings in. You get there and it's gone."

"So, whoever put the body into apartment 1703 presumably took it out of the lift."

Nguyen nodded. "I suppose."

"You suppose."

"Well, yes, that's likely, when you think about it. But how would they know it was in the lift? There's certainly something odd going on."

Forell stared at Nguyen, shook her head.

"You know what? The body could still be in the building. It's either still in the building, or it was loaded into a car. Could someone have hidden it in the garage? What do the video tapes show."

"We haven't got them yet, but Brothers will be going through them as soon as they arrive."

At Forell's look, Nguyen added, "Forensics are getting them to us."

14

"Look at this, boss." Brothers straightened his back and stretched his arms above his head. He had been watching the video screen for almost an hour and a half, focusing on Sunday morning. Nguyen strolled over.

"There are cameras in the lobby, and the basement, but unfortunately none of the foyers have a camera."

Brothers pressed a key and a window opened with a camera view from Basement 1. He flicked some buttons, then at 9:03 two men left a black car, a BMW by the look of it, and walked to the intercom. One of them, the taller, spoke into it.

After a while a lift door opened and a tall fat man half emerged, beckoning them, and the two men joined him in the lift.

"Now this." Brothers pressed another key. At 9:44am the middle lift door opened, and the two men emerged half carrying, half dragging a body.

"Notice—the body has no shirt," Brothers said.

"Play it again."

Brothers pressed a couple more keys, and started the video running at 9:43am. They watched as the two men brought the body out of the lift. One of the men walked across to the black car, backed it out of its lot and drove it to the lift. It was clearly a BMW. They put the body in the boot. The car drove off.

"Can you go back and slow it down, see if we can get the number plate?"

"I can do better. Watch this." Brothers pressed another key, and they saw the rear view of the car waiting for the car park barrier to rise, then exiting the car park. The number plate was visible.

"You beauty!" Nguyen said. He pumped his fist.

Remarkable, thought Brothers. Was that a first? He said, "I've noted the license plate number, and I'll follow it up."

"What about Saturday? Any vision of anyone who could be the dead guy coming into the building? And what about when Makepeace arrived home?"

"If the dead guy lives here, he would go straight in. If he's a visitor, then he would have buzzed and someone will have met him. I've checked the possibilities. And I've found where Makepeace went out and when she arrived home. Here."

Brothers returned to his screen, glanced at some notes on his desk, and played the videos for Saturday evening, at 8 times normal speed. He started with the lobby, and there were flickerings of people coming and going. He paused at one point and they saw Deirdre Makepeace leaving the building at 7:39pm.

"This is where she goes out."

As she was leaving a couple in their twenties, tall man, short woman, entered the lobby and after a time were met at the lifts by a young woman. "The couple must be visitors. And over the next couple of hours there are a few more people coming and going, but no more visitors. Then this."

He jumped to 10pm, and fast-forwarded. At 10:37pm a man dressed in a suit entered the lobby and waited. The left lift door opened and a short thin middle-aged woman emerged and walked over to the man. They spoke, shook hands and together they entered the lift.

"Another visitor. Could he be our man? Though he does have a shirt on."

"It's not a joke, Graham. Anything else? What about when Makepeace gets home?"

Again Brothers fiddled with the keyboard and fast forwarded the images. At 11:23pm a woman entered the lobby with a man. Brothers slowed to normal speed, and confirmed it was Deirdre Makepeace. The man was dressed casually in jeans and a collared shirt. She was unsteady on her feet as she made her way to the lifts, the man holding her up by the upper arm. The man pushed a lift call button. They waited, and Lift

3 arrived and its door opened. Deirdre Makepeace entered the lift, waving at the man, the lift doors shut, and the man walked back out into the street.

"Well, that accounts for Ms Makepeace," Nguyen said. "So, who's the guy at 10:37?"

"No idea," Brothers said. "He's the only other person who was a guest, who needed someone to key him up. No-one else was met by someone in the building."

"Maybe the dead man lived in the building."

"Could be, unless as I said he's the mystery man arriving at 10:37," Brothers said. "Or maybe the dead man was somehow already in the building much earlier on Saturday. But then, we still don't know how he could have got into Deirdre Makepeace's apartment."

"She might have left the door open when she got home. The video shows she was staggering, clearly smashed."

"Could be. Or maybe he was waiting for her in the lobby."

"Double check the lobby again. Maybe he was there earlier, and went up."

Brothers scanned more of the video from 5pm, but there was no sign of a single man on the footage from then until 11:23 pm.

"Can you get me an image of the fat guy who let the two men into the lift in the car park? We'll check with the building manager to see if he knows who it is."

"Sure, Boss." Brothers froze the image at the point the lift in the basement opened, and the man's face was visible. It wasn't all that clear, but they'd have to see if it was good enough to identify him. He took a screen shot and printed it out.

"Thanks, Graham. Can you take it to the manager? Better yet, ring him, and you can email it to him, see if he knows who it is."

"Okay."

"Mr. Smallways? It's Sergeant Graham Brothers from Victoria Police here. We met in your lobby on Sunday morning."

"Oh, yes. About the 'incident'."

"That's right. Listen, I'd like your help on a little matter."

"Of course." Brothers could imagine Smallways relaxing. "Anything to help the boys in blue."

"Well, I'll text you an image. Completely confidential, of course. We believe it may be a resident. Can you let me know who it might be?"

"Of course."

"Don't hang up—you'll get it in a sec. Please take a look while we're on the phone."

Brothers sent the image by text, keeping the phone open. "Have you got it?"

"No. Not yet. Oh, yes. I'll enlarge it — why I think it's Mr. Steenvater."

"Steenvater?"

"Yes—he lives in the penthouse, 2302. He hasn't done anything wrong, has he?"

"No, no. He just may be able to help us with the incident on Sunday. And please keep this to yourself. We wouldn't want to cause any unnecessary embarrassment, would we?"

"Certainly not, Sergeant. Certainly not. You can rely on me."

15

NGUYEN AND BROTHERS BUZZED Apartment 2302 at the intercom outside the lobby. It was answered by a female voice, slightly tremulous, and they held up their badges to the camera.

"Detective John Nguyen from Victoria Police, Ma'am," he said. "May we come up?"

"What's this about?"

"We'll explain when we come up."

"Hmm, okay. Just a minute and I'll come down to key you up."

"That's okay, you don't need to do that. We have a pass from the building manager."

They entered the lobby and Brothers pushed the elevator button. They rode up to the 23rd level and Nguyen knocked. The door opened and a middle-aged woman in white blouse and tan slacks looked out at them.

"I'm Detective John Nguyen and this is Sergeant Graham Brothers."

She seemed as if she wanted to shut the door in their faces, but then nodded, wearily. "I suppose you'd better come in."

"And you are—?"

"Veronica Steenvater." She turned. "Henry!" she called. "There are some police here."

They entered an expansive apartment, and looking up they could see a view across Melbourne from two sides of the large living room.

A man in his fifties came in, dressed in jeans and a pale blue polo shirt.

"This is my husband, Henry. These are the police, dear."

"Yes? What can we do for you? What is this about?" he said.

Nguyen introduced themselves again. "Can we ask you some questions?"

"What about?"

"Last Sunday, Sunday morning. You were here?"

"No, we were out."

Veronica looked startled, and stared at her husband. "But—"

"Out—we went out for brunch."

"What time was that?"

"I don't know. About 9:30. Round about," Steenvater said.

"I see. And Mr. Steenvater. What do you do?"

"I work for Cambridge Bank. CTO."

At the blank look Brothers gave Nguyen, Veronica said, "He's Chief Technology Officer." She smiled with pride.

"What's this about then," Steenvater said. He wasn't smiling.

"We're conducting an investigation. A man has died."

Steenvater, if anything, looked more irritated.

"And?"

"And we want to know what you and your wife were doing last Sunday morning."

"I've told you. We went out to brunch."

"And where was that?"

"Henry—"

"Be quiet, Veronica." Steenvater waved his left hand at his wife, who shut her mouth. "We went to Omelets Are Us."

Seeing their blank looks again, Steenvater said, "It's a cafe. A restaurant."

"What time did you get there?"

"About 10:00, I think."

Nguyen looked at Veronica, who nodded.

"And what time did you get back?"

Steenvater bristled.

"What is this? I don't know when we got back. Veronica?"

"About one-ish, I think," Veronica said, her face relaxing.

"And you were both home before you went out?"

"For God's sake—how could we go out if we weren't at home!" Steenvater burst out.

Nguyen grimaced.

"Look, a man has been killed, and we are asking everyone in the building these questions."

Steenvater did not seem mollified.

"Were you both in on Saturday night?"

"Yes," Steenvater said. He glared at the two of them.

"Who was killed?" Veronica Steenvater asked. "Did the person live in this building?"

"We don't know his name, as yet, Mrs. Steenvater. You've heard nothing?"

"Not a thing about anyone dying. A dead man you say?"

"Yes. Thank you. Thank you. If we have any more questions we'll get back to you."

IN THE LIFT, Brothers said, "I reckon we hit a nerve there."

"Let's check out that restaurant. What was it? Omelets, or something."

Brothers checked his notebook. "Omelets Are Us."

"Where the fuck is that when it's at home?"

After looking at his phone, Brothers said, "In Bridport Street. Albert Park."

"Can you do that, check it out? I'll get back to the office."

Brothers nodded.

"Bloody suspicious. Did you notice how the wife reacted when that arrogant shit said they'd gone out to brunch? God save us."

"Something wrong there, Winner. But what? We've got the video of him letting the two guys into the lift—the same guys who took out the body. He doesn't know we know that—yet."

"Well, if the Omelets place can confirm if and when they were there, that'll give us something to work on. What time is it?"

Brothers checked his watch. "Just after 3.00."

"Too early for a drink. Fancy one later. When we debrief?"

Brothers nodded.

"Okay. Okay." Nguyen rubbed his cheek. "Maybe the so-called corpse wasn't dead after all. Maybe he woke up—he was just knocked out or drunk."

"Maybe."

"Hell, it would explain why we can't find him."

"Yes—but it doesn't explain the guys coming out of Steenvater's apartment. And if he was alive, why they would put him in the boot of their car."

"Okay—off you go. Let's meet at the Vincent. About 5:00pm."

16

BROTHERS GOOGLED OMELETS ARE US, and drove there to Bridport Street in his unmarked police car. He was able to park right outside, in a one-hour zone.

The place was quiet—about to shut for the day. Looking around, Brothers saw it was a breakfast and lunch joint. He entered and ordered a flat white from the barista at the counter, then sat at a table so he could see the door.

The barista, a tattooed man in his twenties, with dark hair in a man bun and stubble on his face, brought the coffee over with a welcoming smile.

"Would you like some water, as well?"

"Thanks." Brothers extended his hand. "I'm Sergeant Graham Brothers with Victoria Police. Were you working yesterday morning?"

The waiter looked at Brothers and shook the hand. "What's this about, then?"

"And you are?"

"Demetri Vassiliki. And yes, I was here on Sunday. So what?"

"We're conducting an investigation. Do you have regulars, who come in on Sundays?"

"Of course. People really like us." He grinned.

Brothers sipped his coffee. It was smooth and delicious.

"I can see why."

Vassaliki smiled again.

Brothers took out his phone, and flicked to photos, where he'd surreptitiously captured the Steenvaters.

"Are these regulars?"

Vassiliki looked at the photo.

"Yeah. They come in from time to time. The guy orders his omelet with egg whites only. No yolks. He acts like a big shot. His wife is nice, though. Quiet."

"And were they here yesterday?"

Vassiliki thought.

"Could be. Not too sure." He paused, looked down at his feet. "The more I think of it, no, I don't think so."

"Was it busy?"

"Pretty normal. Not completely flat out. But, yeah."

"And you would have noticed if they'd come in? For, say brunch?"

"For brunch? Sure. Just for a coffee? Not so much. But if they'd eaten, I would have noticed them. Why? What have they done?"

"Just making enquiries. We do this all the time. Thanks, Demetri." He finished his coffee. Jotted in his notebook, confirming the spelling of Vassiliki.

17

When Brothers got back to the station, a report on his desk identified the owner of the BMW that had been caught on video as Richard Wainwright, of 21 Estony Close, Armadale. Brothers checked the on line reverse directory and came up with a phone number. Feeling excited, he dialed. On the third ring, a cultured voice said, "Hello? Wainright speaking."

"Mr. Wainright, this is Sergeant Graham Brothers from Victoria Police. About your car. A BMW?"

"Oh, great. Thank you, Sergeant. Thank you. Yes, the BMW. I've been waiting for you to call. Quick work."

"Quick—what?"

"Yes. Thank you—where is it?"

"Mr. Wainright, I'm ringing because I thought you would know that."

"You thought I would know? How the hell would I know?" Wainright's voice rose in pitch and in volume.

"Well, it is your car, isn't it?" He read out the number plate.

"Of course it's my car, you—" Wainright paused. Brothers heard deep breathing. Then in a calmer voice, with the words coldly enunciated, "Have you or haven't you got news for me?"

"We're trying to track down your car. Is it with you now?" Brothers thought he must be going mad.

"Of course I haven't got it with me." This time Wainright shouted. "That's why I fucking reported it stolen. And—what's your name again?"

"Brothers, Sergeant Graham Brothers."

"Well, Sergeant Brothers, what the hell are you calling about?"

Brothers took a breath.

"Mr. Wainright. My apologies. I didn't know it had been stolen."

"Then why the hell are you calling me about it?"

"It's been involved in a crime. I'm not from the stolen vehicles area."

"A crime?" Wainright paused. When he spoke again his voice was cooler and less aggressive. "My car was used in a crime?"

"Yes—it was caught on video leaving a building on Sunday morning. We're trying to track it down."

"Well, I reported it missing on Saturday, Saturday morning. Thought you were tracking it down, as you put it. I thought you were ringing to say you'd found it."

"When did you last use it?"

"Last Friday evening. I parked it as per usual in the drive. When I went to go shopping on Saturday morning, it was gone."

"Look, Mr. Wainright, very sorry about the mix up. I'll make sure our traffic people get in touch with you as soon as it's located."

18

John Nguyen knocked on the door of Superintendent Forell's office.

"Come in."

Forell was behind her desk, and looked up from some papers she was reading. She smiled. "So, glad you dropped in. I was about to call you."

"Thought I'd better update you, Boss."

"The missing body caper, eh?" She made it sound like the name of a movie.

"Well, we're now pretty sure there is a body. We have suspicious guys coming into the apartment building, met by the owner of the penthouse. And we've got them coming out of the lift the body was reported in, by Mr. Kraeje. With the body. They put it into the boot of their car We've got its number plate." Nguyen carefully kept his voice even and respectful.

"Do we know who they were visiting? Whose apartment?"

"The Steenvaters. A Henry and Veronica Steenvater. He's an arrogant prick. Chief tech guy at Cambridge Bank. He claimed he and his wife were having brunch on the Sunday morning when we picked up on the video him letting the guys into the car park lift. Get this, Boss. His wife looked surprised when he said they were out to brunch. Brothers is checking it out with the cafe."

"Cafe?"

"Where he said they had brunch. A place called Omelets Are Us. Do you know it?"

"Omelets Are Us?" Forell shook her head. "Never heard of it."

"Brothers will be back shortly. He's also checking out who owns the car. A BMW. Meanwhile Forensics have found traces of blood in the lift. They're doing a DNA check—but that could take a week or so. Unless—" he paused. Raised his eyebrows.

"Yes. Fast track it. I'll approve the budget. This is just the sort of thing that the media will get hold of. Like *Headless Body in Topless Bar*. You know?"

At Nguyen's blank look, Forell said, "It was a headline years ago in the New York Post."

Nguyen smiled. "Is that so. Yeah, well, we certainly don't want the *Missing Body Caper*. Though—" Nguyen gazed at the ceiling.

"Yes? Spit it out."

"Well, let's say we get a bit of grief from the jackals. What if it helps us find the body?"

Forell considered this.

"It will no doubt get out. But let's wait another day. See if something, or rather someone, turns up."

"We could brief them about a crime syndicate that pinched the body—"

She frowned.

"No we won't do that. What have you been smoking? That would make us look even worse fools than they think we are. No, when we brief the media we won't mention any gang or syndicate. That's the last thing we need. We'll say … a body was reported and it's disappeared. We won't mention the women. Keep it simple. A good citizen reported it in the lift of his building as he was going out on his Sunday morning jog."

"Er, bike ride."

"Bike ride. We attended. Body gone. That is if we don't find it by tomorrow. Will Kraeje keep his gob shut?"

"I'll have a word. Yeah, we don't want him running to the media."

"Okay. Keep me in the loop."

As he stood up and was leaving, Forell called him back. "You mentioned the Steenvaters. A senior bank guy. This does raise the possibility that it's not your common or garden street crime. Bloody peculiar."

"Not to mention the body in the bed side of it."

"Exactly. We have to get our version out first, control it. Let me know what you have by midday tomorrow—I'll tee up the PR unit. Meanwhile, check out Henry Steenvater. He's head of tech you say. Cambridge Bank? Banks mean money. And tech is how money moves. And you know what they say about banks?"

Nguyen thought, then meekly said, "What?"

"Banks aren't your friends! So it's not surprising he's arrogant. He'll be making more than a million a year, easy."

"But why would he be involved with a dead body?"

"That, John, is what I want you to find out. If in fact he is involved. Tread carefully. And John?"

"Yes?"

"If you need help interviewing, use uniform. They can do a quick run-down of the people at whatever place this Makepeace woman was at the night before. We can't dismiss the possibility that there's a link there, too."

19

THE VINCENT WAS HALF WAY to being a gastropub. Its Victorian era exterior was preserved, but inside it had had a complete makeover, with walls removed to create a large eating area next to the bar, which had a range of boutique beers on tap, and a line of single malt scotch and specialist gin bottles and other spirits standing against a large mirror.

Nguyen arrived a few minutes after 5:00 and ordered a White Rabbit dark ale. He was served by a young woman with short spiky hair and a diamond stud in one nostril. She reached for a bottle out of the fridge cabinet behind her and unscrewed the bottle top.

"A glass?"

He shook his head, and she passed the bottle to him.

As he sat down, Brothers arrived. "What are you having, Graham? My treat."

"What's that you've got?"

Nguyen held up his bottle of White Rabbit.

"Any good?"

Nguyen nodded. "Does the trick. It's dark—a bit like a stout."

Brothers scratched his belly.

"Hmm, I'll have a Little Creatures."

Nguyen went to the bar and ordered, and gave Brothers his beer.

"So what have we got?"

"It looks like the Steenvaters were telling a porkie." Brothers outlined his visit to Omelets Are Us.

"Interesting. If it was busy, could this guy Demetri have missed them?"

"Possible. But he reckons that if they sat down to eat he would definitely have seen them. They've been there before."

"Makes sense. So why did they lie? By the way, the boss wants to go public tomorrow, see if that flushes out any useful info."

"Well, that'll jam the phones. That arsehole Steenvater—bet he belts his wife. He was lying—covering up those two guys he was greeting at the lift that we caught on video. He must have been home then. Should we tell him we have them on tape?"

"Soon—but let's keep him overconfident for a while. Have you traced the BMW?"

"It belongs to a Richard Wainright, in Armadale."

"Good work. Wainright, eh. Do we know him? He one of the jokers with the body? What did he have to say for himself?"

"He said it was stolen," Brothers said. He raised his beer in a mock toast.

"Shit."

"Yes—and he was not amused when I called him. Thought we'd found his car. Disappointed that we hadn't."

"Any street cameras catch the car?"

"We've got shots of it in the city, going north. Then we lost it."

"When was it stolen?"

"Last Friday night. From Wainright's home. It was parked in his drive."

"How the fuck do they pinch a new BMW? I thought they had all sorts of security built in."

"The tech heads are usually up to speed."

"Tech heads? That rings a bell. Steenvater is a tech head, isn't he?"

"Steenvater? Yeah—but he's management. He's head of tech, not a tech head. I doubt he'd be hands on."

"Not my point. He'd know someone who'd know someone. Anyhow, probably irrelevant." Nguyen shook his head. "Any self-respecting car thief would know."

They finished their drinks.

"Need a lift?" Nguyen asked.

"No, got my own wheels."

"See you in the morning. Depending on what comes back about the fingerprints, I think we may need to speak to the Steenvaters again. And have you talked to Carol McTeish yet?"

"McTeish?"

"Yes—Forell says we can use uniform to help interview the people at, what was it, Glimmers—the bar that had the party. The night before. You know Constable Carol McTeish? She'll help."

"Okay." Carol McTeish was two years in and keen to get into detection.

"And Graham—maybe you should check with Missing Persons. Has the dead guy been reported missing?"

"Good point. See you tomorrow."

JOHN "WINNER" NGUYEN DROVE HOME. His wife Hahn was in the kitchen.

"You're home early. Is there a problem?"

"No—just wanted to see you."

"Yeah. Yeah." Nonetheless she allowed him to hug her and give her a kiss.

"How's Minh?"

"She's asleep." John put his head in to peep at his three-year-old daughter. She was curled up on her side, her face peaceful. He shut the door.

"You been drinking?"

"Just a beer with Brothers. We've got a weird one." He told Hahn about the body in the bed that had gone walkabout. She listened without comment.

"So, what do you reckon?" he said.

"Hmm. Not sure, John. Don't let it get to you."

"Get to me?" He considered this. "The only thing that will get to me is if the Boss gets hot under the collar. Or, rather, cold in the eyes." He laughed. "It'll work out. Just bloody peculiar."

"You sure?" She looked at him, holding his gaze. "Okay. Good." She kissed him. "Let's eat."

20

FRAN DROPPED IN TO Deirdre's apartment that evening.

"How's your day? Any luck with Steve? Feel like pizza?"

Typical Fran. Three questions and not caring about an answer to any of them.

Fran put two pizza boxes on the table. "A capriccioso and a fungi. Is that okay?"

Deirdre nodded, and fetched two plates, put them on the table. Went to the fridge and got out a bottle of white. Poured two glasses.

Fran opened the boxes, and a delicious aroma of hot cheese and oregano filled the room. They both took a slice.

"Yum—just what I needed," Deirdre said. She sipped her wine.

"So—how was work today?"

"I didn't go in—I've got the week off. Actually, Vanessa was pretty understanding. I told her it was a death. I knew she'd be too embarrassed to ask details."

Fran nodded.

"And I caught up with Steve."

Fran's eyes gleamed. "How was he?"

"Actually, very understanding."

"Understanding, eh? What did you talk about?" Fran raised her glass and drank.

"We went through everything that happened. He was very calm. Very helpful. In fact, he's coming over tomorrow night. You know, I think I like him."

Fran grinned. "You are amazing."

"What?"

"After all this, you're ready to 'like' him?"

"Just saying."

"Well, be careful." A thought suddenly occurred to Fran. "What if he did it?"

"Did what?"

"Put the body in your bed."

"Fran. For God's sake be serious."

"I am being serious. Steve is the last person you remember talking to at the party, isn't he?"

Deirdre nodded. She frowned, muttered, "No way. It couldn't be, could it?"

"Well, I mean—what if he spiked your drink, and stuck this guy in your bed?"

Deirdre shook her head several times, a bit like a dog after it has been hosed.

"Fran. Fran. Fran. He's a nice guy. He's a footballer. Why on earth would he do a thing like that?"

"Just saying. Footballers can do some pretty strange things." Seeing Deirdre's expression, she laughed.

"You're the limit. Look. He was really helpful, today. He's not like that at all. And, besides, he's an ex-footballer. He'd never do anything like that."

Fran raised her eyebrows.

"He works for the footy club."

"So?"

"I know all footballers aren't little angels. But he's senior, for godsake, not some wet behind the ears twentysomething. Imagine the nightmare if he did something like that and it got out." She shook her head. "No Fran, he'd never do anything to risk his club."

"Just be careful, okay? You don't really know him. Okay?"

"Okay."

"Now. Why did you invite him over here?"

"Why not?"

"I mean, what message are you trying to give him?"

"Message?"

"You know what I mean. What do you reckon he'll expect, coming here?"

"Nothing. Nothing at all. Just to check out where it happened. Maybe check me out, too. But nothing will happen."

"Yeah. Yeah."

"Fran."

"I know you."

"Well, this is different. I feel different. I must admit, this has thrown me. The last thing I want is to be with anyone at the moment."

"So you invite Steve to dinner."

"Yes. As I keep trying to explain. He's being helpful. I think he's a really nice guy. He's straight. I mean straightforward. Direct. He listens."

"Okay. Okay. I get it. Good luck!" She smiled at Deirdre, and they finished eating. She raised her glass in a mock toast. "Let me know what happens, eh?"

"Will do. And thanks for the pizza. I'll keep you in the loop."

"Okay. See you tomorrow."

Tuesday

21

THE NEXT MORNING DEIRDRE decided to cook a fish curry for her dinner with Steve, and shopped at the South Melbourne Market. She bought some rockling and a packet of basmati rice, knowing that would be easy to cook.

By seven that evening she'd got the rice cooking on low heat, ready to be turned off in twenty minutes, and the fish was in a saucepan with coconut milk and coriander, cooking gently. She turned down the gas so it wouldn't overcook, and whipped off her apron. She went to the bathroom, brushed her teeth, and surveyed herself in the mirror. Hair looked okay. She patted it. Should she change her blouse? No, that looked fine. The white went with her dark pants. Stop it, she thought. I always get anxious. Me. Successful me. Me with a murdered guy in my bed! Who else can claim that?

She went back to the kitchen and turned off the rice, checking the fish. It smelt good. Where was Steve?

She glanced at her watch. Quarter past. She opened a bottle of white, an Italian pinot grigio, and poured herself a glass. Oh well, he's probably held up. She sipped her wine, thinking of Steve. Whatever happened in this bizarre affair, at least she'd met him. Even if he didn't show up tonight.

The intercom buzzed. It was Steve, smiling into the camera.

"Hi. I'll come down to let you up.".

As THE LIFT DOORS OPENED onto the foyer, she saw Steve, carrying a bottle of wine and wearing a dark jacket and pale blue tee shirt with a slogan—there was the letter I, a heart, and a dotted line. Underneath the line, she saw, were the words "fill in name", in brackets. They rode the lift up, without talking. At her door, he gave her the bottle of wine.

She glanced at it and smiled.

"Pinot grigio. Just what I've opened."

Steve came in, and looked around. "Nice."

"Like to see the scene of the crime?" The words were just out of her mouth as she realized she would be taking him into her bedroom. Her cheeks pinked. Why had she said that? How stupid. Oh well.

Steve merely smiled at her, shook his head, but then followed her into the bedroom. He studied the bed.

"Which side was he on?"

"This side." She gestured at the side nearest the door. He seemed focused.

"That would be easiest for whoever. Just plonk him down. No need to walk to the other side." He looked around. She had a dressing table and chair; there were some cosmetics and a couple of postcards on the dresser. Her walk-in closet was shut.

"Let's get out of this room and have a drink," she said, leading the way back to the living room. "Pinot grigio?"

They laughed, and she poured them both a glass, raising hers. He did likewise.

"Have a seat."

She had laid the kitchen table, and they both sat down.

"I haven't made much—a fish curry. I hope you can eat fish?"

"I'm an omnivore," he said. "Eat anything."

"So am I. I mean, not anything. I can't come at chicken feet. Or offal. But most things."

They sipped their wine.

Steve looked at her, a slight smile on his lips. "Now, about this man. The police turn up anything yet?"

"I haven't heard from them."

"Then that means they haven't found him. How would Sherlock Holmes do this?"

"Sherlock Holmes?"

"He'd take seemingly insignificant things, real trivia, and work out a logical explanation for it all."

"Well, that's all well and good. But we don't even have trivial things."

"Are you sure? Let's forget for the moment how he got into your bed. Think about what must have happened after you and your friend stuck him in the lift."

"He disappeared."

"Yes, exactly. Therefore someone else must have known he was in the lift. That someone mightn't have known he was in your flat, here, but they must have known he was in the lift. Otherwise how would they know to get rid of him? And if they knew he was in the lift, how did they know that? Did they just happen to get in the lift and, hey presto! there he was?"

She looked at Steve as he talked. He had dark eyes, and his hair was brushed back.

"So either they monitored the lift cameras—not impossible these days. In fact everyone is doing it. I'm sure there's an app for it. Just hack in and Bob's your uncle."

"Er, I don't think there are lift cameras."

"Oh yeah? Well, never mind. However they found him, they would probably have got him out via the basement. In a car. Or a car boot."

"How does that help us?"

"There'll be video of the basement, surely, in a place like this. Even if there aren't any in the lifts. The cops will have that. Ask the detective—what's his name?"

"Er, Nguyen, I think. John Nguyen."

"Ask him if they have it on video."

"Will he tell me?"

"You can sweet talk him. I'm sure he won't want to, but he'll let you know something."

She thought about it. "But why ask? He'll either tell me, or not. Where does that get us?"

"We'll know whether they are getting anywhere. That itself will be helpful."

"How?"

"Well, it means that the likelihood that he's got some connection to you is the real thing. For you I mean. You didn't recognize him. But maybe he knew you from work or something. I don't know. The important thing is that if it's completely a random thing that got him in your bed, then you don't need to worry."

"But I am worried. What if it happens again?"

"I mean, if he has no reason, no connection to you, then it's likely he was just stuck in the nearest bed, and it happened to be yours."

"That's very comforting."

"Well, more comforting than if you were deliberately chosen."

Deirdre drank some more wine, got up and refilled the glasses.

"I suppose you're right. Let's eat."

She served up rice on each plate and a couple of spoons of the curry on top. The sweet aroma of onion, Thai fish paste and coconut milk wafted from the plates.

"Yum!" Steve said, and tucked in. "You made it yourself! Not takeaway!"

"Yes." Deirdre was absurdly pleased. "Glad you could tell."

"Takeaway doesn't taste like this. Too fresh and … not oily. Also—I can see the saucepans on your stove." He laughed.

"Steve."

"Yes?" He looked back at her.

"You've been asking me all about everything. And you've been so helpful. But I've hardly asked you a question. What do you do?"

He sipped his wine, put the glass down.

"I'm an ex-footballer. And now I'm in marketing, for the Saints. I'm 33. Anything else?" It all came out in a rush. He somehow seemed a bit put out.

"I don't mean to be intrusive. You don't seem like a footballer."

"What's a footballer meant to seem like?"

"I don't know. Sorry. I shouldn't let stereotypes … anyhow, I'm not really a footy type. But, you've been great."

He relaxed and smiled back at her. She put a forkful of curry in her mouth. She liked him looking at her.

After swallowing she said, "Look, I mean it. You've been really helpful. This stuff keeps whirling around inside my head, but you're logical, you're calm, you're—" she paused, thought. "You've calmed me down …"

"Well. The least I could do."

He still seemed a bit uncomfortable. What had she started here?

"I'm not wanting to pry."

"That's okay. Don't mind me."

"Okay. It's just, I want to get to know you a little better."

"Yeah, well. Me too." He was looking her in the eyes, and she glanced away.

They finished eating, and Deirdre got up and made some herbal tea, brought it back to the table. They sipped it.

"What is it?"

"Lemon and ginger. You like it?"

"Yes, it's good." He took another sip. "Look, I'd better be going. I've got an early start tomorrow." He put down his cup. "Thanks for dinner, Deirdre. Make sure you call that detective. And let me know what's happening, eh?"

Deirdre stumbled to her feet.

"Yeah. Okay. Thanks for coming over."

He kissed her on the cheek as she opened the apartment door, then walked to the lift. She waited at the door until the lift came, then waved as got in. He waved back. She closed the door. What had made him suddenly scram? Or was she reading too much into everything? She did like him.

She thought of her relationships. Sudden plunges. Quick endings. Relationships was not the right word. She didn't do relationships. Yet Steve … No. She didn't want … What didn't she want?

At least he had come over. He was helpful. He must like me a bit to do that. She ran her hands through her hair. I'll speak to Fran. She picked up her mobile phone.

"Fran? Hi, it's me."

"This is a bit early. What's happening?"

"Nothing much. Steve's just gone."

"And?"

"I don't know. We had a nice meal. He liked my food. But just left early."

"What did you say?"

"Nothing. I mean we talked about the … case. He made a good suggestion, to call the detective to ask if they have anything. Can tell me anything. You know, to set me at ease."

"Okay, I can understand that. So why did he leave?"

"He did say he had an early start in the morning. But maybe because I asked him about himself. He didn't say much. Seemed to withdraw a bit. I don't know."

"Typical man. Don't worry about it. You're not that good at small talk, are you? Look, if he'd tried to get into your pants, that's when you should be worried."

"But I like him." She realized she sounded wistful.

"Of course you do. He's male, isn't he? Not deformed? It's a good sign that he left early."

"A good sign?"

"He probably doesn't want to get involved."

"And that's a good sign?"

"But, on the other hand if he really doesn't want to get involved, he would have done things differently. Did he ask you to keep in touch, for example?"

Deirdre thought, and remembered that he had.

"Yes."

"So maybe he's been burnt before, and doesn't want to risk it again. Just wants to keep things on the straight and narrow."

"He did peck me on the cheek when he left. But he skedaddled pretty quick smart."

"There you go. Just be patient. Be thankful he likes you enough to be helpful, and not enough to want to get involved with you."

Somehow Fran's twisted logic made a sort of sense.

"Thanks, Fran. See you later."

"See you."

22

Sue Gossiter knocked on John Nguyen's door and entered. Nguyen was behind his desk, staring at his computer screen. He looked up, smiled.

"Hi there, Sue."

"G'day, Winner." She waited until she was sure she had his full attention. "You know the DNA we found in the lift. Got some news for you. Which do you want to hear first—the good or the bad?"

Nguyen grimaced. "Either. I don't care."

"The bad news is that there was nothing in the garage. We didn't find a thing."

"Fuck!" Nguyen said.

"But wait, there's more. The other bad news is that the DNA in the lift doesn't match anything on the state or national DNA database." She looked at Nguyen.

Something in her eyes made him ask, "And?"

"I thought about all the commercial DNA outfits, like Ancestry and My Heritage, and I thought, what if he's tested himself? The good news is we got Ancestry to check it for us."

"Excellent." Finally, something. Nguyen smiled. "That's excellent, Sue. Good thinking."

"The other bad news is he didn't test himself. But."

"Yes?" Why did every conversation with Sue get drawn out like this?

"But they found a likely match with three other people. Two women and a man. Probably relatives. Cousins, maybe. Two are in the US, and one in Sydney."

"So, we know he has relatives. Doesn't everyone have relatives?"

"Yeah, rellies. But you can track them down, hey? They'll know if he's missing, won't they?"

Nguyen jumped up, walked round the desk and hugged her.

"Terrific!"

Sue shrugged him off. "Hey, watch it buddy." Nonetheless she was smiling.

"Thanks, Sue. That's just what we needed. I'll get Brothers onto it straight away. You got the names?"

Sue handed him a sheet of paper. "Here they are."

The three names were Daniel Prosovic, Maria Antwerp and Jelena Smith. According to Ancestry Daniel was in Sydney, Maria in Los Angeles and Jelena in New York.

"A trip to the States, eh?" said Sue.

"Maybe to Sydney, if I'm lucky, knowing our budgets. But we do have the old reliable." He held up his phone, then used it to call Brothers. "Where are you? Can you come in?"

"G'day, mate. I'm downstairs getting coffee. Want one?"

"A flat white. Sue Gossiter's come up with some great news." He looked up at Sue. "Do you want a coffee?"

She shook her head.

"Just the one, for me, thanks." He hung up.

"Should I stay?" she asked.

"Yes, please. Good idea. You'll be better at explaining it."

A few minutes later Graham Brothers walked in carrying two coffees.

"G'day Sue." He looked at the scribbles on the paper cups. "This is yours." He handed it to Nguyen.

"Sue had the brainwave to go outside our normal DNA databases."

Gositter explained how she had found out the three possible relatives for the missing man.

"So," Nguyen said. He handed Brothers the sheet of paper. "Can you find out where they are, and question them? Hopefully they'll know this guy, whoever he is. And whether they've heard from him."

"Right. I'll get on to it." He nodded to Sue. "That's great, mate. Thanks."

"We do our best."

She left, smiling.

"RIGHT, THEN." Brothers looked at the names on the paper. "I'll try to get details on all three. I'll try this Prosovic in Sydney, first."

He went to his desk and entered the name into the national police database. After a short time, it reported no known person. So, no convictions. Hadn't applied for a Working With Children check. Hadn't even had a speeding fine.

He checked White Pages. Immediately several Prosovics came up, including a D P Prosovic in Farnell Street, Curl Curl, New South Wales. Brothers shook his head. Curl Curl?

He dialed the number. It rang and rang, then rang out.

He keyed Daniel Prosovic into Google, and got a reference to Ancestry and My Heritage but nothing else. LinkedIn brought no results. He tried Facebook. Bingo. The photo was of a man in his twenties. He decided to send a query on Messenger. "*Can we talk? This is Sergeant Graham Brothers from Victoria Police. It's a personal matter.*" He added his mobile number. It would probably take a while to get a response, if any. Sometimes people ignored messages from strangers on Messenger.

He phoned Missing Persons, and spoke to Sergeant Molly Ishram. He described the case of the probably murdered man gone missing. "It may be a bit too soon, but have you had anyone ringing in since the weekend? The guy we're looking for is probably in his late 30s or 40s. Caucasian."

"Let me check the database," Ishram said. "Hold on a sec." After a bit she said, "Sorry, Graham. Nothing's come in like that. We've had three females—two teenagers and a woman in her sixties. But no missing men over the weekend, or since."

"Thanks, Molly. If you get a report, a middle-aged man missing, could you let me know?"

"Sure. I'll make a note."

"Thanks again." He hung up.

There was a ping on Brothers' computer. A response on Messenger, from Prosovic: "*You say you're from Victoria Police. What's this about?*"

He thought about what he should reply. He didn't want to put this person off. Maybe being direct was the best option. He typed in, "*We're trying to track down a missing person. Could I phone you to explain? What's your mobile?*"

The typed response came back: "*What missing person? How does it involve me?*"

"*I'll need to talk to you. It's complicated.*"

Brothers sent his mobile number again, and soon Prosovic rang it.

"Hi, Mr. Prosovic. It's Sergeant Graham Brothers here."

"Yes? Daniel Prosovic here. You mentioned a missing person?"

"Well, we think he could be a relative of yours.

"Is this to do with my DNA test?"

"Well, yes, yes it is."

"Thanks so much for calling." He heard Prosovic give out a deep breath. Then he said, "This is amazing. You know, I've just discovered my dad wasn't my dad. You know what I mean?"

"Your dad wasn't your dad?" Was this another nutter? The case seemed to be littered with them.

"That's right. I've just discovered my dad isn't my dad. I mean, he is my dad, but he couldn't have kids. So they had a donor for my mum. It was anonymous, they said. That's how it was done. I always thought something wasn't quite right. You know, growing up. And finally I got up the guts to ask. My parents. I mean, I didn't want to hurt them. But I had to know. And they told me my dad wasn't my real dad. So I took the DNA test." There was a pause. Then a hopeful, "And you think this missing person could be my dad?"

Brothers scratched his head.

"Could be. We don't know. All we know is there's a guy who's missing."

"My dad's missing?"

"A guy is missing," Brothers repeated.

"So how did you get my name?"

Brothers thought about what to say. He didn't want to lie.

"It was through the DNA site. Ancestry.com."

"Wow. Then surely you must know. That's great. Who is it you say is missing? He could be my dad. He could be my dad!" Prosovic's voice rose in both pitch and excitement. "My biological dad, I mean." He quietened down. "My real dad of course is still my real dad, Sergeant. He was scared I wouldn't love him anymore. They both were. Mum and Dad. Scared I'd hate them. But how couldn't I still love them? They brought me up. They were great. They are great. It's all cool. They'll always be my mum and dad. I just want to find out who my biological dad was. I might have other brothers and sisters."

"It could be him. There's certainly a DNA link between the missing man and you."

"So who is he?"

"That's the thing. We don't know."

"You don't know? Then why are you ringing me? Just a minute. Who are you again?"

Brothers felt like screaming.

"Mr. Prosovic, I'm sorry. I'll say it again, and as I said before, I'm Sergeant Graham Brothers. We are investigating a death. The man who died, his DNA is a partial match for yours. He could be your dad, but he also might be a cousin or uncle."

"So he could be my dad? But if you don't know if he is, or if he is a cousin, or, or an uncle? Again—why have you rung me?"

"Er, actually you rang me." Brothers hit his forehead. Why had he said that? "We were hoping that if he was related to you, you'd know him, and might know if he'd gone missing."

"But I'm trying to find him. How could I know if he is missing, when I don't know who he is? And you say that you don't know who he is, either."

Brothers took a deep breath. "That's right. He could be your dad. He definitely seems to be a relative of yours. According to the DNA. We were hoping that you'd know him, if he was related. I mean, we thought you would know if a relative had gone missing."

"But that's why I took the DNA test in the first place."

"Yes. I'm really sorry to have landed this on you like this. Are you okay?"

"Yes. I suppose. It's one thing to find out you're a donut."

"Donut?"

"Donut. That's the word for people like me—a kid from a donor. It's one thing to find out you're a donut, the product of artificial insemination. But then you get in touch and raise my hopes."

"Well, we're going to keep searching. We'll find out who he was."

"That's just it. Don't you see? If you find out he was my dad—he's dead. I've lost him."

"Look we got a couple of other matches, in the States."

"Could they be my dad?"

"Well no. Somehow I don't think so." Brother hesitated. "They're women." Then more heartily, "But they could be your sisters, or aunts or something. And they might lead us to your real dad. This missing guy in Melbourne, like I said, may just be a cousin or something. Not necessarily your dad."

"Will you let me know?"

"Of course. Thanks, Mr. Prosovic. I don't suppose I could talk to your mum or dad?"

"What for?"

"They might be able to help."

"How would they be able to help? The donor was anonymous. They don't know who he was."

"Maybe there are details of where the … sperm came from?"

"I checked—as I say, the donor was anonymous."

"But hasn't the law changed? I mean, don't they have to let you know now?" He was getting out of his depth.

"They just told me the guy was anonymous. I suppose I can understand why. But it's just so frustrating."

"Who did you check with? What was the agency?"

"It's called, um, City Fertility. In Miranda. I already rang them."

"Thanks, Mr. Prosovic. Maybe they'll say more to me. Can I mention your name?"

Prosovic took a while, then said, "Okay." Then more forcefully, "Sure. What have I got to lose?"

"Thanks, again. If we find anything, we'll get straight in touch. And please call me, if you think of anything else, or have any questions. Here's my mobile number again."

23

Brothers walked over and put his head into Nguyen's office.

"Checked out the guy in Sydney, Daniel Prosovic. Would you believe it—calls himself a donut."

"A donut?"

"Yeah—he's from a sperm donor. He doesn't know who his dad is. His real dad, that is. His dad isn't his dad."

"Right," said Nguyen. "Right. So no luck there. A sperm donor. What are the odds? And he actually said he calls himself a donut?"

"That seems to be the term—kids of donors."

"And he hadn't traced his dad?"

"No. He thought I was ringing with the info."

"Well we've got the other two names." Nguyen looked at some papers on his desk. "Maria Antwerp and Jelena Smith. Let's hope they're not donuts too. Have you got their phone numbers?"

"Not yet. They're in the States, New York and LA—do you think calling them from here is a good idea? Assuming I can find out their contact details. I mean, do you reckon Forell might give us the budget to fly over?"

"Fly to the US?" Nguyen thought about it, rubbed his chin. "It's a weird one, isn't it? If it was just some bozo caught up in a street brawl, who got hit and stumbled up into whatshername's apartment, her bed I mean, then there's no way we'd get to fly even to Sydney. But there's more to this one. Those two meeting Steenvater and putting the body into a Beemer. That doesn't sound like a street brawl to me. We'll have to find out more, a lot more, and it better be enough to get the Boss intrigued. I'm sure she'll understand that working with our US colleagues should be the best way get more information."

"Get her intrigued?"

"You know what I mean. I think we'll need to visit the Steenvaters again. Put some pressure on them. Why did they lie about going out to the Omelets place? Why didn't they mention the two men? Were they in on it, whatever it was? Let's go see them again. And we need to follow up on that party that Makepeace was at, last Saturday night. Have you got McTeish interviewing the people there?"

"I've asked her to get the guest list."

"We have to get a move on. When will she get the list?"

Brothers went red. He'd completely forgotten to follow that up. "On to it, Winner."

He walked to his desk. No sign of Constable McTeish. He rang her mobile.

"Constable McTeish." Carol McTeish had a voice pitched in the middle ranges and she sounded older than her 23 years.

"Hi Carol. It's Graham Brothers—where are you? We need to speak."

"I'll be there in a jiffy. Give me five, okay?"

Seven minutes later McTeish walked in, rushed to her desk and put down a package, then walked up to Brothers. "What's up?"

"I need some help checking on some possible witnesses."

"Witnesses? Is this the disappearing act job?"

Brothers groaned. "Word flies around pretty quickly here, doesn't it?"

"So it is that one." She grinned. "What do you need done?"

Brothers briefed her about Deirdre Makepeace and the need to find out who was at the party at Glimmers the night before she had got home apparently drunk. And if anyone knew how she got home.

"You sure she was drunk?" McTeish asked.

"She couldn't remember anything." Brothers thought for a moment. "She could have been drugged."

"Was she tested? You know, a blood test?"

Carol was sharp, Brothers thought. He hadn't even thought to get a fucking blood test.

"No. You're right. We should have."

"If she was drugged with, say, a date drug like Rohypnol," McTeish said, "that would explain why she couldn't remember a thing. Of course," she paused, shut her eyes for a moment, "saying she was drugged could be very convenient for her. A great excuse."

"That's possible. But having met her, I reckon it's unlikely she was pretending. It's certainly possible someone put something in her drink. Anyhow, we need to find out who she talked to at the party. It was at a city bar called Glimmers. Some sort of work function. Can you track that down, and talk to those we can identify? It might come to nothing, but who knows? She mentioned she was talking to some footballer, Steve Dalmatico."

"Steve Dalmatico? The St Kilda star?"

"That's the one."

"He finished playing a couple of years ago, didn't he?"

"Well he's one to have a yarn to. Maybe I'll speak to him. Can you find out who else was there? You do half, I'll do the rest. Okay?"

McTeish nodded. "Who should I get in touch with?"

"Makepeace said she was invited by a guy who works for a company called Red Mustard." He flicked through his notes. "Sorry. Pink Mustard. A guy called Adam Mendoza, does their IT. He's probably a good place to start—he'll know who has the guest list. Why don't you come in with me to talk to him. And we can ask if there were any party crashers. And when you get asked what it's all about, just say it has to do with a possible homicide."

"Got you." McTeish smiled, clearly pleased.

She looked up Pink Mustard on the White Pages app and phoned.

"Can I speak to Adam Mendoza?"

She was put through and just as she heard "Hello, Adam Mendoza" she had a thought. She hung up.

"Sergeant."

Brothers looked up.

"He's there now. Mendoza. At Pink Mustard. I hung up before he knew who was calling."

"Why did you do that?"

"I thought it would be too difficult to explain to him on the phone. We could go and see him now."

Brothers turned around and looked at her. Her eyes were bright. She sure looked eager.

"Good thinking. Okay. Let me see." He checked his diary. "Yes, I'm clear for the rest of the day. Let's go. Where are they again?"

"In Richmond, 306 Lennox Street. Near Swan Street."

THE TRAFFIC WAS HEAVY, with road works on Punt Road slowing everything down. After about half an hour Brothers turned into Lennox Street, and found a place to park about three doors from a Victorian terrace house with the number 306 on a large brass plate attached near the door. It had been turned into an office building that now housed Pink Mustard. They entered into a small reception area. The walls were white, there was glass and chrome and a low desk behind which sat a young man with dreadlocks, keying something into his computer. He looked up.

"Yes? Can I help you?"

"G'day. I'm Sergeant Graham Brothers from Victoria Police. And this is Constable Carol McTeish."

"Yes?"

"Is Adam Mendoza in? We need to speak to him."

"Adam? Yes. Just a sec."

He picked up his phone and pushed a couple of buttons.

"Adam? Er, there are some police here to see you."

"Police? To see me? What's it about?" Mendoza's voice had risen so much that Brothers could hear him through the phone.

The young man grimaced. "Search me."

"Okay, I'll come out."

A short time later a middle-sized man appeared, somewhat overweight with stubble and a shaved head. He was dressed in jeans and a multi-hued shirt. He stopped short and looked at the police, then held out his hand.

"Hello. I'm Adam Mendoza. How can I help you?"

They introduced themselves.

"What's this about? Is it my parking tickets?" His face took on a sheepish smile.

"Parking tickets? No. No. Nothing like that. We're investigating something completely different. A possible homicide. Is there somewhere we can sit, in private?"

"A homicide? What's that to do with me? Sorry. What's your name again?"

"Brothers, Sergeant Graham Brothers."

"Constable McTeish," said Carol.

"What homicide? How can I help?"

"Is there a meeting room …?

"Of course. Come with me."

He led them through a glass door along a short hallway to a small meeting room. There was a table, six chairs in black leather with chrome frames, and a side table, with a tray, a carafe of water and six glasses.

"Would you like tea or coffee?"

"A glass of water would be fine."

"Yes, please, a water for me, too," McTeish said.

Mendoza pick up the phone.

"Ron. Could you bring me in a latte? Thanks."

He poured water into two glasses, then looked up.

"A homicide. Someone dead, you say? Is this about Deirdre Makepeace?"

"Do you know Deirdre Makepeace?"

"Yes. I invited her to our Christmas party."

"Why did you mention her when I said someone was dead?"

"Because she rang me yesterday, and told me—I didn't know whether to believe her at the time—she told me there was a dead man in her bed. After the Christmas party. Is that what this is about?"

"Well, yes. We're talking to everyone who might have some information," Brothers said.

The receptionist came in with a latte in a white cup and saucer.

"Thanks, Ron."

He looked questioningly at the three of them, then left.

"You saw Deirdre at the party, at Glimmers? She did come to the party?" McTeish said.

"Yes. It was quite a night. We hosted our clients."

"She said she was a little drunk. Couldn't remember much. Until the next day."

"Yes. When she rang me, she told me …you know, about the dead man. She said she'd called you lot."

"Yes, she did, Mr. Mendoza. We're checking it out. There's a small chance it might possibly involve one of your party goers."

Adam took a sip of his coffee. Stared at them, apparently waiting for more.

"Apparently the man was not someone she knew, you understand."

Mendoza sat there eyes somewhat glazed. Eventually he said, "So how can I help?"

"Well, it seems the last thing she remembers is being at the party. You said you invited her, didn't you?"

"Yes, I did. She's a client. Does IT for the Bank of Ballarat."

"We're trying to track down people she spoke to at the party. Do you remember when she left?"

Adam thought, shook his head.

"No, I remember talking to her earlier. She was with a group of our other clients. I think she was talking to Steve Dalmatico for a while."

"You didn't see her leave?" Brothers asked.

"No. She was gone when we finished up."

"What time was that?"

"About 11:30. Our deal with the bar meant we had to be out by midnight. I left a bit earlier."

"Were there many still there by then?"

"A few stragglers. You know, those still searching for another drink."

"Was Steve still there?"

"No. He'd gone. I can't remember when."

"Do you have the guest list?"

"I'm sure I can get it for you."

He picked up the phone again.

"Ron? You know our Glimmers party. Can you bring in the guest list, please?" He put the phone down. "He should have it shortly."

"So you didn't notice whether Steve left with Deirdre?"

"Sorry. No. I didn't see either leave. That's a bit strange."

"Strange?"

"Normally Deirdre would come up and thank me for the party. But she didn't. That was not like her at all."

The door opened and the receptionist came in, gave a sheet of paper to Adam.

"Thanks, Ron."

"Anything else?" Ron asked.

"No. That's fine. I'll give you a buzz if we need anything." Adam handed the list to Brothers.

There were around 50 names on the list, including the organizations they worked for and contact details. Seven were from Pink Mustard.

"Thanks. Thanks very much." He passed the list to McTeish, who perused it with care.

"While we're here, can we speak to the other Pink Mustard people who were there?"

"Sure." He picked up the phone again.

BROTHERS AND McTEISH SPOKE to the other employees in turn. None could remember seeing Deirdre leave, nor Steve. There were no strangers who gate-crashed the party.

"Well, let's talk to this Steve Dalmatico." Brothers looked at McTeish. "Do you want to set up the interview?"

She grinned. "On to it, Sarge."

When Carol McTeish rang the St Kilda Football Club she was in luck, and was put straight through to Steve Dalmatico. She explained who she was and why she wanted to see him. He asked if they could meet at a cafe rather than at work, and they agreed to meet in South Melbourne at 10:30am the next day, at a place called Boojums.

Wednesday

24

BROTHERS LET THE DOG outside to do its business, checked there was food and water by its kennel, and left his house in Elwood. His wife, a nurse, had gone to work about an hour earlier. He had plenty of time, so he decided to drive along the beach route. The traffic was light at that time, the sky overcast and the sea a gunmetal grey. With no wind the still water looked as if you could walk on it.

He arrived early and drove down into the car park to his usual spot, and waited for the lift to arrive. He thought of John Nguyen. For a senior partner he was good to work with. He was easy going, didn't want to prove a point all the time. And he backed him up when needed. But this case seemed to be getting under his collar. It wasn't obvious—but working with him for as long as he had—what was it, seven years?—he'd got to know when he got a bit jumpy.

He got out of the lift and walked over to Nguyen's office. Nguyen was already in.

"How'd you go at Pink Mustard?"

"Nothing there, I'm afraid. No one noticed Makepeace leave. And that was odd in itself. But she rang the guy who runs it, one Adam Mendoza, rang him Monday morning, and told him about the body. All the details."

"Did you find out who she talked to at the party?"

"As far as we can work out, a guy called Steve Dalmatico." Brothers looked at Nguyen, who made no response. "He's a former footballer."

"So?"

Brothers shook his head. "Anyway, Carol and I are going to see him this morning."

"Well, that's good. But it's already three days since we discovered, er, didn't discover the body. That's getting too long."

"Any news on the US trip?"

"We'll talk with the boss once you and McTeish are back from seeing, what was his name, Dalmatico."

"Okay."

25

Henry Steenvater was playing Hearts on his PC when he felt someone looking at him. He turned around and saw Veronica. She was standing behind him, twisting her hands together.

"Henry?"

"What?" he said, annoyed.

"You're playing Hearts. What's up?"

He closed the window. "So what?"

"You play Hearts when you're upset."

"I'm not upset."

"Then why did you lie to the police?"

"Lie to the police?"

"About eating brunch. At Omelets Are Us?"

He winced. "Look, dear. I didn't want them to know." He stopped. "You know those two Americans who visited?"

She nodded.

"Well, the sooner we're rid of them the better. It's none of the police's business."

"How will we be rid of them?"

"I mean, as soon as they go back to the States."

"Why. What's the problem? And surely the police will see them."

"See them?"

"On the TV monitors, whatever they're called."

The CCTV? Oh, shit." Steenvater blanched. "I forgot about that. Hmm, would they have seen me? I was only in the car park at the lift."

He stood up, paced back and forth. "Never mind. I'll work something out. Thanks for backing me up about the brunch."

"Who were the men?"

"It's a long story."

"Yes?"

"They represent a syndicate. They're trying to find—good Lord. That's why the police were here."

He stopped pacing, and held out his hands to Veronica. She hugged him.

"What's this about?

"Remember back in 1999, when everyone was concerned about the Millennium Bug?"

"The Millennium Bug?"

"You know, the dates in the computers didn't have the full years, just the last two digits. For example, the year 1999 was keyed in as 99. When the clock rolled round to 2000, would the programs take it as 2000 or go back to 1900? Would they freeze? We were worried the bank system might crash. Planes might fall out of the sky. We had to fix it."

"Oh, yes. I remember now. That." She smiled at him. "But that was ages ago. Wasn't it a complete damp squib?"

"Only because we all made the necessary changes. So, no catastrophes. But. Well, it seems someone had the bright idea to round down every dollar transaction, so a cent was diverted to a special account. This started on January 1, 2000."

"A cent?"

"Multiply that by 1000 transactions and that's ten bucks. There are millions of transactions a day. That's thousands of dollars. Until we picked it up, we reckon close to a billion dollars could've got scammed. But no one cared because it was only a cent a transaction. Or half a cent. No one noticed. A rounding error."

"Where did it go?"

"We're not too sure. It must have been diverted to a different account—probably many accounts, and in fact several diversions, to make it even harder to trace. The belief is the money never got touched. It's still in those accounts, somewhere. Anyhow, those guys represent the syndicate that's trying to recover the money. That's why they were here. Nothing to do with whatever happened in the lift."

"But why would they come to you? And on a Sunday morning? They didn't seem particularly nice men."

"They were trying to heavy me. Fat chance. I know nothing about it, except in principle. They've been after me about accessing the Bank's records." Steenvater paused. "You know, I wonder if we were the only bank? We can't have been. Though--" He thought for a while. "Yes, they would have had to have had someone inside. Maybe it was just us. Anyhow." He smiled. "Nothing for us to worry about."

"But why say we went to Omelets?"

"That was a mistake. I just didn't want this to come up."

"A mistake? Lying to the police? You know what you have to do?"

"What?"

"Ring that detective and tell him you made a mistake."

Steenvater went red in the face, thought about it. Then he said, "Yes, dear."

26

Earlier that Sunday morning there had been a buzz on the Steenvater's intercom.

"Yes?"

"Mr. Steenvater? It's Joe and Pete here. We need to speak."

"Why are you here? This is my home. How did you get my address? Come to my office tomorrow."

"This is important. And we don't want to be seen at your office."

"We could meet somewhere else."

"We need to see you now."

"What about my wife?"

"You ain't got a study?" Geronimo said.

"Okay. Okay. I'll come down to let you up in the lift. Are you in the Lobby?"

"Basement 1, it says here."

"Okay."

The lift arrived at level 23 and Steenvater and the two Americans got out. Steenvater gestured for them to follow him into his apartment. He led them into his study. A moment later Veronica put her head through the door.

"I thought I heard — oh, hello. I'm Veronica Steenvater." She extended her hand.

"Please to meet you. I'm Joseph," the shorter man said, without giving his surname.

"I'm Pete," the other said. He also shook her hand.

She stared at them, then asked, "Would you like a cup of tea or coffee?"

"No, we're fine, dear," Steenvater said, cutting off Pete who was about to ask for a coffee. "We just have a little business to discuss. It won't take long."

Veronica nodded and closed the door.

"Well, gentlemen, take a seat," Steenvater said, indicating two chairs. "What's so urgent?"

"It's Antwerp," Joe said.

"What about him?"

"We think he's close to a breakthrough. With the coding. He called us and said he was visiting you. He come to see you last night?"

"What if he did?"

"Did he find the accounts?"

"It seems he has. At least he said he's identified them."

"Well then?"

"He left in a hurry."

"He doesn't think he can cash in on this without us, does he?"

Steenvater looked at them both, made a decision. "He did offer to cut me in. And you out."

"What do you mean?"

"Just what I said. He's going to fly back to the States, and access the cash. He said he doesn't need you anymore."

"He won't get far," Pete said. "He ought to know by now. What an asswipe."

Joe nodded. "We'll see to that."

"We still need him, don't forget. Without him none of us gets anything," Steenvater said.

"Shit," Joe said.

27

BROTHERS AND MCTEISH ARRIVED at Boojums a few minutes before 10:30 and sat facing the door at a table towards the back. From there they had a clear view of everyone coming in. There were only three other customers. Dalmatico arrived shortly after. He looked around, and McTeish stood up, waved him over.

"Hello. I'm Constable Carol McTeish. We spoke on the phone. And this is Sergeant Graham Brothers." They shook hands, and he joined them at the table.

"Thanks very much for agreeing to see us, Mr. Dalmatico."

"Please call me Steve."

"Steve. What would you like? Tea? Coffee?" she asked.

"Just water."

"A flat white for me, Carol," Brothers said.

She went to the counter and ordered, then came and sat down.

They sat looking at each other for a time.

"I think I know what this is about," Dalmatico said. He seemed at ease, and looked at both of them in turn.

"Yes?" Brothers said.

"Deirdre Makepeace? The missing man?"

"Well, yes," Brothers said. "How did you know?"

"I caught up with Deirdre. She told me all the gories."

"We'd like to ask you a few questions, Mr. Dalmatico."

"Steve. Sure. If I can help."

A waiter arrived carrying a tray with two coffees, three glasses and a bottle of water.

"Who's the skinny latte?"

McTeish nodded.

"And the flat white?"

Brothers pointed at the table in front of him.

"Then the water is for you." He placed a glass in front of Dalmatico and poured water into it, leaving the other two glasses and the bottle on the table.

"Thanks," Brothers said. After the waiter left, he asked, "So, how do you know Ms Makepeace?"

"I met her last Saturday night, at a party, in town."

"At Glimmers?"

"Yes. It was a Christmas party—hosted by Pink Mustard. We deal with them at the club."

"And you met Ms Makepeace there?"

"Yes. We had a chat."

"Just a chat?"

"Yes—we arranged to talk later. In fact, we were going to swap phone numbers."

"Going to swap numbers?"

"She said she had to go to the Ladies, and I never saw her again. That is, not that night."

"So you hadn't known her before?"

"No. As I said, we met at the party. We just talked."

"And did you leave together?"

"No. After she went to the Ladies, I didn't see her."

"When was that, when she left you?"

"I don't know. About 10:00ish, I suppose. Maybe 10:30."

"And what time did you leave?"

"Shortly after that. I may have stayed another ten or twenty minutes."

"But you did meet up afterwards?"

"Yep—but not that night. She rang me on Monday. We had a coffee."

"And?"

"And we had dinner last night, too."

"So what did she say?"

"She told me the whole thing. She was pretty calm about it, considering. It was only a couple of days later, I suppose. But she was bewildered by it all. Actually, bamboozled is a better word. She just doesn't understand what happened. I got her to tell me, and she doesn't even remember leaving the party, let alone getting home. And then waking up with, you know. The body. Actually, she got a bit distressed, now I come to think about it."

"Distressed? Or calm?"

"Well. She was calm most of the time. She did cry at one stage. But she certainly didn't go to pieces. This was over the coffee we had on Monday. Then, in fact, she invited me to dinner so we could discuss it further."

Brothers glanced at McTeish, who was staring at Dalmatico. He raised an eyebrow.

"And was that last night?"

"Yes. She cooked a meal."

"And then you left?"

"Yes, then I left," Dalmatico said. He seemed a bit peeved. "Of course I left. What do you take me for?"

"So, just so I get this straight. You hadn't met her before last Saturday, she rang you on Monday, you met for coffee and then had dinner last night? And then left?"

"That's right."

Brothers stared at Dalmatico for a time.

"Why did she ring you on Monday?"

"She said she remembered talking to me at the party. And she thought I might have noticed something."

"Noticed something? But you'd just met. Why ring you?"

"She said that's about all she could remember from the party—talking to me. She thought I might know when she left, or whether she left with anyone. She said also someone might have spiked her drink."

"Spiked her drink?" McTeish repeated.

"Not me! She was trying to understand why she couldn't remember anything."

"Apart from talking to you."

"Well, yes."

"Was she drunk?"

"Not that I noticed. Not particularly. We certainly had a few. I think she was drinking champagne. Oh, we had a couple of vodka shots. She might have been a little tipsy. It was a Christmas party after all. But she wasn't legless or anything."

"Is there anything else you can tell us?"

"She's pretty upset by it all. She doesn't necessarily show it. She's worried it might happen again."

"What, wake up with another dead man?" Brothers said. McTeish winced.

Dalmatico rolled his eyes. "She's worried she might be in danger."

"Of course," McTeish said. "That would be natural."

"I told her that it was unlikely—unlikely that there'd be another dead body. Or that she was in danger."

"Why was that?" McTeish said.

"I wanted to reassure her, for God's sake. And also, I don't think there will be another dead body. Do you?"

Brothers shrugged. "Unlikely."

"Is there anything else I can help you with?"

"I think that's all for the moment. Thank you, Steve, for your help. If you can think of anything that might help, please call me." Brothers gave him his card.

28

NGUYEN AND BROTHERS WENT to see Superintendent Forell, and outlined where they were with the case. Forell listened calmly. She picked up some papers on her desk, lined them up and put them down next to a pad.

"So," she said. "We have the body in a Beemer. A guy in Sydney and two women in the States who are related to the body. And no one at the bar, what was it called?"

"Glimmers," said Brothers.

"Yes, Glimmers. Ever been there?" Forell glanced at both of them. They shook their heads. "Worth putting your head in. Not bad for a bar. Excellent range of single malts." She glanced down at the pad she had made notes on. "Anyway, no one at Glimmers saw Makepeace leave. And this Steve Dalmatico has caught up with her since. Am I missing anything?"

"The Steenvaters, Boss," said Nguyen. "There is definitely something strange going on there, with Steenvater letting the two guys into the lift, the same ones who later took the body, and drove off with it in the BMW. The stolen BMW."

"Seems to me the two women in the States need following up. If we can find who the stiff was, that'll give us more leverage on the Steenvaters."

Forell gazed at the ceiling, and Nguyen and Brothers said nothing.

"Mmm. As you said, worth talking to the Steenvaters again, anyhow. But these women in the States, what are their names?" She glanced down. "Ah yes, Maria Antwerp and Jelena Smith."

She pondered. Nguyen knew better than to interrupt her musings.

"A phone call could be problematic." She puckered her lips on the word problematic, making a slight plosive popping sound. "Phone calls won't work. They won't get us anywhere. Face to face is much better." She thought for a time. "I suppose we could call on a favour from our mates over there, get them to go talk to them. But—" She thought some more. "No. I think one of you will need to go as well. We need to be there, to talk to the women. We don't want to use up all our favours with our mates, do we? And certainly the courts will prefer if one of us takes the evidence."

She glanced across at them. Both were smiling.

"But only one of you. You hear?"

"Okay, Sup. We hear you," Nguyen said. "One of us. If we can find out who that sucker was …"

"Exactly. This is a most … odd matter. Who knows what we'll uncover? But first, the Steenvaters."

29

"THERE'S A CALL FOR you, Winner. Guess who?" Brothers called to Nguyen. Nguyen put his head out of his office.

"Who?"

"Henry Steenvater."

"I'll take it in here."

Brothers transferred the call.

"Hello. Detective John Nguyen."

"Er, hello, Detective. This is Henry Steenvater. I need to talk to you."

"What's this about?"

"Can we meet?"

"Sure. We can come around. To your office?"

"No, no. My home will be fine."

"When's a good time?"

"How about this afternoon? Does that suit?"

Nguyen had nothing else planned that he couldn't move, and they agreed to meet at 4:00pm.

"Graham. Can you come with me? To see the Steenvaters?"

"WHY DO YOU RECKON he rang us?" Brothers asked Nguyen, as he drove them to The Belvedere.

"We'll find out soon enough. But it makes it easier for us, doesn't it."

"How do you mean?"

"He's wanting something from us. It makes it easier for us to get something from him."

"Winner."

"What?"

"What do you reckon they did with the body? In the car."

"Maybe that's something we can ask Mr. Steenvater. They must have dumped it somewhere. Which reminds me—have we had any reports of where the Beemer went?"

"Nothing that I've seen or heard so far. If it travelled on the freeway, the cameras will have picked it up, but I haven't been informed. Maybe it's somewhere north of the city."

Brothers struck it lucky as they approached The Belvedere. A car pulled out and he pulled in and parked. Nguyen pushed the intercom button for the Steenvaters.

"Ah, Detective, Sergeant. I'll come right down to let you up."

They took the lift to the top floor and Steenvater opened the door to his penthouse.

"Please come in. Sit down." He gestured to the study they had sat in on their first visit. Veronica Steenvater appeared, her face tight and anxious.

"Would you gentlemen like tea or coffee?"

"Coffee, please," Nguyen said.

"How do you take it? We have an espresso machine."

"With milk, please. No sugar."

"The same, please," said Brothers. She relaxed and bustled off.

"Now, Mr. Steenvater," Nguyen began.

"Henry. Please call me Henry."

"Okay, Henry. You said you wanted to talk?"

"Yes. I wasn't completely frank with you the other day."

Nguyen looked at him, saying nothing.

"Yes, we didn't actually go to Omelets Are Us that morning."

"Well why did you say you did?"

Veronica Steenvater appeared with a tray and four coffees.

"Here we are," she said with a bright smile, and handed them out. She sat down, her face expectant.

"Thank you, Mrs. Steenvater. Your husband was about to tell us why you both lied about going to Omelets Are Us." Her face dropped.

"It was me, not Veronica. She didn't lie."

"Well, she didn't correct you. That sounds to me like obstructing justice."

"Yes, but I was the one who said we'd been there."

"Well, why did you lie?"

"I don't know. It was stupid. I had some visitors, and they had nothing to do with any missing man. They were here to see me on business. We had been going to go to the Omelets place, but when they arrived we didn't. I just thought they were a red herring."

"A red herring?" Nguyen glanced at Brothers, who sat, his face impassive. Steenvater said nothing.

"Why a red herring?"

"They came on bank business. I didn't think you'd be interested in them. They had nothing to do with a missing man. A dead man."

"And what did they want, these businessmen? On bank business?"

"Just business."

"What sort of business?"

"To do with the bank."

"And they came on a Sunday morning—do you usually have bank meetings on Sunday mornings?"

"From time to time. They were from the States, and that time suited them."

"Well, think of this. Maybe they aren't a red herring? Maybe they are involved."

"What do you mean? It was purely bank business."

"What sort of bank business?"

"Well, that's confidential. I can't discuss it."

"Mr. Steenvater, this is a murder enquiry."

"Murder? You think it was murder? You said you were investigating the death of a missing man. So now it's murder?"

"It could be. Why do you think they put the dead man in the boot of a car?"

"What? Put a dead man in the boot of a car? Who ..." his voice trailed off.

"Your visitors. I don't think they were much of a red herring, were they?"

"I don't understand," Steenvater said. "They put a dead man into the boot of their car?" His voice rose.

"Henry," Veronica said.

"What?"

"Hadn't you better tell them?"

Henry made an exasperated motion with his hand.

"Yes, Henry. Hadn't you better tell us?" Nguyen said.

"I don't understand what this missing man has to do with anything. Or my visitors. Why would they put a body in a car?"

Neither Nguyen nor Brothers spoke.

Steenvater breathed in deeply, then exhaled with a sigh. "They came to see me about some missing money."

"What missing money?"

"It's to do with the Millennium Bug."

"The Millennium Bug?" Nguyen and Brothers looked puzzled. "What's the Millennium Bug? And what's that to do with a missing dead man?"

"It's complicated," Steenvater said. "Look, remember the late 90s? Well, we were all worried that when 2000 rolled around, the computer software would freeze—the programs wouldn't know whether the date was 2000 or 1900."

"What do you mean?"

"Since COBOL and the other commercial software started back in the 60s, dates were only entered with the last two digits. So 1991 was 91, or 1975 was 75. But come the year 2000, the software might revert to 1900 rather than to 2000? You see what I mean?"

"I understand that—but so what? Nothing happened. The world went on," Nguyen said.

"Only because we fixed it."

"Okay, so you all fixed it. Thanks for the reminder. But what has that to do with the missing man, the dead man?"

"That's where it gets complicated." Steenvater explained how it was thought that somehow someone had used the confusion about the Millennium Bug to strip a cent from each banking transaction.

"A cent, eh? Not the biggest deal. Did you report this to the police?"

"Each cent adds up. What's the expression? Look after the pennies and the pounds look after themselves?"

"Your point being?"

"Our bank does millions of transactions a day. That adds up."

"A million cents is just ten grand," Brothers said.

"Yes, Sergeant. Thank you. That's correct."

Brothers smiled.

"But that's per day. And it's more like ten million transactions a day. Many of them are just round dollar numbers. But many are not. And that's just our bank. Over a couple of weeks that could be more than a million dollars. Over a hundred banks that's tens of millions. In fact I reckon someone's got away with over a billion."

Nguyen and Brothers said nothing. Then Nguyen said, "Who did this? Wouldn't people notice? Are you serious, about a billion dollars?"

"When you buy something for $9.98, you probably expect to be charged $10. There's two cents worth. A billion is just a rough estimate. Could be less, could be more."

"So where do you come in?"

"The thing is, the guys who visited me think the money is still out there somewhere, sitting in a bank account. They think I can help trace where it is."

"Are they right?"

"Good Lord no. It was done years ago. The money would have been coded to slip into some account, then another, perhaps several. I don't know if other banks were affected, but why would someone stop at one?"

"Would it be an inside job?"

"It must have been—how else could someone divert the cents? Someone must have changed the computer code."

"And who might that be? Could it have been an IT expert? Could it have been you?"

"That's what the Yanks want to know. I can tell you it wasn't me. Let me ask you a question, Detective. Do you think that if I had stolen a billion dollars back in 2000 I'd still be here, working for Cambridge Bank?" He shook his head.

Nguyen considered this. "So, if I understand you aright, these men— what were their names?"

"Joe—Joseph Stevenson, and Peter Knight."

Nguyen raised an eyebrow. Brothers frowned.

"These men, then, think you know where the money is, or, maybe, know how to trace it?"

"The latter. Trace it. As head of IT, they think I can authorize the appropriate traces."

"And can you?"

"In theory, yes."

"Why not in practice?"

"It would be very complicated, after all this time."

"Complicated?"

"It would be a major operation. I'd need a team."

"And the dead man?"

"I know nothing about that, nothing at all." He stared at his wife, who sat up, smiled.

"Would anyone like a second cup of coffee?" she asked, glancing at both policemen and her husband. Each shook his head. She sighed and remained seated.

"So how did these Americans get in touch with you?" Nguyen stressed the word 'Americans'.

Steenvater looked pained.

"They sent me a message—wanted to see me."

"How did they 'send you a message'?"

"On my phone."

"Tell me, Henry, why did you, a very senior banker, agree to see them?"

"I saw no harm in it. I thought I could explain that they were on a wild goose chase."

"Can I see the message?"

Steenvater put his hand in his pocket, froze, then took out his phone. He called up his messages and scrolled down.

"Here." He handed Nguyen his phone.

Mr. Steenvater, we need to speak to you. Just a few minutes. This Sunday morning.

Who are you?

It's about the Millennium Bug.

Who are you? Why do you want to see me?

A reminder. It's in your interests.

"Hmm," Nguyen murmured. "And this was enough to get you to agree to see them?"

"Frankly, I was intrigued."

"What aren't you telling us, Mr. Steenvater?"

"Nothing. That's it."

"You do know it's a serious crime to withhold information from us, particularly in a murder case?"

"I'm not withholding information."

"You haven't told us why would they put a dead man into the boot of their car. Strange behavior for bankers, don't you think?"

"I have no idea why they would do that. I didn't even know they had done that, till you told me." He was white in the face.

"We may need to question you again, Mr. Steenvater." Nguyen stood up, and Brothers followed suit.

"Good afternoon to you both," Steenvater said, and led them to the door.

In the lift down, Brothers said, "What a liar!"

Nguyen grinned.

"He'll be shitting himself. He knows we don't believe him."

"Yeah, well, give him enough rope … . By the way, did you notice Mrs. Steenvater?"

"What about her?"

"She's clearly not comfortable. We'll need to speak to her separately. She knows something, too."

"Those guys, the yanks who called in, Stevenson and Knight, they must have something on him. Do you reckon he did a few dodgy things back in the day? Or more recently?"

"As he said, if he had the money, he wouldn't still be working for the bank. He may well have skated close to the edge earlier on. And why wouldn't the bank want to trace transactions from back then? They'd have a chance to get the money back. But why now? I reckon we just let them simmer for a while. With Stevenson and Knight, we've got enough to give the boss now to get the US trip okayed. We know they stuck the dead man in their car. The stolen car. Though he did seem surprised they did that. I'm not completely sure he knew."

"And will you be going to the States?" Brothers grinned.

"I hope so."

30

SUPERINTENDENT FORELL GAZED ACROSS her desk at Nguyen, who sat in a chair facing her.

"So," she said, in her quiet even manner. "You've got the Steenvaters up to something, a possible billion dollars in play, two Americans who were caught on video surveillance putting a dead man into the boot of their car, and two could-be relations in the US. Why don't I feel happy?"

Nguyen said nothing.

"You got nothing from this footballer?"

"Nothing, except he's interested in Ms Makepeace."

"And remind me, how do we know the guy in her bed was a stranger?"

"She said so."

Forell made no comment but stared at Nguyen.

"Well, I believe her."

"And do you believe that the footballer had nothing to do with her getting home? Or that he didn't know the mystery guy?"

Nguyen reflected. It was always interesting to see the Super's reaction to whatever answer you gave.

"I think the guys who dropped in on the Steenvaters are the more likely path to follow. They did, after all, put the body in the car. And if what Steenvater says is true, there could be a very big payoff for us, if we find out who the stiff was."

Forell grimaced.

"The body, I mean."

"Yes—and you say the DNA is linked to these two women in the States."

"That's right. And the donut, too." She grimaced again. "Though of course that's a blank for the moment."

"Okay—make arrangements with our liaison people, with LA and New York. Set up meetings. A quick trip, Detective. Can you do both in a week?"

Nguyen thought for a second. "Yes, boss. The sooner the better, eh?"

"And will Sergeant Brothers be able to keep going at this end?"

"Yes. He's got the help of a young constable, Carol McTeish. She seems competent. And certainly keen."

"McTeish. Do I know her?"

How the hell would I know, Nguyen thought.

"She's helping us, Brothers and me. You suggested getting uniform to help. She's doing a good job. Do you want to meet with both of them before I go?"

"A group meeting? Not a bad idea. Set it up once you've fixed the travel arrangements. And Nguyen."

"Yes?"

"Send the CCTV footage across to our colleagues in the States—the two yanks, what were their names, Stevenson and Knight. Maybe someone over there might recognize them."

Nguyen called Brothers and McTeish together.

"We've got the go ahead from the boss."

"The go ahead?"

"For the US trip."

"That's great. Fantastic. You say we. Who for?" said Brothers.

"I'll be going," Nguyen said.

"Yeah. Okay. Of course." Brothers smiled.

"We need to get in touch with our US colleagues. Through the liaison office. I'll find out what we need to do. Then, Carol, once we have the dates, can you please organise the travel."

"Sure thing, boss. Who do I book it through?"

"The admin people. I'll email you the authority, once we know when and where. And we need to send the images from the CCTV footage across, too. The characters might be known."

31

Steve rang Deirdre.

"Hi there."

"Who's calling?"

"It's me, Steve."

"Oh, Steve. Hi. How are you?"

"Good—thanks for dinner last night."

"No problem. You seemed to leave a bit quickly."

"What? Oh. Yep. I suppose I did. Listen. Can we meet?"

So he still wants to see me. "Okay. When?"

"Are you still off work?"

"Yes. For the rest of the week."

"Then could we meet tomorrow morning? At say, Sixpence?"

Deirdre thought about that. "Okay."

"Would 10 be okay?"

"Yes. That's fine."

"See you then."

He hung up.

Deirdre wondered what was going on? Yes, she liked Steve. But he seemed to be blowing hot and cold. Maybe she was expecting too much.

Thursday

32

STEVE WAS AT SIXPENCE when Deirdre arrived, and he jumped to his feet, kissed her on the cheek, and stood looking at her. She smiled up at him.

"Thanks for coming."

They sat down. The waitress came over, and Deirdre nodded to her. "A latte, please. And some water."

Steve ordered the same.

"The police came to see me yesterday," Steve said. "They asked how I knew you, why you rang me on Monday."

"And?"

"I just thought you should know."

"Know what?"

"That the police are talking to people at the party."

"Well, that's good, isn't it? Maybe they'll find out something. Or someone."

The waitress brought the coffees and water.

"Did you call the detective?" Steve asked. "About whether there was a car used to get the body away?"

"Not yet. I didn't see much point, to be honest. What could he tell me, anyway?"

"I suppose."

"Steve." She stopped, then continued. "What's going on? You have been really helpful. But then you left suddenly, and now you're friendly again."

"Well, I am friendly."

"Is that all it is, friendly?"

"Look, as a former footy player, I have to be careful."

"What do you mean?"

"Lots of people just want me because of the footy. They don't see me. Who I am! They just see a footballer, and one that was famous—well, semi-famous. I am not being obnoxious. I was a good player, and noticed, so the fame, well it made me a target."

"But I'm not into footy. I told you that."

"I know. That's something I like about you. And you're a bit hard to read, too."

"Hard to read? I've just had the most bizarre experience in my life. Horrific. And you reckon I'm hard to read."

"Are you in a relationship?"

"What?" Deirdre laughed. "I don't do relationships."

"Why not? I mean, I'm not in one either." He looked down at his hands. "But what's your excuse?"

Deirdre gazed at him, a smile on her lips, as he looked up. "I do have my reasons."

"Well, let's just say I do, too. I've also learnt the hard the way." He paused. "Look. It's probably none of my business, but what did you learn, the hard way?"

She looked at him again. He did seem serious, concerned.

"I'm just busy with work. I don't have time for a relationship."

"I'd like to see you."

"You are seeing me. Right in front of you."

"I mean, get to know you better. This, what did you call it, bizarre thing has brought us together. I like you."

"Is that what you like? The bizarre?"

Steve slumped in his chair, picked up his coffee and sipped. "That's not what I mean."

"Sorry. I'm being a bit prickly."

"That's okay. Look, the police are interviewing everyone at the party. Maybe they will find out if someone left with you. But I didn't get the impression they were all that hopeful. That's why it might still be worth your while to call that detective, whatshisname, Nguyen?"

Deirdre felt conflicting feelings. She did like Steve, but did she want to start anything, even a brief fling, right now? Yes, you do, she told herself. No, you don't, she reminded herself.

"Deirdre?"

"Yes? What?"

"You seem to be away with the pixies."

"It's just I'm still confused about everything."

Steve took a deep breath. "Tell me about yourself. What do you do?"

"I'm in IT—Bank of Ballarat."

"What does that mean?"

"Well, website stuff. Transactions. Cyber security. You know, IT."

"How did you get the job?"

"Are you saying I'm not qualified?" She laughed. "Or a woman can't get a job in IT?"

"No. Not at all." He laughed too; she liked his laugh. "Nothing like that. I'm just curious, that's all. It must have been really hard to get it. A lot of competition."

She thought about it. "Actually, I was recommended by a friend. Adam Mendoza. I think you know him."

"From Pink Mustard, the guy who had the party at Glimmers?"

"That's the one."

"He invited me, too."

"Well, I used to work for him. This job came up. The bank asked did he know anyone. That was about it. I went in for what they called a chat. And it was just a chat. I suppose checking me out. You know, interpersonal skills. Then I was appointed."

"How long have you been there?"

"About two, no three years. What about you?"

"Well." Steve paused. She could see the wheels turning. "As I said before, I'm doing marketing at the Saints."

"I mean, how did you get that job?"

"After I retired from playing, the Club wanted me to stay on. They knew and trusted me. I was still part of the Saints family. And I'd done some marketing studies in the last years I was playing. I fitted in with what they wanted."

"And you're not with anyone at the moment?" Deirdre laughed at his expression. "Sorry—is that a bit too personal?"

"No. I mean, yes. It is a bit personal. But, no, I'm not with anyone at the moment. Apart from sitting here with you." He grinned.

She reached out her hand and put it on his.

"I'm not sure if I want a relationship right now, but I really like talking to you. Can we be friends, sort of?"

He turned his hand over and held hers.

"Yep. Sort of, eh?"

"You know what I mean."

"You're really not into relationships, are you. You don't want to be?"

"Too busy."

"But you work at a bank. Pretty nine to five isn't it?"

"Nine to five? You've got to be joking. More like seven to seven, when it's busy. And it's usually busy. That's why I'm too busy for a relationship."

"Have you ever had one, a relationship, I mean?"

"Not for a long time." Deirdre thought of Antony, what was it, six years ago? That hadn't ended well. "As I said, work keeps me pretty busy." She sipped her coffee. He was looking at her with a slight smile on his face. "And you? You say you're not in a relationship?" she asked. The phrase was so cumbersome. "Sounds like you might want to be in one." She smiled at him.

"No. I'm not in a relationship. And to be truthful, I'm not really looking for one. So, like you say, let's be friends."

"You've been in one, though?"

"Well, yes." Steve looked glum for a moment, then smiled at her again. "But not for a time. You may not understand it, but as I said before, as a footballer you get all sorts wanting to be with me—but it's their idea of me. They don't see the real me. Footballers can be trophies." He broke off, then said, "I'm not into any of that." He paused. "Anyhow, I just wanted to check up how you were. What with the police and everything."

"Thanks." She looked at him. "Thanks. Thanks for listening to me."

"Look, I've got to go now. Sorry about that. Don't take it the wrong way. It's work. But fancy a movie?"

"When?"

"I don't know. Tomorrow night?"

Deirdre waited a couple of seconds, then said, "Yes. That would be great. What film?"

"There's a Korean movie at the Astor—The Host. Have you seen it?"

"I haven't even heard of it. Korean, you say?"

"South Korean. It's sort of a comedy, sort of science fiction, according to the reviews."

"Okay, then. It might take my mind off things."

"It's on at 7:30pm. Shall I pick you up at say 7:00?"

"You don't want a bite first?"

"We could go to a place nearby. Hanoi Hanna is pretty good. How about 6:00 then?"

"Sounds like a plan."

They stood up to leave. Steve kissed Deirdre on the cheek. Despite his comments she felt tense and a little anxious, and had to force a smile. Did she want a relationship after all? "See you tomorrow," she said.

He smiled at her and strode out of the cafe, leaving her feeling annoyed at herself. She was the one after all who had insisted on them just being friends. And yet she really liked him. It was bewildering. Was a relationship really that terrifying?

Friday

33

DEIRDRE HAD BEEN ANTSY all day. Admit it, she told herself. You're anxious. Why was she feeling jumpy? It was just a guy, for goodness sake. And here she was, dressed up ready and waiting for Steve. Finally. he buzzed her intercom just after 6 on Friday.

"I'll be right down."

She grabbed a coat, checked herself in the mirror, then left her apartment.

Steve was dressed in jeans and an open-necked shirt. He gave her a hug and kissed her on the cheek. Again, Deirdre felt uncomfortable— why, she wasn't sure. Was he taking her for granted? But all he was doing was the standard greeting to a friend. Hug and kiss. And hadn't she agreed to be just friends?

His car was out the front, and they got in. Steve looked at her before starting the engine.

"Are you okay?"

"Yes. I'm fine." She shook her head. "It's just been pretty full on. A pretty crazy time."

"Of course. Sorry."

She smiled, but it was a bleak smile. "Let's go, shall we?"

"O-kay," Steve said, drawing out the last syllable.

He drove in silence to Chapel Street, and found a parking spot outside the Red Stitch theatre company, opposite the Astor.

"We can walk down to Hanoi Hanna from here," he said.

They walked in silence. Deirdre felt—what? On edge. She felt her heart beating. Why was she feeling so uptight?

"Steve —"

"Deirdre —"

They both spoke at once.

Deirdre smiled.

"Sorry, Steve, if I'm being awful."

"What? Don't be silly."

She grabbed him, kissed him on the lips, clung to him. The kiss went on, until Deirdre broke away.

"Phew!" she said.

Steve kissed her again, folding his arms around her. She hugged him to her.

"Let's forget the movie," she said.

He looked at her, smiled. "Okay."

"And Hanoi Hanna."

"Okay."

"Let's go back to my place."

The drive back was also silent. Deirdre kept glancing at Steve, and reddened. He smiled at her.

They parked, and rushed to the lifts. He kissed her in the lift, and she kissed back.

She fumbled for her keys, then led him to her bedroom, where they started to strip off their clothes.

She slipped out of her dress, and was undoing her bra as Steve stepped out of his jeans, and pulled down his boxers. His penis sprung up.

Steve pulled her undies down, kissing her, then her breasts.

They fell on the bed.

He entered her at once, and she moved with him, clasping her to him. About a minute later he came, and lay on her, still inside.

"Gosh," she said.

He murmured something.

"What was that?"

"Nothing. Just, wonderful. You are wonderful."

She moved her hips a little to get more comfortable, and felt him stiffen inside her. This time they moved slowly, and she closed her eyes as she met his thrusts with her own.

"God, you're beautiful," he muttered, licking a nipple.

She felt a surge of desire and held him to her and ground against him.

This time she felt release herself, as Steve came again.

He rolled off her, keeping a leg over hers and his arm under her neck.

"Just a sec," she said, easing the arm out so she could rest her head on the pillow.

She smiled and kissed him again.

"Wow."

"Yes," Steve said. "Wow."

He placed a hand on her crotch.

"Yes," he said, and smiled.

"What?"

"You don't shave down there."

They lay there for a time, their breathing slow and synchronized with each other. Maybe she napped for a little.

Half asleep, she felt Steve turn his head to face her.

"Feeling hungry now?"

She yawned, smiled at him.

"For food, I mean."

"Yes, that too."

He closed his eyes and she looked at him. A fit, healthy man lying next to her. And he was thoughtful, too. She did like him. She hummed to herself.

"Steve?"

He opened his eyes.

"Mmm?"

"We could order Hanoi Hanna take away. They deliver to South Melbourne."

He grinned.

She got up, gave his penis a light pinch and googled the restaurant.

"What would you like?"

"I think they've got a prawn and noodle dish. Maybe some spring rolls. Whatever. You choose."

He closed his eyes.

She placed the order and paid with her card; it would take about 35 minutes.

She looked again at the now sleeping Steve, smiled and snuggled down next to him.

The next thing, she heard the intercom buzzer. She got up and found her clothes on the floor, pulled her dress and undies on.

"I'll be right down," she said.

The delivery guy was waiting with the food in white plastic bags, and when she returned she put out two plates and knives and forks. She took off her dress and grabbed her dressing gown.

"Wake up, sleeping beauty," she called.

Steve turned over on the bed.

She went over and turned his head, kissing him.

"Mmm. What?" he said.

"Dinner is served."

"What? Oh." He smiled up at her, sat up and walked naked to the table.

The food was delicious.

Steve kept looking at her. She saw her dressing gown had fallen open. Was her belly fat? He wasn't looking at her belly. She pulled the gown close.

"Aww," he said.

She looked at him, not saying anything, then stood up and let the dressing gown drop to the floor. She liked the way he gazed at her.

She moved around behind him and put her hands on his shoulders, kissing him on the neck.

He turned and stood up too. She felt his arousal.

"Come back to bed," he said. "Is it too soon?"

She shook her head and, not letting him go, they half walked, half stumbled back to the bed, Steve lying heavily on her.

She pushed him off onto his back, and ran her left hand down his chest. She raised her head to take a look, then lay back down on him, fondling him.

"Very nice," she murmured.

She smiled again, his penis still in her fingers. She raised herself up and took it in her mouth. It tasted salty, of their bodies, and she licked its head. Circumcised. Interesting. She lay back again, and Steve moved down between her legs, licking with a gentleness that aroused her again. She pulled him up, and he entered her.

Deirdre felt as if all the tension and anxiety of the past week had completely dissipated. After a time Steve said, "Deirdre."

"Yes?"

"I just like saying your name." Then, a little later, "You know, you are full of surprises."

"Surprises?"

He sensed she'd tensed. "In the best possible way." He rolled to face her, kissing her. "That was so special."

She kissed him back. He relaxed, lay back and fell asleep.

Lying there quietly, Deirdre stared at the ceiling, lazy feelings flowing through her. Special? Yes. Very special. Oh God. What would happen now? Stop it, part of herself told herself. Just take it as it comes. She giggled as she realized what she had just half-whispered.

Saturday

34

SHE WOKE, and the bed was empty. Had he left? Without saying anything?

She heard the toilet flush.

He put his head through the doorway.

"Like some coffee?"

She nodded. "The coffee is in the cupboard above the machine."

She stretched. She couldn't stop smiling.

"You want a latte?" he called.

"Yes, please."

She heard the noise of the coffee machine, and the aroma of ground coffee drifted in.

He brought two mugs, and sat on the bed next to her.

"Thanks." She put her arm around his waist, sipped the coffee.

He looked down at her, tousled her hair.

"You still look great."

"What do you mean, still?"

"I mean, in the morning. You look gorgeous. In fact, scrumptious."

Oh oh, she thought, grinning up at him. "Let me finish this first." She sipped the coffee.

"Listen. Sorry. I have to go," Steve said.

"What?" She put down her mug. "You're going?"

"The football—my club is playing today. I have to be there."

"Oh." She tried to keep the disappointment off her face. This is what always seemed to happen, whenever she met someone she liked.

He hugged her.

"Don't worry, you silly. I'll be back." Seeing her face, he added, "If you want me to."

"Okay."

"Okay?"

"I mean, yes."

He kissed her. She forced a smile.

"Did you have anything planned for later today?" he asked.

"I was going to see Fran."

"Fran?"

"My friend. You know. She helped me when —" she gestured vaguely. "Last Sunday. With the body."

"Oh. Of course." He took her left hand in his. "When can I see you then?"

"What time does the game finish?"

"I'll be able to leave after about seven. Will you be finished with Fran by then?"

"Yes, I will. Come around when you're ready. Or I could come to you. Where do you live?"

"I'll come back here. If that's okay. My place is a bit of a mess."

Steve stood up, looked around, then picked up his clothes, scattered on the floor. He smiled at her as he dressed.

"Looks like we were in a rush."

"Yes," she said.

"Deirdre."

She looked up at him.

"I really want to see you again. It's just, you know. It's my job."

"I know." She shook her head.

"You know I would rather stay here with you."

She nodded.

"See you tonight, then," he said. He kissed her again, then opened the front door. She followed him and waited until the lift came. He turned and waved.

"Bye," she said to the closing lift door.

She collected the coffee mugs and put them into the dishwasher. Then she decided to have a shower.

The water took a few moments to get hot, then she stepped in, feeling it sluice through her hair and over her body. She used shampoo, rinsed, rubbed in conditioner. She couldn't work him out. Or was it her? It was completely reasonable to go to work, even if it happened to be the footy. Why was she feeling let down? *Maybe I've been burned too much.*

She stepped out of the shower and dried herself, twirled around and gazed at her image in the mirror.

Not too bad. She smiled at herself. Mouthed a kiss. *Fuck it.*

She dressed, then picked up her clothes from the previous night. She smiled again. *Certainly unexpected.*

She made some toast, and as she munched, she picked up her phone and called Fran.

"Deirdre? Do you realize what time it is?"

Deirdre looked.

"What? It's after 10."

"It's Saturday."

"So?"

"Hey." Fran's voice changed. "What's happened?"

"Nothing."

"Come on, I know you."

"Nothing—well, Steve stayed last night."

Fran let out a squeal.

"He didn't."

"Yes—he's just left. Had to go to the footy."

"I'm coming up."

ABOUT TEN MINUTES LATER Fran buzzed her front door, and Deirdre let her in.

Fran grinned and hugged her, then stood back looking at her.

"Well. What's up? Didn't it go okay?"

"Like a coffee? I'm having another one."

"Okay."

They walked to the kitchen and Fran sat down while Deirdre fiddled with the coffee machine, rinsing out the old grounds and spooning in some fresh grind.

"So, tell all."

"It was great." She tried to smile. "He's great."

"Well why the long face, as the barman said to the horse."

"It's silly, I suppose. It's just that he's gone off to the footy."

"Well he does work for a footy club, doesn't he? And it is Saturday. And they are playing. And he does have to be there, doesn't he?"

"Yes, of course. I know I'm being stupid. I was just hoping to spend time with him today."

"What, he's not coming back?"

Deirdre looked shamefaced.

"Well, yes, he is. This evening. After the footy."

"So?" Fran stood up and hugged her. "He must be okay then. Normally you'd boot them straight out the door."

"It's just I wonder if he's all that interested. That's all."

"Do you see the pattern?"

Deirdre sighed. "Pattern?"

"If you like them, they're not interested. If you don't like them, they are. You're just happiest when you're not happy."

"But, I do like him."

"And why do you think he doesn't like you?"

"Arghhh," Deirdre cried out.

"Exactly."

They finished their coffees in silence.

"Well, got to be going. Let me know what happens."

35

DEIRDRE DECIDED HER FLAT needed a tidy up. She changed the sheets, put the used ones in the washing machine, vacuumed the floors, emptied the dishwasher. Okay, that didn't take too much time. She checked the wall clock—just before 1 pm. Better go to the market to get some food. What would he want to eat? Would he in fact come back after the footy? What did she really know about him, anyway? He'd got what he wanted, hadn't he? Her stomach felt empty, and her pulse was racing. Calm down, she told herself. Calm down. So he's gone to the footy. So what?

She flopped down in a chair, grabbed her phone and rolled down the messages. Nothing of interest. She put the phone down. He'll come back, or he won't, she decided. I have to stop getting in a flap about men. This is why I don't do relationships. But I also have to stop trying to push for something after just one night. Snap out of it.

After talking to herself she felt a little better, and decided to go to the market.

LATER THAT AFTERNOON SHE returned to her apartment with bread, vegetables and some lamb chops. An idea occurred to her and she put on the television. The St Kilda game was on. She watched it for a few minutes, then switched it off. She didn't really understand the game, but she saw they were losing.

She thought about it all. Why was she working herself up? Was Fran right? She phoned her.

"How's it going?"

"Hi Deirdre. What's up?"

"What do you mean, what's up?"

"I can tell from your voice."

"Just felt like a chin wag. What are you up to? Care for a coffee?"

"Sure—want to come down here?"

"Okay. See you in five."

DEIRDRE TOOK THE LIFT to Fran's apartment. Fran took one look and said, "Come on, spit it out."

"What do you mean?"

"Something's eating you. What's he done?"

"Done? Nothing. I mean, he's at work, the footy. He's coming back later."

"We went through this this morning."

"So?"

"So why are you feeling anxious?"

"This seems different. I don't know. I feel on edge somehow." She smiled at Fran, a tight grimace. "Have I made a fool of myself?"

Her question hung in the air as Fran made coffee.

"What, you think I have?" Deirdre asked.

"Don't be a silly. You like him, don't you?"

"Yes." She grinned. Then groaned. "What you said earlier. Maybe that's the problem. I do like him. I mean as a person. I want to get to know him. Not just the sex. Maybe I don't know how."

"Yeah, yeah," Fran said. "Perfectly understandable. It just shows you're feeling vulnerable. You're putting yourself out there. That's never comfortable, is it?" She fixed Deirdre with a look. "Hey. When am I going to meet him?"

"I'm not sure I'm ready for that. I'm going to cook another meal for him this evening." Deirdre stood up and paced around the room. "Maybe you could drop in?" At once she felt better about herself. She sat back down and drank her coffee. She looked at Fran.

"So you'll come up later? Maybe, after dinner—but not too late." She grinned. "Just in case I lose it again. Before we end up in bed. I just want to talk, but just us. I don't think it will happen with you there ..." she let the sentence tail off, looking at Fran with hope.

Fran studied her for a moment, and smiled, then nodded. "Okay. Not too late it is."

"Thanks. Oh—got to go. Steve is supposed to be coming and I still have to cook."

36

STEVE RANG A BIT after 7 pm. "Hi Dee," he said.

Dee? She thought. Hmm.

"Hi Stee," she said.

He laughed. "I'm finished here. We still on? Shall I come around?"

"You'd better," she said, without thinking. "I mean, I've cooked. Lamb chops. Can you bring some wine?"

"On my way." He hung up.

She put on some music and hummed to herself, laying the table.

Some twenty minutes later Steve buzzed at the intercom, and she went down to let him up. He kissed her as he got into the lift, giving her a hug. When they entered her apartment, he put a bottle of wine into her hands. "Will this do?"

She looked at it. Heathcote Shiraz. "Good choice. Um, how was the footy. I saw they were losing."

"You watched?"

"Just a little. You know, footy isn't my thing."

"Yeah, we fought back, but couldn't do it. There's always next week." He kissed her again.

She served the food and they sat looking at each other.

"What?" she said.

"Nothing. A cat can look at a, er, queen, can't he?"

She took a mouthful of mashed potato.

"You look great," he said. He picked up a chop by its bone and took a bite. "You don't mind if I use my fingers? It's a bad habit I've never grown out of."

"Be my guest."

They ate for a time. Then Steve said, "Any thoughts about the situation?"

"Situation? Us?" Deirdre felt her stomach drop.

"No, no—the dead man. We're okay, aren't we?" He stared at her, and she felt herself blush.

"I just hope you're okay with it all. I was thinking, you know, PSD, post whatever, you know, you might still be in shock sort of. I just want to help. If I can."

She breathed a sigh of relief.

"To tell the truth, I do still wonder how he got into my bed. I mean, how did he even get into my flat? Was I that drunk?"

"Have you worked out how you got home?"

"I found a uber receipt on my phone."

"Have you told the police?"

"Should I?"

"Of course you should. You were ... somewhat out of it, weren't you? Whoever drove you is important. Maybe the guy in your bed was the uber driver!"

Deirdre sat stunned. "The uber driver?"

"Forget it. Just a stupid joke. But anyway, the driver will know when you got home. That will help the police understand the timing of it all."

"Steve—" she stopped. She looked at him, noticing his eyes were dark brown with tiny grey specks. "You're right. I will call the police." She stood up, picked up her phone.

"I don't mean right now. It's Saturday night."

"No time like the present. The detective did say to call any time."

"Will he be there?"

"We'll see. I'll call his mobile." She found his card and dialed.

"Detective Inspector John Nguyen." The voice was calm.

"Hello?"

"Who is this?"

"It's Deirdre Makepeace. From Sunday? You said I should ring if I remember anything."

"Yes? Ms Makepeace? How are you? What is it? Has something happened?"

In the background Deirdre could hear baby sounds.

"No, nothing's happened. Sorry to trouble you in the evening, but I've just remembered that I took an uber home after the party. On the Saturday night. I thought I should let you know. I have the receipt. It was emailed to my phone. You should be able to find the driver. Could that be helpful?"

"An uber? Yes it is. That certainly would be helpful. Very helpful, so thank you for calling. And don't worry. My wife is used to me getting calls at all hours. Can you forward me the receipt?" He gave her his email address.

"Sure, will do."

"Do you remember anything about him?"

"Who, the uber driver?"

"Yes. Was the driver a man? Or a woman?"

"Sorry, I don't remember—I just saw this receipt on my phone." She paused. "The man, the body. It couldn't be the uber driver, could it?"

"What on earth makes you think that?"

"Oh, nothing. Just a thought. Forget it."

"No, we'll check it out. We'll get back to you."

She found the email and forwarded it.

Steve came up and hugged her. "Sorry. I shouldn't have raised that."

"No, you're right. I'm glad I rang him. It might help." She breathed deeply. "And it's been good being with you." There, she'd got it out.

He grinned, kissed her again. "Me too. Or maybe that's not the right expression these days."

"What? Oh, yeah."

Her phone rang.

"That was quick," Steve said.

"Hi," said Fran. "I'm outside and wondered if you'd like a drink?"

"It's not the police. It's my friend Fran," she told Steve, and went to the door.

Fran came in carrying a bottle of wine. She had changed her clothes since the afternoon, and wore jeans and a white blouse that, Deirdre thought, accentuated her figure.

"You must be the mysterious Steve," she said, reaching out her hand. "I'm Fran."

"Pleased to meet you. Mysterious? How?"

"Oh, just a figure of speech."

Deirdre saw them assessing each other. "Can I pour you a red?" she said to Fran. "Come and sit down. We've just finished eating." She realized this was a mistake.

"Thanks. Here's a red too, a Pinot Noir." Fran handed over a bottle from the Mornington Peninsula.

Steve sat down next to Deirdre on the couch, and Fran sat facing them.

"Cheers!" They raised their glasses.

"Fran's my best friend," she told Steve. "She helped me when the body was … found."

"Helped get it into the lift!" Fran let out a high-pitched squeal. "Also, washed up the pillow slip. If you ever need a good disposal service …" Fran suddenly stopped. "Sorry. You had to be there."

"How do you feel about it all, now?" Steve asked.

"I worry a bit for Deirdre. There must be some reason she was chosen. But why? A complete stranger."

"We were just talking about it. In fact, Deirdre has sent the details of the uber who drove her home to the police. Maybe that will shed some light on it all."

"Could he have been driven home with you? The dead man, I mean. Did you go anywhere else after the party?" Fran said.

"I just don't know. But if he came home with me, where was his shirt, and why was he dead?" Deirdre was breathing quickly, shallow pants. Steve placed a hand on her knee. She smiled gratefully at him.

"Let's look at this logically," Steve said. "Deirdre, you were either drunk or you were drugged —" Deirdre winced. "Sorry," he said. He grinned. "But you must have been out of it, weren't you?"

After a moment, she nodded.

"And an uber drove you home. Either the dead guy rode with you, or he got in some other way. If he came home with you, it still doesn't explain how he came to be dead. And how he came to be shirtless. So let's assume he didn't come home with you. That doesn't seem likely."

"O-kay," Fran said, drawing out the word.

"So the real question is, how was he able to get inside this apartment."

"And who killed him," Fran said. "Don't forget that. Hey—what if the dead man was the uber driver?" Fran laughed again. It was infectious and Deirdre couldn't help smiling.

Steve looked irritated. "We already talked about that. I presume whoever killed him put him in the bed. That's why I reckon we can rule out a guy coming home with you," he looked at Deirdre. "And rule out the uber driver."

Fran laughed her squeal again. Deirdre could see the thoughts going on in her head. "Why rule out the uber driver?"

"Well, what would be his connection with Deirdre, or with the dead man? I presume it was a male uber driver? Was it?"

"I've no idea," Deirdre said, shaking her head.

"No, probably not. The car would be downstairs somewhere, wouldn't it?"

"If," said Deirdre, "if the uber driver is the dead man, and it's a big if, how come he didn't have a shirt on?"

"Look, let's keep our feet on the ground," Steve said. "It's simply too weird for a uber driver to be killed in your bed. Who killed him? Let's forget the fucking uber driver."

"Right. Not the uber driver," Fran said. "And the dead man didn't come home with you, either, did he? Because someone else killed him." She shuddered in a theatrical way. "Maybe the uber driver did?" She squealed again. "Sorry. I know this isn't a laughing matter—" she burst into laughter again.

Both Deirdre and Steve waited for her to get her breath under control.

"Sorry," she gasped.

Deirdre got up, patted her on the shoulder, sat down again.

After a pause, Deirdre said, "So. Looking at it logically, we can rule out the uber driver, rule out the dead man being in the uber with me, so we're still left with, who is he? Not just who is he, but how did he get in here, into my bed, and who killed him? Where's logic got us?" She looked up at both of them.

"Hmm," Steve said.

Fran had regained her composure and was sipping at her wine. She swallowed and said, "The police will work it out. Won't they?"

"I suppose. It does freak me out, though. What if it happens again?"

"It won't happen again," Steve said.

"How can you be so confident?"

"It's just too weird. The more I think about it, the more it seems a coincidence."

"A coincidence?"

"Wrong man, wrong bed."

"But how did he get in here in the first place?" Despite herself, she started sobbing. Where did that come from? Steve put his arm around her.

"Sorry. I'm sure there's some good explanation—that has nothing to do with you."

She liked his arm around her shoulders, and lent against him.

"Maybe I should change the door lock."

"If it makes you feel better—good idea. I can do that, if you like."

Fran picked up her glass and gestured with it.

"Do you want a top up?" Deirdre said.

"Thanks—I'll get it," Fran said.

She poured wine into each of the glasses, took a sip of hers, and watched Deirdre and Steve for a moment.

"Well, you know what they say about three ..." Fran drained her glass.

"What's that?" Steve said.

"A crowd."

"Don't be silly," Deirdre said.

"No—I'll see you later. Good to meet you, Steve." And she was out the door.

Sunday

37

NGUYEN PHONED THEIR LA contact, a Detective Nat Turner, who told him he had tracked down Maria Antwerp, and confirmed she was recorded as living in Venice Beach. The New York counterpart, Detective April Martinez, had similarly located Jelena Smith, in Brooklyn.

"Hi, Detective, John Nguyen here," Nguyen said.

"Hi John. And remember, you were to call me Nat."

"Okay, Nat. Thanks for doing the ground work for us."

Nguyen gave him an update of the case. Turner listened without comment, until he mentioned the possibility of a billion dollars.

"A billion? Whooh boy! Do you suppose any of that could be over here?"

"Well, it seems like a couple of your citizens are involved." Nguyen explained about the video of the men putting the body into the BMW. "The guys who drove off with the body were American, according to our witness."

"And the DNA of the dead guy is linked to this Maria Antwerp?"

"So Ancestry.com tells us. We thought it best to meet face to face."

"Hold on a sec. I'll check her out—see if she's still living there."

"If she is, I'll be on a plane arriving on Monday morning."

There was a pause, then Turner said, "Okay, give me a few moments, I'll check a few other things. You don't have to come all this way to find out she's not around."

The hold music was the Beatles "Help".

Two or three minutes later, Turner was back on the phone.

"You're in luck. She still lives in the address in Venice Beach that I located, and she's in town."

"How did you find that out so quickly? You must have one hell of a database."

"I rang her."

Nguyen laughed. "That's great. What did you say?"

"Pretended it was a misdial.

"I'm on my way."

He gave Turner the flight details.

"We'll send a car to meet you."

Monday Morning–USA

38

THE FLIGHT OVER WAS in premium economy, so he had a bit of extra leg room, and despite the seats not inclining flat, he had caught some sleep.

Nevertheless he felt a little dazed as he emerged from the baggage area into the LAX arrival's hall trundling his bag, and looked around for his contact. He saw a few people holding up signs with names on them, but none was his. He glanced at his watch. It was just 2:10. The plane had landed early. He looked around again, saw a Starbucks, and bought a coffee. Not up to Melbourne standards, but a step up from the over-brewed stuff he'd had on an earlier trip to the States.

Sipping it, he walked back near the exit doors to the street. Still no sign, as people milled around in a steady stream.

Two police walked in, and Nguyen looked at them with a smile. They strode past him without a glance. Clearly not Nat Turner.

Then he saw a small, wiry man with a baseball cap, holding up a sign with Nguyen written on it. He hurried over.

"Detective Turner?" he said.

"What? No way, man." The man grinned. "He out in the car. Follow me." He didn't introduce himself, and didn't offer to help with his bag. Nguyen followed him.

At the curb was a black and white Ford Interceptor utility. The door opened and a big black man stepped out, hand stretched in greeting.

"Nat Turner."

"John Nguyen." He shook the hand. "Thanks for meeting me."

"How was the flight?" Before Nguyen could answer, Turner continued, "I thought we could call in to see this Antwerp woman on the way—save you some time."

"Well, thanks."

The smaller man who had met Nguyen waited while Turner slipped a note into his hand. He glanced at it. "Thanks, pal. Any time." Then walked off to join three other men who, Nguyen now saw, filled the function generated by the fact that there was no standing at the curb.

"So, the flight?" Turner said, wheeling the car into the traffic.

"It was okay—got a bit of sleep. Saw a couple of movies. We had a tail wind, so we were a bit early."

"And this Antwerp woman—she's linked to your missing man?"

"We sure hope so. If she knows who the match is, we might have the guy."

He told Turner about the dead-end of the possibility in Sydney, with the donut. At Turner's quizzical look, Nguyen explained about the sperm donor business, and Turner laughed.

"Donut, you say? I'll have to think twice now about eating those suckers." He patted his belly, keeping the other hand on the steering wheel. "It won't be too long. She lives fairly close." He started fiddling with the GPS. He keyed in the address as they drove down the Lincoln Boulevard.

"It's Horizon Avenue, right?" Nguyen said. "I haven't been to LA before. Is it far?"

"Pretty convenient. About ten minutes away, now. That's why I thought we'd save time by dropping in before hitting my base."

"Did you get the video we sent?"

"Video?"

"From the CCTV cameras. The two men—Americans who put the body in the boot. Um, in the trunk. We're told their names are Joseph Stevenson and Peter Knight."

"Yes. We've sent them to be checked using the specialist software. Facial recognition. We'll know directly if we know anything about them."

"How soon is that?"

"Depends on how many are backed up in line. It's quick, once they feed it in."

"Has it got, like, priority?"

Turner smiled at Nguyen.

"With a billion dollars, you betcha."

A few minutes later, Turner said, "You mentioned that guy in Sydney. What you called the donut."

"He called himself that."

"Well, in any case, he's linked to this Antwerp woman, isn't he?"

"Yes—through his father, the donor," Nguyen said.

"So, does that mean Antwerp's father is also this guy's dad?"

"Maybe. Or uncle. Or cousin."

"But she's American. So, how did her dad or uncle or cousin or whatever get to donate in Sydney? And if the dead man's American, what's he doing dead in Melbourne?" Turner said.

"That's what we are trying to find out."

Monday

39

THEY DROVE UP TO a two storey house, and parked outside. Nguyen and Turner got out, and Turner knocked on the door. After a few moments, they heard footsteps, and the door was opened.

"Yes?" A woman in her forties peered at them through the grill. Her eyes widened as Turner held up his badge for her inspection. "Police? How can I help?"

"Well ma'am," Turner said. "My colleague here is all the way from Australia, just come to see you."

"Me?"

"Excuse me, ma'am. Are you Maria Antwerp?"

"Yes, that's me."

"I'm Detective John Nguyen, with Victoria Police." At her blank stare he added, "From Melbourne, Australia."

She unlocked the grill. "Come on in. What's this about?"

Maria Antwerp was slim and about as tall as Nguyen, She brushed her hair away from her face as she turned and led them into a large front room, furnished with a couch, armchairs, a Persian rug and a huge flat screen TV. The late afternoon light flooded in through two large windows.

She gestured for them to sit, and looked at Nguyen expectantly.

Nguyen had thought hard about how to explain the situation.

"We're trying to trace a missing man, back in Melbourne, and we wondered whether you have any relatives there. We're hoping there might be a link."

"In Australia? A missing man? My cousin Freddie Antwerp lives in Melbourne. He's the only person I know in Melbourne. Is Freddie missing?"

Nguyen smiled. The trip seemed to be paying off.

"Why are you smiling?" Maria Antwerp asked.

"Sorry. I was just relieved. It may be that your cousin is missing. That's all. Do you have any contact details for Freddie? That's his name, Freddie Antwerp?"

"Yes—Freddie. Let me check his details." Maria Antwerp took out her mobile phone and searched. "Here's his email address."

Nguyen took down the details.

"Do you have a phone number or street address?"

She looked further.

"Yes, I do. He lives in East Melbourne. And here's his cell. It's an Aussie number." And she gave Nguyen the information.

"How long since you have seen him, ma'am?" Turner asked.

"Oh, it must be just last year. I think he was back here, let me see. Actually, we kept in touch last Christmas."

"Was that here, or in Melbourne?"

"Here. In LA."

"Was he here on holiday?"

"No, he was here on business, I think. He'd just got this job down under, and he was back for Christmas. The Aussies seem to have a big break at Christmas. We had a meal together, here in Venice Beach."

"Do you have any other family here?" Nguyen asked.

"No. My parents live in Beverly Hills. We're Hollywood people— except my sister now lives in New York."

"Hollywood people? What does that mean?"

"We're all in the movie business."

"Movies!" Nguyen said. "What do you do?"

"I'm a location manager."

"Oh, you manage properties?"

"No." She laughed. "I find them. For the movies. For television. They all need locations. They come to me."

Maria Antwerp smiled. She seemed happy that Nguyen was confused.

"And what business is your cousin Freddie in? He in movies too?"

"No. Movies? Not Freddie. He's a banker."

"Do you know who with?"

"An Aussie bank. What is it? Like a British university. Cambridge. That's it. Cambridge Bank."

"And does he have family?"

"He's divorced. He has a son and daughter. They're with his ex."

"Are they in Australia, too?"

"No—they live in New York."

"I don't suppose you have their details?"

She checked her phone.

"It's been a while, you know. Sorry, I don't have them."

"Not to worry. Thank you very much. You've been most helpful."

"Hang on a minute," Antwerp said. "Why is he missing? How long for? And how do you know it's Freddie who's missing?"

"We don't know if he is the one who's missing. But now we can check. If he's okay, then he gets eliminated."

"Eliminated?" Antwerp gasped.

"If it's not him, we can rule him out of our enquiries. We have to find out who else it might be."

"But why do you think he's missing? Why come to me—all the way from Australia?"

"There's a DNA link. There's a dead man, and we're trying to identify him."

"A dead man. What about the missing man? You mean there are two men?" She stiffened. "Could I see your identification, please?"

Turner took out his badge.

"Sorry, ma'am. The dead man is the missing man. That's who we're trying to identify."

"Surely someone in Australia can identify him. I don't understand why *you* need to come to LA." She pointed at Nguyen.

"That's the thing. The body has disappeared. But we do have his DNA. And we got a match with yours. Meaning you could be related. If it is Freddie. As I say, we'll check. If he's okay, we'll scratch him from our enquiries."

"How did you get my DNA?"

"Through Ancestry.com. They have your DNA on file."

Before he could finish answering, Maria Antwerp had her phone to her ear.

"I'm calling Freddie," she said.

They watched her. After a minute she put the phone down. She stood up, took a few paces, then sat back down.

"It went to voicemail." She wrung her hands. "Does this mean he could be dead?" she whispered. Her face paled.

"Look, what time is it in Melbourne?" Nguyen checked his phone. "There's about a 17 hour time difference, so it's around 8:00am in Melbourne, tomorrow, Tuesday. If he works for a bank he could be in a meeting. He could be driving. He could be talking to someone else. His mobile phone could be switched off."

"He could be dead." She raised her voice. "What if he's the missing man. The dead man. This is terrible." She shut her eyes, shivered.

"We'll let you know as soon as we find out anything. I'm sorry if this has upset you," Nguyen said.

"What did you expect? Of course I'm upset, if Freddie is dead."

"We don't know that yet. Please be patient."

"Another thing, Ms Antwerp," Turner said. "Did your father ever visit Australia?"

"My father? He went to Sydney in the 90s. He was working on a movie there."

"What did he do?"

"He's a set designer." She smiled, then grimaced.

"Is that how you got into the movie business?"

"I grew up in it. He used to take us onto the sets all the time, when we were young. We got to meet the stars. But why the interest in my dad?"

"He is also a DNA link," Nguyen said.

"But he's alive and well here in LA. He's still very much working."

"He must be Freddie's uncle."

"Yes. He is."

"Thanks for your help, Ms Antwerp."

They both stood up.

"Ma'am, if anything comes to mind, can you please call me?" Turner handed her his card. "Any time."

They left her, slack-jawed, at the door.

Monday late evening–U.S.A.

40

NGUYEN PHONED BROTHERS; accounting for the time difference, it was Tuesday morning in Melbourne.

"Good news, Graham—we may have a match. A Freddie Antwerp. Turns out he's the cousin of Maria Antwerp. And he's a banker. And would you believe it, he works for Cambridge Bank—he joined them about six months ago."

"That's Steenvater's bank. Another thing that fat bastard didn't tell us."

"That's the one. You better talk to him again. But see if you can locate Antwerp—I got his mobile number from Maria. When I tried it, it went to voicemail, so it's possible he's no longer around."

"Maybe it was just switched off, John, or he was in a meeting."

"But it was his DNA in the lift. And his body dumped in the boot of the Beemer. I don't think he is in any meeting. Or if he is, it's not one I'd want to be attending." Nguyen laughed. "Can you check which telco he's with? I'll text you his number."

"Sure, boss. Once we know that, we can find out when he last used it."

"And maybe we can find his phone. It could be with the body. If I'm not getting ahead of myself."

"Okay." Brothers noted the details. "The phone company can tell us that. I'll have to get a warrant," he muttered. "That shouldn't be too hard. And what about the other link, Jelena Smith? Are you still going to speak to her?"

"Is there any point? Though I would like to see New York again."

"Winner. What if Freddie Antwerp turns out to be alive and kicking?"

"What, you reckon he was alive when they stuck him in the boot?"

"Anything's possible, isn't it?"

"I'm still booked to fly to New York tomorrow evening. Seeing that I'm over here, I may as well. And, I reckon we can forget Freddie Antwerp still being alive. I'm hoping Jelena Smith will know more about him, and what he's been up to. It might be a wild goose chase, but we can't overlook the opportunity. And you could be right. Imagine if things went pear-shaped, and I hadn't spoken to Jelena Smith while I was over here."

"Well, I'll check with the telcos about this phone number, and get back to you later today. It'll probably be late, your time, when I call you. That okay?"

"Sure. And I'll let Forell know, too," Nguyen said. He sent a text to Forell that a possible match had been found, and that Brothers was following up the lead.

BROTHERS SPOKE TO MCTEISH, and asked her to research the telecommunication companies. After three searches, she discovered the phone was with Vodafone, and confirmed that Frederick Antwerp lived in East Melbourne. She googled him, and he came up on LinkedIn. She immediately turned to Brothers.

"And the boss was right. He does work for Cambridge Bank!" she called out.

Brothers came over, looked at the screen.

"Well, well, well. This confirms what the Antwerp woman in LA told John. I think Mr. Henry Steenvater has been a naughty boy. Holding back information."

"Do you reckon he knows the dead man is Antwerp?" McTeish said, staring at Brothers. Her eyes gleamed. "In fact, do we know that Antwerp is the guy? I mean, is he even dead?"

"Christ, Carol. Don't ruin a good day! It was his DNA in the lift, wasn't it?"

"So it seems, but don't you think we should check with the bank, in any case? Find out if he's missing? And if so, for how long?"

"Why don't you do just that," Brothers said, somewhat embarrassed that he hadn't thought of that himself.

McTeish checked on Google, then rang Cambridge Bank's general number. After listening for the various options stated by a fake friendly computer voice, she selected button 5 and heard music, then an assurance that the Bank valued customers highly, and an apology for the delay. When the music resumed, she put her phone on loudspeaker and went back to her computer to search more about Frederick Antwerp. The message about valuing customers sounded again, as she saw that Antwerp worked in the IT section, in charge of cyber security.

"Sergeant," she called. Brothers turned to her.

"This Antwerp guy works in cyber security—isn't that what Deirdre Makepeace does, too?"

At that moment the music on her phone chopped off, and she heard a Filipino voice ask how she could help.

Picking up her handset, McTeish said, "Can you please put me through to Mr. Freddie Antwerp. He's in IT."

"Freddie Antwerp? Hold the line, please." The music resumed. "Putting you through now." Then a ringing tone, then:

"This is the voicemail of Freddie Antwerp. Please leave a message after the tone, and I'll get back to you as soon as possible."

"Any luck?" asked Brothers.

"Voicemail." She hung up, cursing under her breath.

"You mentioned cyber security?"

"Yes. Maybe we could ask Ms Makepeace whether she knows him? Small world, and all that."

"Good idea." Brothers halted himself in time from saying, "You're not just a pretty face". Language was so difficult these days. What was the expression—PC? He checked his notebook, then dialed.

"Ms Makepeace? Graham Brothers here. Sergeant Brothers."

"Oh, hello, Sergeant. How can I help you? Have you found out about the uber driver?"

"The uber driver?"

"I emailed the details to Detective Nguyen."

"I haven't got them yet. An uber driver, you say?"

"The one who drove me home that Saturday night."

Nguyen had put that on his list. Shit. "Oh. Yes—we're on to that. Sorry to bother you, but I'm ringing about something else. Can I confirm you work in cyber security?"

"Yes—what's this about then?"

"Do you know the cyber security people at Cambridge Bank?"

"They've got a couple of guys there, I think. I can't remember their names. I may have met them at a conference or somewhere. But I can't recall."

"A Freddie Antwerp?"

"Antwerp? I think that rings a bell. But I can't put a face to the name."

You'd be surprised, thought Brothers—if Antwerp was the guy she had found in her bed.

"You don't have a business card, his number, do you?"

"No. I may have met him, but I can't recall when or where."

"What about Henry Steenvater?"

"Steenvater—he's CTO, isn't he?"

"CTO?"

"Chief Technology Officer—runs the bank's IT."

"That's the one. Do you know him?"

"Not personally. I've seen him speak. You know, at a conference. Why do you want to know? Have they got anything to do with—" she broke off and he heard a faint sob.

"Just making enquiries. Thanks, Ms Makepeace."

"But is he connected to the dead man, the one that went missing?"

"We don't know. I'll let you know when we have something definite."

"Well, okay. Thanks, I suppose. By the way, did you find anything on the video cameras?"

"What cameras?"

"You know, the cameras here at The Belvedere. The ones that monitor the foyer and the basement garage. Did they pick up what happened to the body?"

Brothers thought for a moment. What harm was there in sharing some info?

"Well, we did pick up that the body was taken to the basement and put into a car, and was driven away. But where, we don't know yet."

"So, he was taken away in a car."

"Yes. We're trying to locate it."

"Do you have its number plate?"

"Yes—we know who owns it. But it was stolen."

"Oh."

"If anything else comes to mind about Frederick Antwerp, can you please call me?"

"Of course. But I don't think I ever met him. And you will let me know if you have any luck with the uber driver, won't you? Or is it too soon?"

"We're still following that up. We'll get back to you. And, thanks again, Ms Makepeace."

Brothers hung up. He turned to McTeish. "I forgot—Makepeace rang John and told him she used an uber on Saturday night. John emailed me the receipt. Could you follow it up, see if the driver knows anything?" Brothers forwarded the email.

"Sure, Sarge."

"You know, it seems it's about time we visited Cambridge Bank." He smiled at McTeish.

She nodded, smiled back. "Hey, do we know any of their security people? Could maybe some of them be former police?"

"Good point, Carol. I don't know who would know that. Let's go to their headquarters rather than spending more time farting around with their telephone system. Where are they, again?"

"Collins Place, in the city."

Brothers shook his head. She was certainly spot on.

"I'll get on to the uber after that, okay?"

41

BROTHERS AND MCTEISH DROVE up and parked in a No Standing space, and walked into the Collins Place plaza. Cambridge Bank was the major tenant in one of the towers. They entered the revolving door, and asked at the reception desk for Cambridge Bank's security.

Bruno, according to his name tag, a heavyset man in a too-tight suit, gazed at them for a moment, then checked Brothers' identification.

"Who in security?" His voice was an unexpectedly high tenor.

"Mr. Fredrick Antwerp."

"Just a moment, please."

Bruno checked on his screen, and dialed a number.

"Visitors for Mr. Antwerp."

He waited, listened, then hung up.

"Mr. Antwerp is out."

"Then we need to speak to his boss. His manager."

Bruno checked his screen again.

"That would be Dr Grainger."

"Could you let him know we are here?"

Bruno dialed again.

"She's sending someone down to you. Could you please put these on?" He handed them two visitor tags.

Brothers and McTeish sat on a leather couch, facing the turnstiles to the lifts. People milled about, some coming and going into the retail branch of the bank, some coming and going to the lifts.

A young woman approached them, dressed in a navy suit with large white lapels of her blouse framing her neck. She was petite and shorter than McTeish. She smiled and said, "Sergeant Brothers? Niki sent me down to collect you."

"Niki?"

"Dr Grainger."

They stood up and followed her; she passed them through the turnstile with her card, and they took a lift to the 26th floor. She took them through a security door, and led them to a corner office, with windows that looked over south east Melbourne. A tall, elegant woman of about forty stood up from behind her desk and came around to meet them. She wore an immaculate tailored suit and a haughty, superior expression. She had hazel eyes that inspected them as if they were laboratory specimens. They exchanged names.

"How can I help?"

"Thanks for seeing us, Dr Grainger. It's actually Frederick Antwerp that we want to see. Is he in?"

"Freddie? I haven't seen him the last few days. Olivia!" she called.

The young woman who had collected them put her head in the door.

"Do you know where Freddie is?"

"He hasn't been in this week. Not last week, either, I don't think."

"Not at all?"

"No. Not as far as I know. And he hasn't rung in, either. He's not travelling?"

"Not that I know of." She turned to Brothers and McTeish, seemed to acknowledge them properly for the first time. "Please take a seat, Officers."

They sat in two chairs in front of her desk.

"Hold on a second."

She glanced at her desktop screen, pressed a button, then studied her calendar.

"That's odd." She looked puzzled. "Olivia, could you please check whether any of Freddie's team are around?"

Olivia hurried off, and returned shortly with a heavyset man with a ponytail. His suit pants were shiny and he wore white sneakers.

"Yes, Niki?"

She didn't introduce the police to him.

"Have you seen Freddie this week?"

"He hasn't been in. Nor last week. I tried to call him, but his phone goes to voicemail. I thought he must be on a project for you."

"Yes, yes. That's all. Thank you, Brian."

He left, glancing at the two police on his way out.

"So no Freddie," Grainger said. "What's up? Why do you want to see him?"

"So you haven't seen him for a week and a half?"

"I give my people independence."

"It may be a bit too early to tell, but he seems to have gone missing," Brothers said. "You're sure he hasn't been in the office and you just didn't see him? You know, since he doesn't have to report in to you, but went on his merry way?" He marveled at her lack of awareness. Nguyen would know like a shot if he was just one day out of the office.

"He runs his own team. We were due for a catch up—" she consulted her calendar, "—tomorrow, in fact. At 9:00am. He may be off on a frolic of his own."

"A frolic?"

"Well, he chases up stuff—his judgement, of course. He keeps me in the loop."

Brothers raised his eyebrows.

"That's what tomorrow's meeting is about. Reporting progress."

"Well, we're investigating the death of a man. And it might be that it's Mr. Antwerp," McTeish said.

"Freddie? Dead?"

"Some CCTV cameras showed a dead man being shoved into the boot of a car. A black BMW. And it looks increasingly likely that that dead man is Mr. Antwerp."

"Good God," Grainger said. She went back behind her desk and slumped into her chair. "Freddie, dead?" she repeated, as if trying to comprehend.

"We found some DNA. It's linked to him."

"Could I have a look at your ID again, please?"

Brothers handed his across. Grainger looked at it, holding it up to the light. Then she grimaced.

"Sorry. In our job you have to make sure."

"Make sure?"

"There are all sorts of scams, imposters, frauds."

"Dr Grainger, this is serious. This is a murder inquiry."

"What? Of course. It just threw me, you saying Freddie is dead."

"What sort of man was he?"

"So you're sure he's dead?"

"Not sure, but it does seem that that could be the case. And he was like, what?"

"Well, what can I say? He was American. From New York."

"How old would you say?"

"About 40 or so. He's been with us for six months or so."

"Did you recruit him?"

"Why, yes. He was running the cyber security team. They're not thick on the ground. We were lucky to find him." She shook her head. "Dead and gone. Where will I find a replacement?"

Brothers glanced at McTeish, who looked out the window.

"Can you find out when anyone last saw him? In fact, when did you last see him?"

Grainger put her hands on the desk, picked up a pen, put it down. "I saw him Friday a week ago. In the morning. We had a meeting."

"Friday week ago? You mean Friday a week and a half ago, not last Friday?"

"Yes. Friday week ago." She picked up her phone and dialed. "Nihal, could you come over? Yes, now, please, if that's okay."

She put the phone down.

"Nihal is Freddie's deputy."

A few minutes later a tall man in his thirties put his head in the door.

"Niki. You wanted to see me?" He clasped his hands in front of him, nodded to the visitors.

"These are police officers. They have some questions about Freddie."

Brothers and McTeish introduced themselves.

"I'm Nihal Patel." He shook their hands. "Is Freddie okay? He hasn't been in for more than a week. And he hasn't been answering his phone."

"You didn't see fit to let me know that?" Grainger said.

"Well, you know Freddie. He gets the job done. You know how he visits the branches, to check on things."

Grainger pursed her lips. "It appears that Freddie is dead, from what these officers are telling me."

"Dead?" Patel blanched. "Freddie, dead?" He sat down heavily on a chair beside McTeish

"We think so. When did you last see him, or talk to him?" Brothers said.

"On Friday, week before last. Freddie dead," he repeated. "How terrible. What happened to him? When did he die?"

"Last Saturday week, we think," Brothers said.

"Well, for fuck's sake," Grainger said. "Why in hell didn't you let us know earlier?" She glared at Brothers. "Why have you been sitting on this?"

"We only found out ourselves this morning that it was Mr. Antwerp," Brothers said.

Grainger stood up and paced behind her desk. "This is ridiculous. He's dead. You say he died Saturday week ago, but you only found out this morning? God help us all."

"We just didn't know he was Freddie, er, who the missing man was— until today."

"You didn't know he was Freddie," she muttered. "God help us all," she said again.

Patel stood up and walked around the desk, put his arm around Grainger.

"Niki, what do you need done?"

Grainger shrugged off the arm, scowled at Patel and sat down again. Patel, trying to hide his embarrassment, returned to his chair.

"Yes, Niki, what *do* you need done?" Brothers asked.

154

She frowned at Brothers, then turned to Patel. "Give me a report on where the various projects are at. And set up a meeting for tomorrow morning with me and your team, so we can debrief first thing."

"Can you let us know what projects he was working on?" Brothers asked.

"That's bank business, Sergeant."

"In fact, it is our business, Ms Grainger. Seeing this is very likely a murder investigation."

"It's *Dr* Grainger, if you don't mind. Nihal, when can you have the report?"

"Close of business today—just broad brush. That okay?"

"I'll email you then, Sergeant. Will that do?"

"Thanks. Broad brush will be fine. Until then, *Dr* Grainger." He gave her his card and stood up.

"One other thing," McTeish said. Both Grainger and Brothers looked at her. "Do you have Mr. Antwerp's address?"

"We don't give out personal details of our employees—" Grainger began to say, then stopped. "I'll see to it. Later today okay?"

"Yes, please."

They left the building, Olivia showing them out.

"Well, Carol. What a world we live in, eh?"

"What do you mean, Sarge?"

"Look at Grainger. One of her senior people is dead, and is she concerned? Only about how to find a replacement! And that guy who works for Antwerp, what's his name, Patel. He didn't even know his boss was missing. Nor did Grainger. Does something happen when you get paid a lot of money?"

"To be fair, he hadn't been there long. Crikey, what am I saying? You're right, Sarge. Completely right."

"Or is it something about IT, cybersecurity. Does it attract nutters with no empathy at all?"

"Low EQ, Sarge?"

"Eh?"

"Emotional intelligence."

"Yeah. Right. I suppose that's the buzz word these days."

"When Winner gets back, we need to have another conversation with Grainger. Find out what exactly Antwerp was working on—if it's not in the report she's going to give us. But I have a feeling—" Brothers scratched his belly "—we're going to have to chase her for the full picture."

"You reckon there are links here with what Steenvater was on about?"

"To quote Sue Gossiter, is the Pope a Catholic? Has to be."

"So could the Americans have knocked him off?"

"That certainly is a possibility. Was he helping them, or the reverse? If he was the obstacle, that could explain things. But as Winner would say, let's not get ahead of ourselves."

"Sarge—you should also talk to Steenvater again. He must know Antwerp—and Grainger works for him, doesn't she?"

"Yes, she does."

"When does the boss get back?"

"He's probably about to fly to New York as we speak. Should be back on the weekend."

"So," McTeish sounded uncharacteristically unsure of the next step. "Do you think we should we wait till next week? What about we check with him about us seeing Steenvater tomorrow?"

Brothers thought about it.

"Good idea. What's the time there? Must be around midnight last night. He'll still be in LA." He immediately sent him a text.

To his surprise, his phone rang.

"Winner? How come you're not on the plane?"

"About to board," came the voice, loud and clear. "I see from your text you want to talk to Steenvater again."

Brothers explained the response they had received from Steenvater's team at Cambridge.

"Grainger has probably spoken to Steenvater already. But, you know, it won't hurt to put the pressure on. Take McTeish with you."

Brothers hung up, nodded to McTeish.

"We'll see him tomorrow."

She raised her eyebrows. "We?"

"Yes, you, too."

"When you talked to Steenvater, was it here, or at his home?"

"At his home. Both times." Brothers rubbed his chin. "These banker guys seem to have a lot of flexibility. I'll ring him now and set up a time tomorrow."

He searched through his notebook, found the number and rang it.

Steenvater answered promptly.

"Hullo? Steenvater here."

"Mr. Steenvater?"

"Yes. That's what I said. Who is this?"

"Sergeant Brothers, sir. Graham Brothers. From Victoria Police."

"Yes, Sergeant?"

"We need a few minutes of your time. When can we see you tomorrow? We can come to your office."

There was silence for a time, then Steenvater said, "Around 9, 9:30 tomorrow morning."

"Okay, let's make it 9:30. We'll see you then—at Collins Place."

"Yes. Collins Place. Good bye."

"Well," Brothers said to McTeish, "we're seeing his nibs tomorrow at 9:30. At Collins Place."

He texted the information to Nguyen.

"Oh, and Carol. Good point to ask for Antwerp's address." She beamed at the praise. "Let's have a look at his place tomorrow as well."

42

BACK AT THE OFFICE McTeish studied the uber receipt that had been printed from Nguyen's email and left on Brothers' desk. Makepeace had been picked up from 111 Russell Street in the city at 11:07pm, and arrived at The Belvedere at 11:22pm, for a cost of $27.36 including a 1.5 surge charge. There was a map of the route. The driver was Sam. She noted his number plate and accreditation number. First she checked the database for who owned the car. Up popped the name Samarth Govinda Chowdhury. The car was a RAV hybrid. She noted the address, and checked for a phone number. A mobile came up, and she rang it.

"Sam here," a confident voice said.

"Uh, Mr. Chowdery?"

"Yes?"

"Constable Carol McTeish here, from Victoria Police."

"Yes?" The voice seemed to lose some of its confidence.

"We're checking up on a customer you drove last Saturday night."

"What's wrong? Is there a problem? Has there been a complaint? All my trips get 5 star ratings, I'll be having you know."

"No complaints. When can I meet you? Where are you now?"

"I am in the city."

"Can you drive to the St Kilda Road station?" She gave the address.

"What, now? I have work to do."

"Yes, sir. We need to speak to you now. It won't take long. Or if you prefer I could come to you at your home."

There was a pause.

"No, no. I'll drive to you." She heard faint music in the background. "Should be there in twenty minutes. Who should I ask for again?"

"McTeish, Constable Carol McTeish. Tell you what, to make it quicker, when you arrive, call this number."

"Okay. Constable McTeish, is it?" he said.

NINETEEN MINUTES LATER HER phone rang. "Constable McTeish? This is Sam Chowdhury—I am out the front. There are no parks."

"Thanks, Mr. Chowdhury. Hang on, I'll come out and we can talk in the car."

"Okay. I am waiting out the front for you."

As she left the building she saw the white RAV hybrid she had been expecting, idling in a No Parking zone. She opened the front passenger door and got in.

"Sam," the driver said to her, holding out his hand.

"Carol McTeish," she said. "Can you drive up the road a bit till you get a park?"

When he'd found a spot, about 150 metres up the road, he pulled over and switched off the engine.

"How can I help you, Constable? You said it wasn't a complaint?"

"Last Saturday night you drove home a Deirdre Makepeace, from the city to South Melbourne. It was just before midnight."

He thought for a while. "Last Saturday night? Ah, yes. I remember her. Drunk. Picked her up in the city, outside Glimmers, in Russell Street. You know it?" He smiled at her, then his face fell. "What's she say I did?"

McTeish looked at him speculatively. "Nothing, nothing at all. We just want to check a few things. Was there anyone with her?"

"No, she was by herself. When I say drunk, she was very drunk. Completely out of it. I got her safely to her apartment."

"What do you mean?"

"She could hardly walk. I parked out the front, got out and helped her into the lobby, made sure she was in safely."

McTeish raised her eyebrows.

"Only to the lifts. Once she got there I went back to the car. Quick smart."

"You didn't go up?"

"No way. Why would I go up? What's going on? Is it a crime to help people?"

"No, of course not. That was very considerate of you."

"I need to get good ratings."

She again raised her eyebrows.

"If you get poor ratings, you lose business," Chowdhury said. "Uber can strike you off."

"And what did you do next?"

"I had another customer. Hang on." He checked his phone. "To Brighton. You can check with uber. I picked them up a bit after midnight."

McTeish thought for a while, then said, "So you drove her to her apartment block, helped her to the lifts, then went back to your car. That all?"

He nodded.

"Thank you, Mr. Chowdhury. And thank you for looking after Ms Makepeace on Saturday."

"Is that all?"

"Yes—don't worry about driving me back."

"You sure?"

"Saves you turning around, and I need a short walk. Thank you again."

Chowdhury gave her a card, "If you are needing an uber, any time, give me a call. Very good service."

McTeish took it. "Thank you, Sam."

She got out and walked back, turning the conversation around in her head. When she got to her desk she saw Brothers.

"Just finished speaking to the uber driver."

"What uber driver?"

"The one who drove Makepeace home on Saturday night—guy named Sam Chowdhury. It looks like she was really out of it when he got her home. On the surface he seems in the clear."

"Okay, so she did get home drunk. Where's the body come in? Maybe we'll get a clue at Antwerp's home—has the bank sent though his address yet?"

McTeish checked her emails. "Not yet."

Late that afternoon, at 5:15pm, an email from Grainger arrived, with a list of Freddie Antwerp's current projects, and his address. Cambridge Bank had arranged his accommodation and it also included a contact at Wilsons, the estate agent handling the rental.

Brothers printed out the project list, and handed it to McTeish.

"See what you can make of this. And Grainger has now confirmed that he lived in East Melbourne, an apartment in Albert Road. Can you call the agent"—he checked—"Jessie—about getting a key?"

"Okay." McTeish scanned the projects. "No mention of the Millennium Bug. I think we'll need to talk to whatsisname, Patel, to get a sense of what these projects mean. There looks like at least two currency fraud items he was working on."

McTeish rang Wilsons, the agent, and asked to be put through to Jessie Morgan. She was still in, and listened without comment as McTeish explained about the possible death of her client, Freddie Antwerp, and gained her agreement to hand over a set of keys in the morning.

Wednesday

43

CAROL MCTEISH SUGGESTED PICKING up the keys before their appointment with Steenvater.

"Their office is in St Kilda, so it'll only be a short detour. Is that okay?"

"Good thinking," Brothers said. "Do you mind driving?"

She drove them to Wilson's office in Fitzroy St and pulled up outside.

"I'll just pop in," she said, leaving the engine running. She was back in about three minutes, waggling a set of keys at Brothers as she got back in the car.

As she drove to Collins Place, she said, "You know, just thinking about the two men Steenvater met, being Americans. Do you think there is a connection with Antwerp being American, too?"

"How do you mean?"

"It just seems a bit convenient." McTeish said. "Convenient that Antwerp was new to the job, and this whole Millennium Bug thing has been dead until now. Just saying."

"That reminds me. Let's hope the video is good enough so our US mates can find a match with their facial recognition stuff. I wonder if that will show a link between them and Antwerp."

The security guy at the desk was expecting them, issued passes and called upstairs. A different young woman presently emerged from a lift and approached them.

"Hi," she said. "You the police for Mr. Steenvater? I'm Carmen, Mr. Steenvater's PA."

"Sergeant Graham Brothers and Constable Carol McTeish," Brothers said.

"I'll escort you up to level 31."

She led them to the lifts then, as the lift ascended, stood, barely acknowledging them. When they arrived at his floor, she indicated an area with two leather couches and said, "Please wait here." As they sat down, Carmen knocked on a door, poked her head in, nodded, and then withdrew.

A moment later Henry Steenvater emerged, glanced across at them, and gestured for them to come inside.

"Good morning," he said. "I don't have much time. Will this be quick?"

"It shouldn't take too long," Brothers said.

"Where's Detective Nguyen?"

"He's on a special trip."

Steenvater looked questioningly at them, but neither spoke.

"So, how can I help?" He pointed at the two chairs in front of his desk. They sat down.

"Mr. Steenvater—"

"Henry."

"Er, Henry. What can you tell us about Freddie Antwerp?"

"Freddie? He works for me. Looks after cybersecurity. What about him?"

"We think he may be the dead man."

"What? Freddie, dead? You must be joking." His eyes lidded and he drummed his fingers on the desk.

"No joke. He seems to be the man found in your apartment block last Sunday morning. When did you last see him?"

"Freddie dead?" He said again, and shook his head. "How could that be? When did I last see him? The week before last. Thursday or Friday. Friday, I think. Why do you think the dead man was Freddie?"

"You mentioned that you had two US visitors that Sunday morning."

"Yes. And as I told you, that it was on bank business."

"And we told you they were seen on camera putting a body into their car."

"Yes. You told me that. As I said, I know nothing about that. Nothing at all. You should speak to them."

"Good idea. Do you have their phone numbers?"

Steenvater shook his head. "No, I don't."

"They might be on your phone—on the text message they sent you. Can you please let us have a look again?"

"What? Oh. Okay." Steenvater took his phone out of his pocket, unlocked it and handed it across to Brothers, who gave it to McTeish. She checked it.

"No luck—no caller ID."

"Well, Mr. Steenvater, if you don't have their numbers, how do you explain that the body they put into the boot of their car was Mr. Antwerp? And that it was a stolen car? Does that sound like they're bankers?"

"They did what?"

"We have them on video. They took the body to the basement."

"Good Lord," Steenvater said. He gasped, breathed deeply. "I've no idea."

"Mr. Steenvater. Henry. I don't think they were just seeing you on bank business, were they?"

"I already told you they were trying to trace the money from New Year's Eve back in 2000."

"So what has Mr. Antwerp got to do with that? He worked for you."

Steenvater was silent.

"What was he meant to have been doing last week?"

"What do you mean, last week? Didn't you just say he was dead."

"That's right. That's what we think. Let me put it this way. He works for you. Yet you say you haven't seen him for nearly two weeks. What did you think he was doing?"

"He runs his own show. I'm not a helicopter manager. He works in one of my teams. You should speak to his boss, Niki Grainger."

"We have spoken to her. How did you come to employ him?"

"Niki found him. We were looking for an expert. Cyber security is changing all the time. He's a top man in the field." Steenvater broke off. "Was a top man."

"And when did he start?"

"About six months ago. I can get the exact date, if you need it."

"No. That's okay. I'll let you know if we need it."

McTeish spoke up. "Mr. Steenvater, who were the two Americans."

"I told Detective Nguyen. They said their names were Joseph Stevenson and Peter Knight. That's what they told me. That's all I know."

"Come on, Mr. Steenvater. They were in your apartment and straight after they left you they put the body of Mr. Antwerp into the car."

Steenvater said nothing.

"It can't just have been bank business, can it now?

"For heaven's sake. I've got no idea what they were doing with Freddie. They were on at me about finding the missing money. That's all."

"And yet they came to see you in a stolen car."

"That's got nothing to do with me."

"Obstructing a police investigation is a serious offence."

"I am not obstructing your investigation. I've told you all I know. And if you don't mind, I have other things to worry about today." He stood up and opened the door.

"Thank you for your time," McTeish said.

"That's given him a shake up," Brothers said, as they descended in the lift.

"Yes, Sarge. It really is odd, isn't it. A guy who works for him is put into the boot of a car by people he says he doesn't know who have just visited him—on a Sunday! And he doesn't seem to care about it at all."

"Not even about the stolen car."

"Do you still want to go to Albert Street, check out Antwerp's apartment?"

Brothers checked his phone for messages.

"Yes—let's do that now. It's close enough. We'll go back to the station afterwards. Maybe our US buddies will have some news for us. Maybe they can identify those two men. Let's hope."

Brothers thought that at last things were moving. Though in which direction he wasn't too sure. First Antwerp's apartment. What would that throw up?

44

THE ALBERT STREET APARTMENT BUILDING was a tower, built about the same time as The Belvedere and, like it, well maintained. Brothers gazed up at it for a moment. "Not cheap rent here," he said.

They used the electronic tag with the keys to enter the lobby, and took a lift up to the 17th floor. There were four apartments. Antwerp's was 23. McTeish switched on a light, and they saw a small living room with a kitchen. There was a large TV but no books or magazines, a couch, two chairs, a table and lamp. Brothers looked at the kitchen. It had an island bench that was clean and bare. It looked unused.

"Better than I've got at home," McTeish said.

She opened the fridge. There was a carton of milk, and that was all. She checked the use by date, screwed up her nose, and poured the contents down the sink. She checked the freezer compartment. Apart from a tray of ice blocks it too was empty.

A tall cupboard beside the fridge was a sort of pantry. There was a half a loaf of sliced bread, jars of honey and of raspberry jam, a packet of muesli, salt and pepper shakers, a packet of unopened biscuits, a small bottle of chili sauce.

"He must have eaten out a lot—or used Deliveroo. What do you reckon, Sarge?"

Brothers grunted, possibly in agreement.

Behind the kitchen was a study and a bedroom, and he put his head in each.

"Hello," he said. "Excellent!" On the desk was a laptop. He switched it on, and of course a password was required. "Carol —" he called out.

"There's a laptop. Take it back with us. The IT guys will be able to crack the password."

There were papers and folders on the desk. He flicked through them. Bank documents, for the most. There was a drawer, and in it he found a passport in the name of Frederik Jerome Antwerp. There was no entry stamp.

"Probably an electronic visa," he said, half to himself.

McTeish came in, picked up the laptop and looked over his shoulder at the passport. "We'll need Home Security to read the chip for us—see when he entered the country."

She noticed a wheeled bag in the corner, the size you could take aboard airlines.

"Ah ha!" She unzipped it. "Damn. Empty." She rolled it across to the desk. "I'll put all these papers in it," she said, scooping them up.

They checked the bedroom. There were two suits in the wardrobe, underwear, three shirts with collars, a couple of Tees, a pair of jeans, a pair of Teva sandals. She checked the pockets of the suits. Nothing.

"He sure travelled light," she said.

"Let's hope the laptop has some good stuff on it."

They both did another quick scan of the rooms, then left with the laptop and wheelie bag full of papers.

45

NGUYEN FLEW INTO JFK on Wednesday morning. The plane arrived at 7am and docked at Terminal 8. He'd managed a couple of hours sleep and the jet lag seemed to be in abeyance.

Before he'd left L.A., he'd spoken to Detective April Martinez from the NYPD Computer Crimes Squad, who said she would send a car to meet him. And sure enough there was a sign with his name on it, held by a tall policewoman, who smiled as he walked up.

"Detective Nguyen?"

"Yes. Detective Martinez?"

"You got it," she laughed. "I'm April."

"John."

"G'day, John. Is that how you say it?"

He nodded. "No wuz."

"What the?"

"That's another Aussie expression. No wuz—no worries."

She laughed.

"No wuz, is that it? I always wanted to visit Australia. I suppose this will be the closest I get. Welcome to the Big Apple."

"Thanks."

Before he could say anything further, she grabbed his wheeled bag and led the way.

"I can manage that," he said, but she turned her head, smiled, and otherwise ignored him. He trotted after her.

She led him through to the police car park next to the Red Lot. A policeman was waiting at the car.

"This is my partner, Jamo Krassberg."

Krassberg was in his thirties, burly, about the same height as Martinez, and going bald. He looked Nguyen up and down, then shook his outstretched hand.

"You from Nam?" his voice wasn't friendly.

"My family was. Boat people."

"My dad was there." He abruptly turned and opened the driver's door. "Get in—we can talk on the way in."

Nguyen got in the back, while Martinez slid into the front. Krassberg started the car and they drove off.

"Now, tell me more," Martinez said, once they were under way. "This Jelena Smith. How does she fit in again?"

"She might be a cousin to our missing man." Nguyen told her in detail what he had outlined yesterday on the phone. "We are hoping she can shed some light on Freddie Antwerp. My colleagues back in Melbourne have just confirmed he's our missing man."

"Well, Smith lives in Brooklyn. How long are you here?"

"I'm flying back tomorrow afternoon."

Krassberg grunted.

"Well let's see if we can talk to her today. I've already spoken to her, and she works in Hell's Kitchen. She said we can meet her near her work."

"How did she sound?"

"Curious."

"Okay. Where are we meeting?"

"She suggested Blue Dog, on West 50th. It's near her office."

"What does she do?" Nguyen asked.

"She's at Universal Pictures. Don't know what she does there. It'll take us about an hour to get into Manhattan, so I'll call her, let her know we're on our way. Did they feed you on the plane?"

"I suppose you could call it that."

"Well, Jamo and I could go a breakfast, so we'll eat at Blue Dog, and then get Smith to join us." She dialed a number.

"Jelena? This is April Martinez."

She listened a moment.

"Would it be convenient for you to meet at around 9.30? At where you suggested, Blue Dog?"

She turned to Nguyen. "That's fixed."

Blue Dog was classy, with wooden tables, napkins in rings at each place. Not your typical diner. It was two thirds full, clearly doing well. A waitress, 20-something with one side of her head shorn, a pony tail and eyebrow rings, smiled and offered them menus.

"How y'all doin' today. Coffee all around?" she asked. To Nguyen's ear she had a lilting Southern accent.

They all nodded.

When Nguyen looked at the "Famous Health Conscious Brunch Menu" he saw he could have almost been in Melbourne. He ordered a Breakfast Burrito—scrambled eggs with jalapeños, salsa, mushrooms and cheese. Martinez ordered a Croque Madame and Krassberg a Cheesus Christ, a burger with a choice of eight cheeses.

"Cholesterol City," he said.

The coffee arrived in three mugs, with a small jug of milk on the side. Then the breakfasts, and they all tucked in.

Swallowing a mouthful, Nguyen asked, "Do know anything else about Jelena Smith?"

"Apart from her working at Universal? Nothing came up. No record. Not even a parking ticket. She's a clean skin."

"Hmm. We already know that the murdered man is Freddie Antwerp. I hope she can help fill in more about why he went to Australia."

Krassberg picked up his burger and chomped into it.

"What do you want from this woman, anyway?" he asked while chewing. "Seems you know all you need to know already."

"Just going by the book. You never know what might turn up."

46

JUST BEFORE 9:30 AM a woman in her 30s dressed in a business suit opened the door to the restaurant and looked around, glancing at the various tables. Nguyen noted her gaze passed over them, then came back. She walked over.

"Detective Martinez?"

"Jelena Smith?" Martinez stood up and smiled, they shook hands, and she gestured to the empty seat at the table.

Nguyen had also stood up, and reached out his hand. Jelena Smith shook it, looking him in the eye. She was tall, dark haired and elegant. Graceful, even. She looked both weary and a little irritated.

He introduced himself, and they sat down.

"Thanks for coming out to see us," Martinez said.

"Will this take long?"

"Detective Nguyen here is all the way from Australia."

Smith raised an eyebrow. Her face relaxed.

"So this is about the DNA test, right?"

"Well, sort of."

"I knew it! I knew I had relatives down under."

Looking at their faces she added, "My dad was a bit of a wild one." She smiled. "Am I right, or am I right?"

Seeing the blank looks on the faces of Martinez and Krassberg, she said. "So it's not just the DNA, is it. What did you mean, 'sort of', Detective?" she asked Nguyen.

"Freddie Antwerp. Do you know him?"

"Freddie? Of course. He's my cousin. But he's from here. I already know that. Hey, just a minute," she said. "Why would that bring you to New York?"

At that moment the waitress appeared, looking questioningly at Jelena Smith. "Can I get you something?"

"I'm investigating the death of Freddie Antwerp," Nguyen said.

The waitress gasped, raised her hand holding her pad to her mouth.

"Dead, you say?" Smith clenched her fists.

"What's that?"

Smith took her eyes off Nguyen and looked up at the waitress.

"What did you say?"

"Can I get you something? A coffee? Something to eat?"

"Coffee. With milk." She turned back to Nguyen. "Freddie? Freddie dead?"

"I'm afraid so."

The waitress' eyes widened, but she kept her mouth closed, lowered her pad and went off, shaking her head.

Smith rubbed her cheek. She breathed out deeply.

"What happened?" A thought seemed to occur to her. "I asked you why are you here. You could have rung, you know. Wouldn't that have been simpler? So, because you are here, I'm thinking it wasn't just an accident, was it? And not a heart attack."

"He was killed." Nguyen winced when he saw her reaction. "I needed to talk to you, and I thought face to face was best."

"Face to fucking face?" she said. "Er, face to face?"

People at the next table looked up, then went back to their conversation.

She muttered, "All the way from Australia. Face to face." Then to Nguyen, "You could've Zoomed me. How did it happen?"

"We don't know."

Smith stared at him, her eyes narrowing.

"We know he was killed, and then his body was taken. We haven't located it yet."

"But why would you come to see me? I don't understand. Why are you here? You said it 'sort of' had something to do with DNA."

"I know this is a shock. It's through the DNA that we managed to identify him. And that's how we found you. We need to find out more about him. Do you know anything about why he went to Australia?"

"He got a job there. Last year. With an Australian bank. He's in IT."

"Yes—but why Australia? Surely bank IT jobs are in demand here, too? Did he say anything about Australia to you?"

"No. I don't think so." She thought. "Actually, he did mention my dad—his uncle. He'd talked about Australia. I don't know if that was a factor."

"When was your dad in Australia?"

"He worked on a couple of movies there. In Melbourne and Sydney, I think. In the 90s."

Nguyen made a note.

"When did you last hear from Freddie?"

"Actually, about three weeks ago. We talked by phone. We're not that close, but we keep in touch. He was just the same as ever. Who would want to kill him?"

"Did he say why he called you? Did he mention anything in particular?"

The waitress brought coffee over. Krassberg made a gesture and she cleared the plates.

"He said he was on a new project. He was excited. He said he was going to be here next week."

"In New York?"

"Yes. That's why he was calling. His ex is here, with his kids. He wanted to catch up. She won't speak to him, and he wanted me to see if I could arrange a visit."

"Was he coming just for that?"

"Well, he did say it was business. And he'd wanted me to know he wanted to see the kids."

"Did he say what sort of business?"

"No. But then I've got no idea what he does. Except it's got to do with IT in the bank."

"Did you set up a meeting with the ex-wife?"

"No. She wasn't keen, to put it bluntly."

"Could I have her, ah, cell number? What's her name?"

"Diane. She goes by her maiden name, Montroso." She checked her phone, read out the number.

"Thanks." Nguyen jotted it down, then asked, "What sort of guy was he? Freddie?"

"How do you mean?"

"Did he have any enemies?"

"He was always a bit on the edge, you know, pushed the boundaries. But he was a good guy. Sort of a nerd. I remember when we were young, he was really into games. Computer games. But enemies? No way. At least none I'm aware of. But then, as I said, we didn't see much of each other." She cast her eyes down, then said quietly, "I can't imagine anyone wanting to kill Freddie."

Martinez asked, "Jelena, what do you do? I know you said you're at Universal."

She looked up. "Yes I am. I'm a producer."

"A producer? You mean you make films?" Nguyen said.

"Films and television. These days TV is where it's all happening."

"I thought all producers are in Hollywood. Yet here you are."

"A lot of TV is done here in New York. Anywhere really. But I love New York."

"What are you working on? Anything we'd know back in Australia?" Nguyen inwardly chastised himself for being non-professional.

"A new series. Family Games."

"Sorry—I don't know it. Some sort of game show?"

"No, not a game show." She laughed. "It's a drama series. I certainly hope you don't know about it in Australia. It's not showing yet. Coming out next year."

"What's it about?" Krassberg asked. He sat up, eyeing Smith eagerly.

"That would be telling."

"Oh." Krassberg slumped back in his chair.

"Just kidding."

"What the —?" He sat up again.

"It's about the Borgias. You know, fifteenth century Italy. Murder, power, religion, politics, sex. You name it, they did it." Smith smiled. "It's going well."

"Who's in it?" Nguyen asked.

"Actually, we do have a couple of Aussies—Russell Crowe and Cate Blanchett. You know them?"

He nodded. "You could say that. I mean, I've seen them."

"Can you believe it, Rusty plays Pope Alexander. And Cate plays Lucrezia, his daughter."

"The Pope had a daughter?" Krassberg frowned. "You got to be kidding."

"And several sons."

"What the fuck?"

"Those were different times, Detective, you might say."

Nguyen thought, no wonder this was television. Then he had another thought.

"But aren't they about the same age? I mean, Russell Crowe may be a couple of years older than Cate. But playing her father?"

"She plays the grown up Lucrezia. He plays the naughty Pope. Different periods."

"I'd really like to see that." Nguyen saw Krassberg looking at him and pulled himself together. "Back to business. I met your sister, Maria."

"Maria? In LA?"

"Yes. Seems she's in the same line as you."

"It's a big world. We grew up together in LA. It's in our blood. Hey, she must have told you about Freddie. Why come to me?"

"She did, and was very helpful. But I have to cover all bases. I'll call Ms Montroso."

"Is that all?"

"For the moment. Thank you for your time, Ms Smith."

Martinez asked, "Did your husband know Freddie?"

Smith paused. "He's met him. But we're not together anymore." Her eyes hardened and her smile was forced. "Is there anything else? I do have to get back to work."

"Thank you," Martinez said.

They all stood up, and Jelena Smith left, without looking back at them.

The three sat down again.

"Did that help you?" Krassberg asked. "I don't mean her TV show." He grinned.

Nguyen nodded. "Yes. Thanks for setting it up. At the very least we got Freddie's wife's name and number." Nguyen thought for a moment. "Amazing, isn't it, she's doing a US show, set in Italy with two Aussie actors?"

"What have you got on for the rest of your time here?" Martinez asked.

"I want to speak to his ex. That's about all."

"Give her a call," Krassberg said. "She needs to hear the news of her ex's death. She'll need to let the kids know. There's probably stuff she'll have to follow up."

Nguyen entered the number and called it. It rang out.

"Voicemail," he said, and hung up.

"Here," Martinez said. "Let me dial. She's more likely to call a New York number. It'd be more difficult with yours." She also keyed in the number, phoned and left a message to call her back.

"Do you want to look at our station while you're here?" she asked. "Our office is on 50th."

"Yes, thanks, April. That would be great. Can I get this?"

"No way, Jose. This is on us." Martinez called for the check.

The waitress arrived promptly, and Martinez glanced at it, left money on the table, took the check as a receipt.

"Thanks," Nguyen said.

"No wuz, as you would say," Martinez said.

"No wuz?" Krassberg looked perplexed.

Martinez grinned. "It's an Aussie expression."

"Whatever," Krassberg said, and stood up, leading the way out to the car.

"We're not far from here," he said as they got in.

"And can I drop my bag at my hotel?"

"Where are you booked?"

"The Grand Hyatt. East 42nd Street."

"You cool to do that after the station?"

"Sure."

"We'll drop you there, then."

47

THE STATION ON WEST 50TH was not that far from Blue Dog, and there was an underground garage. Krassberg parked on basement level 2. They ascended in a lift, and entered at level 3, an open plan series of desks, cabinets, phones, people and noise.

Martinez took Nguyen on a quick tour, pointing out people, whether they were police or detectives, greeting some of them, and then led him into a small meeting room, her partner following.

"Do you want to debrief?"

"We can go over things, but I'd really like to get in touch with Diane Montroso."

"She'll call back. Patience, my friend," Martinez said.

"But will she call today?"

"Hopefully. Why not? So let's debrief."

Nguyen went over the case, pointing out that Diane Montrose could be critical in finding out more about Freddie Antwerp, whether she'd heard from him recently. "And is it possible to track down the two Americans who visited the bank boss, Steenvater, in Melbourne? I'll get my guys in Melbourne to contact our Australian Border Security people—they should have their arrival details. Do you have contacts with your Home Security, who should have their departure info?"

At that moment Nguyen's phone rang.

"John? This is Nat, Nat Turner. LAPD."

"G'day, Nat."

"You still in New York?"

"Yes—I fly home tomorrow afternoon."

"Well, those photos you gave us. Got some matches, courtesy of our friends at the FBI. They are known to us—middle management."

"Middle management?"

"The Mob. Names of Al Geronimo and Pauli Desica. Those names you gave us were fake. They're both originally from Chicago, but they've been in LA and New York off and on. Typical stand over men. But up for more."

"Geronimo? Is that Italian?"

Turner laughed. "No. Not the name. That's Apache. You know, the war leader? But Al Geronimo is. Or rather, his family is, came from Sicily."

"And any idea why they are in Australia?"

"You need to get in touch with the FBI about that."

Nguyen thought for a moment. "Do you have a contact?"

"Here or in New York?"

"New York would be good, seeing as I'm here."

"Okay. Give me a sec."

While they were speaking Martinez' phone rang. She listened for a moment. "Ms Montroso? Thanks for calling back."

"Hey, Nat. Can I call you back in five?" Nguyen said.

"Sure."

"No, you've done nothing wrong," Martinez was saying. "No, I can assure you. No. No. What? We need to talk to you. About your ex-husband. Yes, I know. Can I put on a colleague? He's from Australia?" She rolled her eyes and gave the phone to Nguyen. He put it on speaker.

"Ms. Montroso? This is Detective John Nguyen. I'm from Melbourne, Australia."

"From Australia?" Nguyen heard a low-pitched melodic voice.

"Yes. I need to ask you a few questions about your ex-husband, Freddie Antwerp."

"That louse. What's he done now?"

"That's what I need to speak to you about. Can we visit you today? Are you at work?"

"No, I'm at home. Could you get here before the kids get home from school?"

"Sure. Where are you?" He took down the details. "Brooklyn," he mouthed. "Would half past two suit you?" He glanced at Martinez, who nodded.

"That'll be fine. This isn't about his alimony or child support, is it?" Montroso said.

"No, no, nothing like that. See you then. Thank you." He handed the phone back to Martinez.

"She lives in Brooklyn. East 16th Street in Flatbush."

"Okay with that?" she asked Krassberg, who shrugged.

"Sounds like a plan," he said.

"I'll just call Nat Turner back. He's LAPD and getting me an FBI contact," Ngyuen said. He rang, and Nat picked up straight away.

"John, you want to talk to Special Agent Harry Brownovski. He's in the Intelligence Branch, handles organized crime." He gave Nguyen the phone details. "I'm emailing him about you. He'll expect a call. We go back a ways."

"Do you know Harry Brownovski?" Nguyen asked Martinez and Krassberg.

"Who's he?" Krassberg asked.

"He's with the FBI, based here in New York. Nat Turner, my LAPD contact, said Brownovski could be helpful."

"No, I don't know him." Martinez looked at Krassberg, who shook his head. "What's his area?"

"Turner said he's in the Intelligence branch."

"Interesting."

"It seems the two guys who might have murdered Antwerp are Mafia. Turner said Brownovski might be able to help with that."

"The FBI should have background on them. Hope they share."

Nguyen rang the number Turner had given him.

"Harry Brownovski."

"This is Detective John Nguyen from the Victoria Police in Australia."

"Yes? Australia?" The voice was non-committal.

"Nat Turner gave me your number, said he'd be emailing you."

"Nat, you say? Well, I just got back in. I'll check my emails. Can you wait a moment?"

"Sure."

After a few seconds Brownovski came back on the line, his voice no longer guarded. "Detective—"

"John."

"Hi John. And it's Harry. I got Nat's message. How can I help?"

Nguyen gave Brownovski a rundown of the case, including the names of the two American mafia men, and their aliases in Australia, Joseph Stevenson and Peter Knight

"Al Geronimo and Pauli Desica. I'll just pull up the database."

Nguyen waited a few more seconds.

"Here we go. Yes. Yes. Two of our choice customers. You say they're down under?"

"Yes—we caught them on video putting a corpse in the boot— trunk of a car. Our missing man, Freddie Antwerp."

"Glad they're your problem. Hey, let me check on Antwerp, too."

He came back a little later, "No, he seems to be clean, at least from our perspective."

"What can you tell me about Geronimo and Desica?"

"Why don't you come round here. I'll get some extracts from our files. In the meantime, give me your email."

Nguyen did so.

"These guys—Geronimo's a hit man, Desica's a money man," Brownovski said. "They both work between here and LA, usually. Australia is not in their normal comfort zone."

"If they're in your data base, how come they got through our Border Security? Or yours?" Nguyen said.

"You're presuming they were using their own names. They were probably using the fake names, Stevenson and Knight. So when do you think you can come over to the office?

"I should be free about 4 o'clock. Does that suit you?"

"Sure." Brownovski gave him the address.

Nguyen hung up, and turned to Martinez. "Is it okay to drop my bags at my hotel now?"

"Sure. Plenty of time," Martinez said. Krassberg nodded. It was 11:20.

"You'll have time to freshen up before we go see Montroso," she said.

"Not sure I'll be able to do that—the check in time is 2pm."

"Let's see, eh? We do have some influence in this town."

Krassberg and Martinez drove Nguyen to the Grand Hyatt, and Krassberg waited in the car while Martinez went in with Nguyen to the reception desk. They waited a minute until they were served, by a young woman with short dark hair, who checked her computer and said, "I'm afraid there's nothing ready until 2pm."

Martinez showed her badge.

"Let me check again, see what I can do." After a brief search she smiled. "We do have a room available, but it's on level 5. Is that okay?"

"Sure—I'm only here for a night."

"Okay, sir. It's been paid for, but I'll need your credit card, for any room service or the minibar." She got Nguyen to sign the paperwork.

Martinez said, "Let's see—will we pick you up at say one pm? We can grab a quick meal on the way."

"Thanks. See you at one."

Nguyen took his key, took his smaller bag and ascended to level 5. A bellboy was already there with his bag, a man in his fifties or sixties, and he opened the door to the room.

"Anything you need, sir—just buzz me." He indicated a button. "I'm Wallace."

Nguyen tipped him five dollars as he shut the door. He glanced around. A king size bed. Time for a shower.

48

Promptly at one, Nguyen was waiting on the sidewalk outside the Hyatt. Presently, Martinez and Krassberg drove up.

"We'll take you to Katz's—they make the best pastrami sandwiches. And it's on the way."

"Sounds good to me," Nguyen said. He grinned. Pastrami on rye, New York style. "Great!"

Krassberg parked in Ludlow Street, and they entered the deli. Nguyen noticed a faded framed sign on a wall—send a salami to your boy in the army.

"That must be pretty old," he said.

"Their slogan during World War II," Krassberg said. "The owner's sons were enlisted. The Pastrami is good, but I recommend the hot Reuben Sandwich."

"What's in that?"

"Corned beef, cheese, sauerkraut. You can add pastrami if you want."

"I'm having the Turkey," Martinez said.

"I'll go the Pastrami," Nguyen said. "Something to tell the family back home. And let me look after these, please. You did breakfast, and I do have a small expense account."

Krassberg nodded, and placed their order. Nguyen offered his credit card, and they sat at a table. As they ate they talked about the case, and Krassberg appeared to relax from his earlier grumpiness.

"Well," Martinez said, when they'd finished eating. "We need to get out to Flatbush. You driving?" she asked Krassberg, who nodded.

They left Katz's Deli and drove over the Manhattan Bridge. Nguyen, looking out the right-hand window, saw the Statue of Liberty in the distance. The traffic was moving and they arrived at East 16th Street in twenty-five minutes, parking outside a timber house with red brick frontage.

Martinez knocked on the door, and it was immediately opened by a woman in her early 40s with hair cut short, and dressed in a pink pant suit. She had dark eyes which squinted at the three visitors.

Martinez introduced them. "Ms Montroso, you talked to my Australian colleague, Detective Nguyen, earlier today."

"How do you do," Nguyen said. "Thank you for seeing me. Seeing us."

"That's okay. I'm fine," she said. "Just very curious about Freddie and why you are here all the way from Australia. Come on in."

The house was light and airy, and she led them into a large room with polished wood floors, a Mexican rug, and three Danish-style chairs and two couches.

"Can I get you anything?" she asked.

"No thanks," Nguyen said. The others also shook their heads.

"So. Please take a seat." She gestured to the chairs. "What's the scum bag done now?"

Nguyen kept his face blank. "I'm afraid he's dead."

Montroso laughed. "Dead? Couldn't happen to a nicer guy."

"I know you divorced—"

"And thank God for that. He was a bully. Complete narcissist. Fooled his family. Charming son of a bitch. I'd use a stronger word, but you're a policeman. And an Aussie. So I'm being polite."

"You don't seem surprised?"

"He had it coming."

"How do you mean?"

"The people he was mixed up with. Why do you think he went to Australia?"

"A job? An IT job?"

"Well, yes, but why go to the end of the world?" Seeing Nguyen's expression she laughed again. "Excuse me, Detective. To the other side of the world."

Nguyen said nothing, and both Martinez and Krassberg also kept silent.

"He was getting away from the people he was dealing with here," Montrose said.

"Which people?"

"I don't know who they are, but they were up to no good. To say Mafia sounds paranoid, conspiracy land, but that's who they were."

"And why was he involved with these people?"

"I don't know. But I tell you, Detective. He was scared. And that was not in Freddie's character. Being scared, I mean. That's why he took off."

Nguyen wrote in his notebook.

"So how did he die?" she asked.

"We're not sure. We do know his body was driven away by two men. We think they were his killers."

"And when did this happen?"

"A week and a half ago."

"Have you notified his parents?"

"They are still living?"

"Yes, here in New York."

"We only found out who it was three days ago. That it was Freddie, I mean."

Montroso looked Nguyen up and down. She laughed again, a deep throaty sound.

"And you got to New York in three days, to see me? Come off it, Detective. I wasn't born yesterday." She looked at the two New York detectives. "You in on this, too?"

"How do you mean, Ma'am?" Krassberg asked.

"I know it takes a day and a night to fly from Australia. You should have heard Freddie complain. So what's really going on?"

"We're just helping our colleague," Martinez said.

"And I should explain," Nguyen said.

"Yes, you should explain. That would be a good start."

"We knew a man was dead two weeks ago. We just didn't know it was your ex, till three days ago. Does that make sense?"

"So you flew here, not knowing who he was? To see me?" She laughed again.

"We had DNA." Nguyen told her more of the saga. "I was coming to talk to his cousins, Maria in LA and Jelena here in New York; they helped us identify him. And seeing I was here, and you live here, I thought I'd talk to you, too. Jelena gave me your cell number."

Montroso sat silently for a while. He could see she was pondering what he'd told her.

"So what do you want to ask me?"

"Just about what sort of person he was. You've told us a bit. Can you add anything more? How did you meet, for example?"

"Oh, God. I was 29, he was in his 30s. We met at one of Jelena's parties. A launch of a show, I think. As I say, he fools people. He certainly charmed me. I wanted children. Actually, so did Freddie. We hit it off. I got pregnant. We married. Then." She paused, shook her head. "Then I discovered he's a control freak. It started bit by bit. He'd get angry about something I did, shout at me. Then he'd apologize. I just thought he was stressed at work. That's what he said, anyhow. We disagreed on how to bring up Angelina. That's my first." She smiled. "He wouldn't set boundaries for her, spoiled her rotten—unless he got angry. We fought about that. Anyhow, we split up before Tommy was born."

"Is Tommy his?"

"What? Of course he is. What do you take me for?"

"You did say you broke up before he was born …"

"Oh, I see what you mean. He left when I was eight months—about to have Tommy. Would you believe it?"

"Did he have someone else? Was he cheating?"

"You know, that was strange. I don't think there was another woman."

"And, sorry to ask this, no one else for you?"

"With two kids? You've got to be joking." She laughed again. "No. I don't think he could stand being with us anymore. Angelina has a mouth on her, too." She smiled. "We fought over the money. But he let me have the house. I mean, I insisted on having this house. We finally agreed. That was six years ago."

"Did you see much of him after that?"

"Well, yes. Of course. He saw the kids. He looked after them some weekends. Until about six months ago, when he left for overseas. For down under."

"What did he say about the Mafia?"

"He didn't. I worked that out."

"How was that," Krassberg asked, sitting up.

"I put two and two together. Freddie was in cyber security, you know?"

"Yes."

"Well, if you work for a bank and you want to get through the security systems, what's the simplest way? A hacker? No way. You deal with the expert. And my louse of an ex was the expert. So when he got stressed, and left for Australia. It seemed obvious to me."

She smiled at them. "I wonder if he made a will," she said.

Nguyen sat back, glanced at Martinez and Krassberg, who keep straight faces.

"How will you find out?" he asked eventually.

"I'll check with his lawyer." She raised her eyebrows at Nguyen's expression. "The one I had to deal with in the divorce."

"Could you give me his name, please?"

"He's here in Brooklyn. I've got his card here somewhere." She stood up and went over to a bureau in the corner of the room, searched for a minute and came back with a business card. "The firm is Curley, Milstein and Vittoria. And the lawyer is W. Barry Bilson. He's a slime too, like my ex." She looked across at Martinez. "If you have to deal with him, honey, wash your hands afterwards." She handed the card to Nguyen, who wrote down the details and gave it back.

"Thanks, Ms. Montroso."

"You're welcome," she said, and stood up to usher them out.

Putting up a hand to stop her, Martinez asked, "Do you have Mr. Antwerp's parents' details, too? And do you have a photo of Mr. Antwerp?"

"Just a moment." She checked her phone and gave her the details, then went back to the bureau, pulled out a drawer. She took out a framed photo, and gave it to Nguyen. A man in his 30s with dark hair in an open necked shirt stared out at him.

"Thank you. I'll make sure you get it back."

"You can keep it." She laughed her throaty laugh.

The three of them left.

49

As they got into the car, Martinez said, "We've got plenty of time to drop you at the FBI by four. Do you want us to come there with you?"

"Do you have time?"

"Well," said Krassberg, "this case seems to be involving some of our good citizens, so we may as well tag along. If you don't mind?"

"That would be great."

Krassberg said, "The FBI are in Federal Plaza. Not too far from where we were."

They drove back to Manhattan the way they had come, using the Manhattan Bridge again.

"By the way," Nguyen said. "I wonder if that lawyer is available? Bilson. I'm flying back tomorrow, and I wonder, maybe I can catch him tomorrow morning." He checked the business card that Diane Montroso had given him and rang the number.

Barry Bilson, his assistant said, was unavailable to take the call. He was in conference. But he could be available to meet Nguyen at nine the following morning.

"Can you guys come with me?" he asked.

"Can't wait to see you washing your hands afterwards," Krassberg said to Martinez. "Wouldn't miss that for the world."

The FBI building was a towering skyscraper, and Krassberg was able to park underground off Worth Street. They rode a lift to the lobby, where the three were signed in by an elderly man in a dark suit, who rang up to check they were expected and gave them visitor passes.

Harry Brownovski came down to meet them. He was over six foot and he shook their hands, looking carefully at each as he did so.

"I see you've brought back-up," he said to Nguyen. His voice was Bostonian, clipped.

"These are my pals from the NYPD. They've been really helpful."

Both Martinez and Krassberg nodded, and Krassberg shrugged his shoulders.

"I'm up on 53rd," Brownovski said, leading them to the bank of lifts.

BROWNOVSKI DIRECTED THEM INTO a meeting room, with a dark wooden table and six chairs. There was a computer and printer on a side table. A window looked out towards Jersey City.

"Well, Detective Nguyen. Nat Turner has emailed me a little about your case. And Detectives –" he looked at Martinez and Krassberg— "could I ask what area you are in?"

"Computer Crime," Martinez said. "This Antwerp guy seems to be part of a billion-dollar heist."

"So Nat mentioned. Tell me more."

Both Martinez and Krassberg looked at Nguyen.

"So," Nguyen said. "You know the Millennium Bug." And he went on to explain how a Melbourne bank seemed to have been scammed back in 1999 or 2000. And how its current IT guy had recruited Antwerp from the US just six months ago, and how, oddly enough, Al Geronimo and Paul Desica had followed him to Australia.

"And as I said to you on the phone, it's likely they bumped him. They boosted a car, and dumped him in the trunk and drove off."

"Well, John, I've checked up on Geronimo and Desica. I can give you their cell phone numbers. That should be some help."

"Thanks. Though of course they may well have new phones in Australia."

"And you might be able to check their movements with their visas. Can your border security help there?"

"Thanks. But Jesus," Nguyen said. "I don't know what it's like here, but back down under Border Force class us with the enemy." Brownovski smiled. Martinez gave him a thumbs up.

"Hang on," Brownovski said. "I can check with Homeland Security here. They may have something on these two guys." He dialed a number that was shortly answered.

"Hey! How are you, Sally? Don't call me your man!"

Brownovski outlined what he wanted. "Our persons of interest are Al Geronimo and Paul Desica. Any international movements?"

He listened, covered the mouthpiece of the phone. "She's checking her computer," he said in a whisper.

"What? They what? Thanks very much, Sally. I owe you." He hung up, and looked at Nguyen, rubbing his chin.

Nguyen waited, rising his eyebrows.

"You won't believe it."

"What?"

"Geronimo and Desica. They're here in our good old US of A."

"Here? That's odd. But were they in Australia?" Nguyen asked.

"Not according to what I was just told." Brownovski scratched the back of his left hand. "That's not to say they didn't travel under false passports. Under their fake names? Yeah, must have."

"Shit. Can you get us more info on them? I'd like to get good photos to our border people so they can be picked up if they try to leave. We've got the photos from the security cameras, but they're not the best."

"Just a moment." Brownovski went to the side table, logged into the computer and printed out some pages which he handed to Nguyen. "Here are actual copies. What's your email? I'll forward these plus some other images."

Nguyen glanced at the papers. They included mug shots of the two men.

"Thanks. These are great. I'll get our Federal police to put out a red flag to stop them leaving. In fact, I should do that straight away."

Nguyen heard a ping and checked his phone. "I've got the photos. Thanks again, Harry."

He had a quick read of the pages Brownovski had given him, typed a message and forwarded the email with the photos. "Hopefully my Aussie team will get on to that pronto."

"Listen—I'll put out a brief to Interpol myself," Brownovski said. Those suckers have committed a serious felony, travelling with false names and passports. I want them when you're finished with them."

50

"Well, John," Martinez said as they were leaving the building. "It's your last night in the Big Apple. Care for a drink?"

"I'm all free now, till tomorrow morning. A drink would be great."

"You Aussies like beer, right?" she asked.

He nodded. "We have been known to sip the amber fluid."

"Let's try Blind Tiger then. They have what they call craft beer."

"Sounds good to me."

"It's on Bleeker Street, not too far from your hotel. You in, Jamo?"

"I've got to get home to the kids," Krassberg said.

"Come on, Jamo. You sure?"

"I'm sure. My turn to cook, and going out for drinks … ."

"Okay. A guy's got to do what a guy's got to do, I suppose."

"You got it. How about I drop you both at the bar. Where is it again?"

"281 Bleeker Street."

"Gotcha."

Ten minutes later he dropped them at Blind Tiger.

"I'll see you in the morning, April, at the station. We can pick John up a bit after eight, to go to see the slime."

As they entered Blind Tiger, Nguyen said to Martinez, "You keen on animals?"

"Animals? What do you mean?"

"Well, this morning we had breakfast at Blue Dog, and now here we are at Blind Tiger."

Martinez laughed. "I never thought of that. You didn't like Blue Dog?"

"No, No. It was good. Excellent—reminded me a bit of some Melbourne cafes. The food was tops."

"Well, you'll like this bar too, I hope. Animals are just a coincidence. Anyhow, Blue Dog was Jelena Smith's idea. I'd never been there before, either." She nudged his shoulder. "Now, more importantly, what do want to drink?"

Nguyen looked at the drink list. There was a bewildering range.

"What in hell is *Industrial Arts Pocket Wrench*, or, get this–" he read it out slowly—"*Other Half x Gigantic BBA Wilfred's Paradox?*"

"No idea—haven't tried those yet. I did have a *Smuttynose Wood Chip* the other day—it's a chocolate stout."

"My God." Nguyen read down further. "I'll have a *Victory Prima Pils*—at least it sounds like a regular beer."

Martinez ordered two *Victory Prima Pils*, and took them to a table near the wall where Nguyen had seated himself.

"A toast," she said. "To victory with the Antwerp case!"

"I'll drink to that." Nguyen raised his glass and clinked it against hers, then took a gulp. "Not bad," he said, and took another mouthful. "In fact, this *Victory* is damn good."

"Tell me," Martinez said, after swallowing. "You mentioned family some time before. I take it you're married?"

"Yes. And we've got a daughter." He smiled. "And you?"

"No kids. I was married. But it's just too hard with the job. How in hell do you manage it?"

"I don't know. Found the right person, perhaps. She understands if I'm not home when I said I would be."

"Yeah, that's a problem." She took a drink. "He slept around, too." She looked at him for a time. "No, you don't seem to be that type." She smiled.

He felt himself redden. "No. No, I'm not. There's work, and there's family. Keep the two apart, my dad said."

She drained her beer. "Feel like another one?"

"I'm not much of a drinker," he said. "But another would be good. That hit the spot. Here, I'll get it. The same again?"

"Sure."

He went to the bar and returned with two more bottles of *Victorys*.

"How did you get into Computer Crime?" he asked.

"I was a bit of an IT nerd."

"You don't look like a nerd at all."

It was her turn to pink. "I don't look like a nerd? What does a nerd look like?"

"Sorry. Dunno. Someone mousy, maybe, or shy, or … you're right. Those are just stereotypes. Anyhow, you don't look like that. At all."

She looked thoughtfully at him. "And you're happily married …"

"Yes, I am."

Seeing his expression she laughed.

"Look," Nguyen said, "we've got an early start tomorrow, and I'm still a bit jet lagged. Maybe we should call it a night?"

"You don't want to eat? The food here's good."

"Okay. But I am pretty done in."

There was a food menu on the table, and Nguyen picked it up.

"The Caesar Salad is good," Martinez said, studying the menu. "I'll have that with chicken on the side. What about you?"

The list was short, some salads, all quite exotic, including something called a Golden Goddess. That, he thought, might give the wrong signal. "I'll have the Steakhouse Sandwich."

"Okay. I'll get them." She went to the bar, placed the order and returned. "They'll be here soon."

They sat sipping their beers for a few moments in silence. Then they both started to speak at the same time, and laughed.

"You go," Nguyen said.

"Just wanted to say, I'm just the friendly type. Don't make anything of it."

"Me too," he said. They both grinned.

"Okay."

A waiter brought the food and they started eating. The Steak Sandwich had creamed spinach, onions and horse radish on tender roast beef.

"You like it?"

"Pretty damn good," he said with his mouth full.

"Just a small sample of what we have to offer a visiting cop from down under."

"You'll have to come to Melbourne, we have some great food, too."

"That's tempting. A pity this billion-dollar case won't fund me and Jamo a visit to you. I've travelled a little, but I don't think he's ever been out of New York."

They finished eating, and Martinez stood up. "You're right. Time for an early night. I live near here and I'll walk. You can catch a cab—it's not far to the Hyatt. Should be about ten minutes."

In the street he hailed a Yellow Cab.

"See you tomorrow morning, John. We'll pick you up about 8:15," Martinez said, giving him a wave.

"Thanks, April. See you in the morning."

51

Martinez and Krassberg picked him up on the dot of 8:15, and they drove back to Brooklyn, arriving at the offices of Curley, Milstein and Vittoria.

"How's the jet lag?" Krassberg asked. "You sleep okay?" He smirked.

"I woke at about one," Nguyen said. "Wide awake, then sort of dozed, off and on for the rest of the night. But I must've fallen asleep because my alarm woke me at 6:30."

"How was Blind Tiger? Did you stay late?"

"No, we were good girls and boys," Martinez said. "I got to bed before ten."

Krassberg grinned, nudged her.

"My bed, Jamo."

"Yeah, yeah." Krassberg said. "Of course."

"By myself."

Nguyen laughed. "You ever have dealings with this Barry Bilson, or his law firm?" he asked.

"No, but there's always a first time," Krassberg said.

The building was a refurbished brownstone, with a swanky reception area. A young woman with lacquered makeup, red stripes through her hair and long false eyelashes sat behind a desk painted gold, keying into a laptop. She looked up.

"Can I help you?" Her drawl was pure Brooklyn.

"We're here to see Mr. Bilson," Nguyen said.

"Ah, you must be the guy from Australia." She glanced at Martinez and Krassberg. "You're colleagues?"

"We're New York born and bred," Krassberg said. "And colleagues."

She smiled, and in doing so seemed to flutter her eyelashes. "Just a moment," she picked up her phone. "The cops are here, Barry." She listened, nodded, hung up. "Please follow me."

She stood up on five-inch heels. Krassberg watched carefully as they followed her, shaking his head and mouthing "Wow" to Martinez.

A short man with a dwindling hairline and his belt fastened under a bulging belly greeted them. "Come on in, Detectives. I wasn't expecting three of you, but the more the merrier."

They introduced themselves.

"Call me Barry," Bilson said. "Oh, and Charlene," he said to the receptionist, "did you offer our guests coffee?"

Charlene looked at each of them, her eyebrows raised.

"No thanks," Nguyen and Martinez said simultaneously.

"Yeah, thank you," said Krassberg. "With a drop of milk, please."

She tottered off, and at Bilson's invitation they sat down around the coffee table in his office.

"What's this about? I understand you're all the way from Australia," he said to Nguyen. "Which is why I changed my schedule to fit you in. Always happy to oblige officers of the law."

Nguyen glanced at Martinez, who nodded. "We understand you represent Mr. Frederick Antwerp, Mr. Bilson."

"Freddie? Yes I do. What's he up and done."

"I'm afraid he's up and gone," Krassberg said.

"To Australia? I know that."

"No," Nguyen said. "I'm afraid he's dead."

"My God," Bilson said. "Dead? How did that happen?"

"He was found dead in Melbourne, in Australia—my home town. I'm here investigating his possible murder."

"Murder? Freddie murdered? Jesus. So what's this got to do with me?"

"Nothing at all, I hope. We're just interviewing anyone who might be able to shed some light on what Mr. Antwerp was doing."

"Look, I know he was in Australia. He told me he had a job with a bank down there. He was paying his alimony, wasn't he?"

"Alimony is not what we're here about, Mr. Bilson," Martinez said

"Barry. Please."

"Barry. Did he tell you what he was working on?"

"We didn't talk about that, Officer." He smiled at Martinez. "He was in, you know, IT, cyber security. I presume that's what he was hired to do. And now he's got himself murdered. Wowsers. You can never tell, can you?"

"And you've heard nothing from him since he went down under?" Martinez said.

"Not a peep. But murdered, you say? Who would want to do that?" His glance went over her.

"That's a good question. Have you any ideas?"

"He certainly had his moments ... but murder?"

"No organized crime links that you're aware of?" Krassberg asked.

"What the?" Bilson shook his head. "No way. Not that I know of." He thought, still eyeing Martinez. "What?" he said. "You think the mafia was involved? In Australia?"

"Just asking."

"Well, I may have my networks. I may be well connected," Bilson smiled. "But not in Australia. Are the mafia in Australia, too?" he asked Nguyen.

"I think they're most places these days."

"Nothing else you can tell us?" Martinez said.

Bilson still appeared to be thinking. "No. Nothing more. Don't think so."

"Well, if you do think of anything, please let me or Detective Krassberg know. We'll make sure it gets to Detective Nguyen." She gave Bilson her card.

"Detective April Martinez. I most certainly will call you, if there is anything. But, if there's nothing else, I am rather busy ..." He stood up.

"Did he leave a will?" she asked, as they also stood up.

"Yes, as a matter of fact he did. Before he left for down under. I have it here in our safe. It's quite secure."

"You might like to get it out, let his ex-wife know, and his parents. And anyone else involved."

"Will do, April," he said.

As THEY GOT INTO the car, Martinez said, "I can see what Diane Montrose meant."

Krassberg said, "I didn't see anything I didn't expect to see." He laughed.

She punched him on the shoulder.

"Well, you need anything else while you're here, John?"

"No. Nothing much from Bilson. Just confirmed what we already know. I think he was lying about the mafia, though."

"That's for sure," Krassberg said. "Anyone with eyes and ears in this town knows the mafia are everywhere."

"What time's your flight?" Martinez said.

"I need to be at JFK by 2:30. Just need to get back to the hotel, call back to the office and set up a couple of things."

"We'll drop you at the hotel. Need a lift to JFK?" Martinez said.

"Have you got time? You've both already been so helpful."

"No worries, as you Aussies would say," she said.

"Yeah—how about we pick you up from the Hyatt at 1:15? Okay?" Krassberg said.

"Okay. That would be great. Thanks."

Thursday

52

DEIRDRE RANG STEVE. "I just remembered something. The police sergeant, Brothers, he asked me whether I knew Freddie Antwerp, or Henry Steenvater."

"Who are they?" Steve said.

"They work in IT, at Cambridge Bank."

"What are their names again?"

"Antwerp and Steenvater."

"So why did he ask you, I wonder?"

"I bet they're connected to the dead man. Don't forget, I work in IT, too—also in banking.

"So maybe you should have a chat to them. Maybe they'll be able to fill in some missing blanks for you."

"That's a great idea. Thanks. I hadn't thought of that," Deirdre said.

"Cambridge Bank, you say?"

"Yes. I'll ring them, set up appointments."

"Will they see you?"

"Well, I work in cyber security, too. Would you mind coming with me when I see them?"

"Of course. Just let me know when."

She hung up, then checked the number for Cambridge Bank, rang it.

When she finally got through to a human voice, she asked to be put through to Freddie Antwerp.

"Yes?" The phone was answered by an impatient voice. "Freddie Antwerp? I'm afraid he no longer works here."

"When did he leave?"

"He stopped working here a week or so ago."

"Why did he leave—sorry, I shouldn't ask that."

"That's okay—he didn't get fired. Or resign. He's passed."

"He's passed? Passed what?"

"I mean he's, er, deceased."

Deirdre understood what it meant to say your jaw dropped, even though she knew it was still attached to her face. "He's dead?"

"So the police say."

"Well, thanks." She hung up.

Was that why Sergeant Brothers had mentioned those names? Freddie Antwerp was dead. Was he the man in her bed? But why? She rang the bank again, and after the interminable options and music, asked to speak to Henry Steenvater. She was put through to another voice.

"Mr. Steenvater's office. Carmen speaking."

"Could I speak to Mr. Steenvater, please?"

"Who may I say is calling?" Well at least it didn't sound like *he* was dead.

"Deirdre Makepeace."

"Where are you from, Ms. Makepeace?"

"Bank of Ballarat."

"Does he know you?"

"Well, we have met."

"I'll see if he's available."

After about 30 seconds she was put through.

"Steenvater speaking."

"Oh yes, Mr. Steenvater. This is Deirdre Makepeace, from the Bank of Ballarat."

"Do I know you?"

"Not really. It's about Freddie Antwerp."

The line went quiet. She could hear him breathing.

"What about Freddie Antwerp?" The voice was guarded.

"I'd like to come to see you. I don't want to talk about it over the phone."

"Hmm." She heard the breathing again.

"Could we meet for a coffee?"

"A coffee?" There was another pause. "Yes, that's a good idea. What's your name again? Deirdre …?"

"Makepeace."

"When, Ms Makepeace?"

"When are you free?"

"Let's see." Another pause. "How about tomorrow afternoon, at three."

"That's good for me."

"Can you come here to Collins Place? Let's meet at Ambrosia. Do you know it?"

"I'll find it. Thank you. See you at three."

Yes! she thought. Yes!

She rang Steve, explained about Antwerp. "He's dead."

"Antwerp's dead?"

"His assistant said passed, then deceased. So, dead, yes. He must be the guy in my bed."

"Jesus. And he worked with this guy Steenvater. What time are you meeting him?"

"Three o'clock tomorrow."

They agreed to meet at Ambrosia at 10 to 3.

"Maybe you'll finally get to the bottom of things."

"Let's hope so. See you at ten to."

Friday

53

AMBROSIA WAS A BRIGHTLY lit cafe in the Collins Place arcade. It did not look gourmet, in fact for an upmarket locale like Collins Place it was distinctly down market. No sign of artisan pastries or single origin coffee.

Deirdre and Steve ordered coffee at the bar. Deirdre led them to a table near the rear so they could see when Steenvater arrived.

"So," Steve said, "You reckon this Antwerp could be the guy in your bed."

"Yes. He could be. He's dead. But how come he worked for Steenvater."

"Does it seem odd that he agreed to meet you so readily?"

"Well, I work in cyber security, too."

"Yes, but you mentioned Antwerp. And Steenvater must know he's dead."

"We'll find out soon enough."

A tall man in his fifties, in a dark grey suit that didn't conceal a generous waistline, entered the cafe and peered around.

"That's him," Deirdre whispered, and stood up to greet him.

"Mr. Steenvater?"

"Ms. Makepeace? Hello."

"Deirdre." She beckoned him over to their table. "I hope you don't mind. I brought a friend. Steve Dalmatico."

Steve stood up, shook the man's hand.

"You play footy?" he asked.

"Yep," Steve smiled. "For St Kilda."

"Ah yes." Steenvater looked him over, assessing him. "You played forward, didn't you?"

"Forward, wing, midfield. It changed a bit."

"Quite. Quite." Steenvater sat down, eyeing them warily. "You wanted to speak to me, Ms Makepeace, about Freddie Antwerp?"

"Well, yes," Deirdre said. "Would you like a coffee?"

Steenvater shook his head. "Just a glass of water."

Deirdre went to the bar and poured a glass of water, gave it to Steenvater, then handed him her business card. "I work for the Bank of Ballarat."

Steenvater took a business card from his coat jacket and gave it to Deirdre. As she glanced at it, Steve asked, "How did he die?"

Steenvater jerked his head, glared at Steve, then took a breath, as if he'd made a decision. "I don't know. The police asked me the same question. How do you know him?" he asked Steve.

"I don't."

"Pardon?" Steenvater sat up straighter. His eyes hardened. "You don't know him?"

"No. Never spoke to him."

"Then why are we meeting?"

Deirdre spoke. "I saw him on the day he died. At The Belvedere in South Melbourne."

"The Belvedere? You were at The Belvedere? Why were you there?" A thought seemed to have occurred to him. "Do you live there, too?"

"Yes, I do. And you said 'too'—so, do you live there?"

"I've got the penthouse." He relaxed a little and smiled complacently.

"Look, I work in cyber security. And I know Freddie did. And so do you."

Steenvater shrugged. "IT, really. But, yes, that does include cyber security. So what?"

"So what was Freddie doing that got him killed?"

"I've no idea. The last I saw of him he was alive and kicking."

"But what was he doing for you," Steve asked.

"What's your interest in all this? A bit different to football, isn't it?"

"I'm a friend of Deirdre's." He patted her hand. She pulled it away and reached for her coffee.

Steenvater looked around, then eyed them both. "I've already told the police. Antwerp was trying to find some money, for the bank."

"What money," Steve asked.

"I've told this to the police. You know the Millennium Bug?" Steenvater explained how a huge amount of money had been skimmed off, from millions and millions of transactions. "He was trying to find what happened to it."

Deirdre nodded. "Did he find it?"

"No. He was getting somewhere, but no."

"Is that why he died?"

Again, Steenvater looked around. He bent forward. "There were a couple of mafia guys, out from the States. They were after the money, too."

"What. Did they kill him?" Steve said.

"Who knows?" Steenvater shrugged.

"Can you please explain this business of how the money got skimmed off, again?" Steve asked.

"It's a rounding up algorithm," Steenvater said. "The money was diverted into other accounts. That's what Freddie was trying to track down. I still don't understand how you come into all this. Or," he muttered, "why I'm telling you this." He eyed Deirdre. "How do you know when he died?"

"I found him dead. In my bed," Deirdre said.

"What?" Steenvater jerked upright. "I thought you said you didn't know him." He looked at her in disgust.

"Hang on, buddy," Steve said. "She found him in her bed. He was already dead. She didn't sleep with him. She didn't know him, didn't even know who he was."

Steenvater frowned, sipped his water. "In your bed?"

"Yes—on Sunday morning. The Sunday before last. So, I think I have a right to know what's going on."

He stood up. "Nice meeting you both," he said, and stalked out of the cafe.

Steve and Deirdre exchanged glances.

"Well," Deirdre said. "Was that helpful. Or was it helpful?"

"At least we know that Steenvater was using Antwerp to find the money. How much, do you reckon?"

"What did he say—rounding up? That means there'd be around a half cent on average where rounding up would work. How many zillions of transitions have taken place since then?"

"Whew." Steve started counting to himself. "A shitload, don't you reckon?"

"That would explain the mafia," Deirdre said. She sat there for a time, contemplating the situation. "A very large shitload."

"What do you want to do now?" Steve asked.

"Find that money!" Deirdre grinned.

Steve gazed at Deirdre; she saw confusion on his face, which changed to a smile, perhaps of understanding. "Find the money," he repeated.

"Yes—Antwerp's no longer in the picture. I reckon I'm as good at IT as anyone. So—I'll finish what he started."

"How ...?" Steve's question faded out.

"With difficulty!"

Looking at his face, she added, "We'll need to get pompous arse on board."

"And how do we do that? He looked pretty rattled."

"Yes—but he said stuff he didn't need to say. I reckon he was there for more than one reason."

"What do you mean?" Steve frowned.

"He was curious, for a start. And because I work for another bank, in IT, I reckon he might be thinking of his future."

"What—going to work for another bank?"

She shook her head, smiled. "No, you idiot. If Antwerp is dead, he needs another expert to help him."

Steve blinked. "So?"

"So, I could be the next Freddie Antwerp."

"And get yourself killed?"

"If I get involved, no one will know. He mentioned the mafia. They don't know me."

"They'll find out."

"How? I'm just a lil ol' Aussie bank worker."

"Well I want you to be a lil ol' *live* Aussie bank worker."

"Come on," she stood up.

"Come on where?"

"I want to see where you live."

"But I told you. It's a mess."

"Come on." She grabbed his hand. "A mess I can handle. Let's just forget about all of this and get to your place."

THEY CAUGHT AN UBER to Steve's apartment, on Beaconsfield Parade in St Kilda. It was on the top floor of a four-storey block overlooking the beach. It was full of light, white, lots of glass, a tiled floor in the main kitchen cum living room, with a pale green rug on the floor.

"Wow—makes my place look pretty small."

"Being a footballer does have a few benefits."

He showed her around. There were three bedrooms, one clearly slept in, one set up as a study, and one spare. The bathroom had a full-size bath, white tiles up the walls, the floor tiled in a dark grey.

"I thought you said it was a mess," Deirdre said.

"Well." Steve shrugged. Then, "Would you like a drink? Another coffee? A glass of something?"

"Water will be fine."

They sat on stools at the kitchen bench.

"So how do you get the money?" Steve asked.

"I'll check my Ballarat Bank first—see if there were any suss transactions back in 2000—or even if there are any still today. Then—" she paused.

"Then?"

"Then, if the syphoning occurred, or if it is still occurring, I'll find out which account it's been fed into. Or still being fed into." She had a thought. "It'd be funny, wouldn't it, if somehow after someone went to all the trouble to set this up, no one ever accessed the cash."

"Hmm. And if you can't find anything at your bank?"

"Yeah, it's unlikely to have happened at Ballarat. If there's nothing there, we speak to Steenvater."

Steve gazed at Deirdre in admiration. "Sounds like a plan."

"You know, if Steenvater can give me access, I should be able to follow the rabbits down their burrows, remotely. I wouldn't need to go into the bank itself."

"Can you do that for Ballarat Bank, too?"

"Of course. I already work remotely from time to time."

"What do you do if you find the money?"

"Hmm." She eyed Steve speculatively. "You said you."

"Well, it's your idea."

"We could turn it in. I say we, because you're part of this now, aren't you?" She gazed at him, and he smiled back. She relaxed. "But no one will know, will they. We could keep it. Or some of it."

"Why, what would you do with it?"

"I could stop working, I suppose." An image of a tropical beach floated in her mind's eye. A waiter dressed in white offering her a gin and tonic, made from artisan international award-winning Tasmanian gin.

Steve nudged her. "Hey."

She blinked, looked at him. "What?"

"Think it through. If you suddenly stop working, won't that be suspicious? What would you tell Fran, or your other friends? Wouldn't the police keep an eye on you?"

"Don't be a wet blanket," Deirdre said. "I could say I won the lottery."

"Well, yeah. There's that. Would anyone check?"

"Damn. You know, you're right. People would ask questions."

"Maybe you could get a finder's fee. Put a proposal in first, to the bank. Be vague—you don't want to give anyone else the big idea."

"A finder's fee? Not bad. Not bad. Yes, I needn't mention the Millennium Bug. But, if we go to Steenvater, would he go along with that?"

"Maybe he's the sort of guy who could authorize the finder's fee. He'd be doing his own bank a service. He could probably grab a chunk himself. Five percent of a billion is 50 million dollars. That would do me!"

"He'd be a management hero—and he would pocket at least 10% himself, to boot."

"Well, that just leaves one thing to do," Steve said.

"What's that?"

He stood up, kissed her. "Come here," he said.

54

"You know," Deirdre said, lolling in bed besides a sleepy Steve, "I think I'll get onto this now. Can I use your computer?"

"What?" Steve said. He opened his eyes, smiled at her, lifted himself up to give her a kiss. "Computer? It's in the study."

She got up, twirled around. "Can I use the shower?"

"Sure—I'll get you a towel." He cuddled her, got out of bed and then led her to the bathroom.

"Here." He took a fluffy white towel out of a cupboard, then kissed her again.

"Thanks." She pushed him away. "Later."

The shower had a large rainwater head above her, plus a hand held spray. She waited for the hot water to come through, then stood under the heavy stream. She felt it sluice through her hair, down her body, as if it were also washing any cares away.

Drying herself, she walked back to the bedroom and pulled on her clothes. Steve was lying in bed, and he looked up.

"Okay? My turn." He got up as she dressed.

She walked into the study. The computer was on the desk.

"Does it need a password?"

"You won't need it for the browser," he called back from the bathroom.

She keyed in her details on the Ballarat Bank site, and waited till her connection was confirmed. She thought for a while. Then she searched the daily master file, to see if the records from the year 2000 were accessible.

She felt a hand on her shoulder, glanced up, and pushed it off. "Later, Steve. I've got to concentrate."

"Like a coffee?"

"No, I'm okay."

She delved back into the files, absorbed. After a time, she shook her head and sat up.

"Steve?"

"Yep," he called from the kitchen.

"I can't find anything yet. That's not to say there isn't anything. But it'll take me a lot longer to rule it out completely. I suspect I'll have to get access to the archived files. I think we might need to go back to Steenvater."

"You reckon? How were you searching?"

She stood up and stretched, walked and sat down next to Steve at the kitchen island bench.

"Look, it's difficult to do, let alone explain. I've been trying to find any coded instruction to round numbers up or down. It's a bit of a nightmare. They might be there, or they might not. But I'm not sure I know what I'm looking for. That's why Steenvater might be able to point me in the right direction. He'll need someone to help. I think that's why he agreed to meet today—to check me out. I did say I worked in IT at a bank."

"Give him a call tomorrow. It's important to meet him, face to face again."

"Yeah, you're right. Just a phone call won't work."

"If he's interested, you'll need some agreement. Make sure it's in writing."

"If he's interested, the question is, will he do it officially. With a finder's fee. Or will he be greedy and want the lot for himself? Even with some small payment to me."

"If it's official, he can organize the paperwork."

"And if it's not?"

Steve looked up, stared at her, his face serious. "If it's not going to be official, I reckon you should walk away from it all." He nodded his head, as if settling an unspoken argument. "And, you should tell the police. That will put you in the clear."

"What would I tell the police?"

"Exactly what you wanted to do. That you offered to try to track down the money, for a finder's fee, and he said no."

Deirdre thought about this. "It would keep me in the clear, wouldn't it?" Then she added, "But there'd be no more billion dollars." There was a wistful tone in her voice.

"Dee?" Steve jabbed her.

"Ow. What?"

"Do you agree?"

"About what?"

"Doing something criminal is not the basis of a relationship. Or rather, not the basis of one I want to be part of."

"Relationship." He'd said the word. "Hmm," she said. "Making conditions, are we?" She wasn't sure whether she was amused or irritated.

"Yep." He smiled.

"It would be fun, though, wouldn't it?"

He shook his head, them said, "Beware brief delight and lasting shame."

Again she felt a slight annoyance, but then she laughed, and kissed him. "Okay. Nothing illegal!"

He tickled her below the ribs.

"Hey!"

She ran into the bedroom, grabbed a pillow and stood behind the door. As Steve came in she tried to thump him across the shoulders. Missed. Damn, he was too tall.

He whisked the pillow from her, picked her up and threw her face down on the bed. She rolled over and reached for him. Uh oh, she thought. Here goes the evening.

Saturday

55

DEIRDRE WOKE UP, stretched and looked around. She was alone in the bed. Her head was clear and the world was good. She got up, felt a little giddy and stumbled to the toilet.

She emerged to the smell of espresso coffee, and wafted after it into the kitchen, where Steve had just poured two cups.

"You like a flat white, don't you, Dee?" he asked.

"Yes, Stee," she said, sipping it.

"Are you still up to calling Steenvater?" he asked.

She sipped some more. "Yes—have you got any toast?"

"Coming right up. Feel like bacon and eggs?"

She nodded. "Yes please. No toast?"

"Coming up. With toast."

She thought about the call she would make, and checked her phone; it was 7:38. "I'll call him after 8," she said. "Catch him early."

SHE RETRIEVED STEENVATER'S CARD from her handbag, studied it and dialed.

"Steenvater speaking." The voice was pompous, impatient.

"Hi Mr. Steenvater. This is Deirdre Makepeace. We met yesterday."

"Ms. Makepeace. Do we have anything further to say to each other?" he said.

"Well, I thought I might be able to help you find the money."

"What are you talking about?"

"I'm in IT, too, you know. I reckon I'm pretty damn good. Probably better than Antwerp. So, maybe I can help."

For a time Steenvater said nothing.

"Hello?" Deirdre said.

"Hold on. I'm thinking."

"Could we meet again?"

He said nothing.

"Just the two of us. I want to explain my idea, without interruptions."

"Your idea? Hmm." There was silence again. Then, after a time, he said, "Very well. You say you live in The Belvedere?"

"Yes."

"Well, come up to my penthouse tomorrow evening—say around 8."

"Okay. Eight o'clock, tomorrow evening. Yes. That's the top floor, isn't it?"

"Yes—apartment 2302."

"I'll see you tomorrow night, then."

She put her phone down and gave a thumbs up to Steve.

"I'll see him tomorrow night at 8 o'clock."

"How did he sound?"

"At first his usual pompous self. But I think he wants to find the money. I reckon that's why he's seeing me again."

"Well, be careful when you see him."

56

Nguyen's flight arrived at Tullamarine on Saturday morning. He'd managed to get some sleep, and after passing through customs—which was very slow because the electronic passport readers were down and he'd had to queue—he'd collected his bag and caught a cab home.

Hahn welcomed him at the door, his daughter Minh standing at her side, arms outreached towards him. He kissed Hahn, lifted Minh up and hugged the two of them.

"Good flight?" Hahn asked.

"Yes, but too long. I'm glad to be home." He lugged his bag inside, and they sat around the kitchen table.

"Did you get what you wanted? Was the trip worth it?"

"I think so. We certainly know a lot more than before I went." He rarely talked about work at home, but he'd let Hahn know the broad details of why he'd had to fly to the States.

"Any jet lag?"

"It'll probably kick in later today."

"Feel like breakfast? I've made some bánh cuốn."

"They did feed me on the plane."

"But, daddy. It's yummy," Minh said, picking up a set of chopsticks and pushing them across to him.

Nguyen smiled and took the chopsticks from his daughter, pointed at the bánh cuốn. She pushed the dish across to him, and Hahn put several pieces on his plate. He sniffed them, his eyes on his daughter as she gazed at him. He tousled her hair and ate two pieces before saying, "You're right, Minh. Yum yum!"

Hahn watched him eat. "I bet they didn't have that on the plane," she said.

He nodded, chewing. Hahn was such a good cook.

Sunday

57

On Sunday morning Nguyen was back in the office, with Brothers. Commander Forell had approved the overtime because of the Antwerp case. Like most Sundays, it was quiet. They sipped coffee, and Nguyen told Brothers about his trip.

"You know those two guys Steenvater met? They're Mafia. The FBI identified them. Al Geronimo and Pauli Desica. I emailed you the details."

"Yeah. You reckoned Geronimo and Desica must have flown under the fake names and passports. Stevenson and Knight."

Nguyen nodded. "I've arranged for an Interpol red flag in case they try to travel again."

"I wonder how important they are, in the Mafia."

"How do you mean?"

"Well—if they flew out here just to bump off Antwerp, they wouldn't be the most senior players, would they?"

"So?"

"So, would their bosses care that much if they're picked up? Or would they be hiding them?"

Nguyen gazed at Brothers, sipped some more coffee. Maybe he was still jet lagged. Never thought of that. "You're right. Hopefully they'll be found. I'm sure Forell will be pleased with what we've got so far. The trip has certainly paid off. Not only do we know the names of the possible killers, but we also know the name of the victim!"

"Did our US buddies look after you?"

"Too right. Very helpful."

"When are you briefing Forell?" Brothers asked.

"We'll brief her together on Monday. You can bring her up to date on the Melbourne end, and I'll fill her in on the US trip."

BROTHERS TOOK THE CALL at 9:58am. "A body in the lift, you say? And where are you? In the lift? Where's the lift?" Brothers thought he recognized the voice, but couldn't immediately place it.

"The Belvedere Apartments."

"The Belvedere?" Brothers shouted.

"Yes, The Belvedere, in South Melbourne. This is beyond a joke. I rang before. Two weeks ago. I'm Gerald Kraeje. I think it's the same body."

"The same body?"

"As last time."

"Hang on a sec, Mr. Kraeje." Brothers put the phone down, his face white. He stood up and threw a scrunched-up piece of paper through the door at Nguyen, who turned around. "There's a body in a lift at The Belvedere. Again."

Nguyen looked up. "What are you playing at, mate. I'm still jet lagged."

"Kraeje's on the phone—he's found another body in the lift."

"Gerald Kraeje?"

"The same."

"In the lift?"

"The same." Brothers wasn't sure whether he should laugh or scream.

"Tell him to wait in the fucking foyer."

"Mr. Kraeje, we'll be there straight away. Can you please wait in the foyer? And please don't touch anything."

Brothers had just hung up when the phone rang again. He answered it impatiently.

"Yes? What now?" His voice changed. "Winner—it's for you. The Feds."

"Can you take down the details? Tell them I'll call them back. We've got to go to The Belvedere. I can't speak now."

58

WHEN NGUYEN AND BROTHERS arrived at The Belvedere, Gerald Kraeje, again dressed in lycra, was pacing up and down.

"Hello, Mr. Kraeje," Nguyen said.

Kraeje simply pointed to the middle lift, the door of which was open.

"I put my backpack there. Kept the door ajar." Kraeje smiled helpfully.

They approached the lift and looked in. A man without a shirt lay slumped in the corner.

"I was doing what I do every Sunday, going for my bike ride," Kraeje said. "I just got into the lift—and there he was."

Nguyen and Brothers ignored him and peered at the body. The eyes were open, blank. The face looked like the photo he had been given by Diane Montroso. "Freddie Antwerp," he whispered.

Brothers was already calling Sue Gossiter on his phone. "Sue? We need you. Yes, straight away. We've found Freddie Antwerp. We think. At The Belvedere."

"What the fuck?"

"Yes. The body in the lift. The middle lift. The same middle lift."

Nguyen snatched the phone. "Hi Sue. Can you and your team get here pronto? We'll stay here to make sure it doesn't go walkabout again." He turned to face the agitated man. "Thank you again, Mr. Kraeje."

Kraeje looked from one to the other. "Just doing what any good citizen would do."

"Well, unfortunately not everyone is as civic minded as you."

"How can this happen? It's the same body, isn't it?"

"Maybe he had a twin," Brothers said.

"A twin?" Kraeje looked appalled.

"You never know."

Kraeje contemplated the two police, unsure what to say.

"This must be a shock, Mr. Kraeje. Can we do anything for you?" Nguyen said.

Kraeje thought for a while. "No, it's okay. I'll just go for my ride. That'll clear the cobwebs. Is that okay? Do you need a statement or something?"

"Sergeant Brothers here will take some notes. That okay with you?"

Kraeje nodded.

While Brothers asked a series of questions and jotted down the answers, Nguyen called Deirdre Makepeace.

"Ms. Makepeace? Detective John Nguyen here."

"Hello, Detective. Can I help you?"

"Actually, you can. Are you at home at the moment?"

"No. I'm out with a friend."

"Would you mind coming back to The Belvedere?"

"Why? I can of course, if it's important, but why? On a Sunday?"

"It is important, Ms. Makepeace. Very important. It's best if I explain when you get here. Are you far away?"

"You mean you are there? At The Belvedere?"

"Yes. Will it take you long to get here?"

"Maybe a quarter of an hour."

"Thank you very much. I really appreciate it. I'll meet you in the foyer."

About 12 minutes later a uber pulled up outside The Belvedere and Deirdre Makepeace got out. She entered the foyer, saw Nguyen and approached him.

"Hello, Detective. How can I help you?"

"Ahh … we've found a body. In the lift."

"What?" Deirdre gasped. Her arms flew up and she grabbed her hair. "Another body? Why do you want to see me?"

"We need you to tell us if it's the same person who was in your bed."

"But how could that possibly be? That was two weeks ago. I don't understand. Wasn't that Freddie Antwerp?"

"You know about Freddie Antwerp?"

"Sergeant Brothers told me he was dead."

"I'm sorry, this is not very pleasant. But please take a look. See if you recognize him."

She saw that the middle lift was open, with two people standing nearby. Nguyen led her to it, and she peered in. A body without a shirt lay slumped in the corner. She gasped again, put her hand to her mouth. She looked at the face, saw the pants and shoes.

"My God. That's him!"

"You're sure?"

"Yes. That's the man who was in my bed." She swayed, and Nguyen grabbed her arm, steadying her. "So that's Freddie Antwerp!"

"You're sure?" he said.

"But why is he in the lift—again? How could that be? He was dead two weeks ago. I'm sure he was dead."

"We don't know yet. We'll find out, I can assure you."

"This is awful, awful. What's going on?"

"I know it's very distressing. Ms. Makepeace, thank you so much for coming here. I'm sorry to press you, but are you definitely sure it's the same man?"

"I'm sure," she muttered. "I don't feel well. Do you need me anymore?"

"No. Thank you. Thank you for your help."

"I need to go home upstairs and sit down," she said.

"Of course. I'm really sorry this has upset you."

BACK IN HER APARTMENT, Makepeace flopped on her couch. The dead man, the man she and Fran had put in the lift, was back, two weeks later. It didn't make sense. She found her phone and called Steve.

"Steve," she sobbed.

"What is it, Dee?"

"The reason the police wanted me to come back here is that the body has turned up in the same lift again." She stifled her sobs.

"What? The same man?"

"Yes. Freddie Antwerp. And in the same lift, too."

"That's ridiculous. I'm coming over."

"Thank you. Thank you." She hung up.

She dried her eyes, poured herself a drink of water. How could Antwerp turn up in the same lift again?

59

Three quarters of an hour after Nguyen and Brothers rang from The Belvedere, Sue Gossiter and her team arrived. She waved at Nguyen and Brothers and strode past them straight to the lift. She stood staring with hands on hips, then shook her head and whistled. She used her phone, took some photos, called over her shoulder to an assistant, "Get the gurney!"

The assistant, a man in his 20s in a white lab coat, ran off, and returned shortly with a silver gurney and another two men in their 20s, one carrying a case.

Gossiter was kneeling down scrutinizing the body without touching it. She sniffed it.

"Nothing immediately obvious apart from that dried blood on the head. Let's get it out of here. Tony, you check for prints and DNA. Got it?"

One of the men opened his case.

The other two nodded, and grasped the body under the armpits and the legs, heaved it onto the gurney. It was still dressed with trousers, socks and shoes, but no shirt or other clothing above the waist. Gossiter inspected it again. She half rolled the body and checked the back, raised the arms, examined the head.

"Sue," Nguyen called.

She looked up.

"Results ASAP, okay?"

She shrugged, and smiled. "Top priority. Should have some prelim results tomorrow—possibly later today. Depending if it's complicated."

"Complicated? A corpse disappears, then shows up in the same spot a fortnight later. I'd say complicated is a fucking good word."

"Well, there's no sign of any trauma apart from the back of the head. But there is something else strange here."

"What's that?"

"There's no smell. It's been a fortnight. It should be off, rotting. I'll let you know more once I find out."

Sue gave instructions. Tony and another of her aides started collecting evidence in the lift. She turned and followed the gurney being wheeled by the third man.

"WINNER, KNOCK, KNOCK," Gossiter said to Nguyen at the door to his office. It was just past 4 o'clock. "This is a real bizarro. I thought you should know straight away."

Nguyen looked at her, kept his face blank. She was right—bizarro was a good word. He was still jet lagged, and sick of the whole Antwerp business. And Sue wasn't displaying her usual jokiness.

"You've got news? What do you reckon?"

"Looks like he died from a subdural hematoma," she said.

"What's that when it's at home?"

"It's bleedin' obvious, innit?" She said this in a Cockney accent.

"Not to me."

"Bleeding on the brain, Winner. From a knock to the head. Or a fall."

He called out to Brothers. "Come in in here, Graham. You'd better hear this. And bring in McTeish."

They stepped into the office, saw Gossiter and both nodded a greeting. Nguyen gestured to her to continue.

"Antwerp died from a sub—" she corrected herself "—from bleeding on the brain."

"What does that mean?" asked Brothers.

"Well, he suffered trauma to the brain that caused bleeding. His head may have been hit directly, maybe a punch, or he was knocked over and hit his head on something hard. That creates a hemorrhage that can kill you."

Nguyen whistled. "A king hit. Um, coward punch."

"Or he may have simply fallen. Same result. There's no bruising to the jaw or the rest of the head. There are slight abrasions where the body has been dragged, but the only damage to the head seems to be from just one blow, at the back. And if he hit his head, or someone hit him, he wouldn't have died straight away. These things usually take hours."

"You mean he could have been pushed over and hit his head?"

"Pushed, shoved, yes. Possibly punched, but I think that's less likely, unless the punch caused him to fall."

"Well we know the Yanks stuck his body in the boot of a car."

"Yes. But we don't know whether it was an accident or deliberate."

"It's not deliberate putting a body into the boot of a car, a stolen car?" Brothers said, his voice rising.

"I mean," Gossiter said, "we don't know whether his death, the hitting of the head on a hard surface, was an accident or deliberate. Not putting him in the boot."

"Why would the Yanks get involved if it was an accident? And if it was an accident, how did he end up in Makepeace's bed?" Nguyen said.

"That's for you to know and me to find out, Winner."

"But I don't know! That's the problem."

"How come the body didn't stink?" McTeish asked.

"Now there's a good question," Gossiter said. "The body seems to have been dead for only about a day. So either he wasn't killed a fortnight ago—"

"But he was found in that girl's bed. And in the lift," Brothers said.

"He could have been unconscious. Who'd have known? Maybe he just woke up yesterday morning."

"What, and ambled down to The Belvedere, so he could off himself in the lift? Jesus!" Brothers wiped his brow.

"Or?" said McTeish.

Gossiter glanced appraisingly at McTeish.

"You've got a bright one here, Winner. Or—" Gossiter paused, smiled. "Actually, I'm teasing you. We reckon he was indeed killed a fortnight ago, but someone tried a little amateur cryogenics. Stuck him in cold storage, put him a fridge."

"Why the fuck would anyone do that? How are we going to explain that to the boss?" Nguyen said. He had a thought. "Maybe they're trying to play games with us. Devious bastards. But why?"

NGUYEN REALIZED HE NEEDED to bring Forell into the loop, and rang her.

"John? Where are you calling from?"

"Hi boss. Here—the office."

"You back already?"

"Got home yesterday."

"Then you know this is Sunday. What's so important you have to call me on a Sunday?"

"Ah, the body turned up."

"Well, that's good, isn't it? Now we don't have a missing body. Makes things so much better when we have to deal with the reptiles."

"But it's where it turned up."

Forell said nothing. He could imagine her lips tightening. Finally she said, "Where did it turn up?"

"In the lift, at The Belvedere. Where it went missing."

"The Belvedere? What the fuck is going on? Tell me you're joking." He heard the gasp of an intake of air, and then it's expulsion. "No, you don't do jokes, do you?"

"Boss—the same guy found it and reported it. The guy who found him two weeks ago."

"Is he part of it, do you reckon? Surely that can't be a coincidence."

"Don't think so. He's just the unlucky stiff who found the … stiff."

"Don't start making jokes this late in your career," Forell said, but there was some warmth in her voice.

"I think he's okay, not involved. And we've already got forensics checking it out."

"Who have you got?"

"Sue Gossiter."

"Ah, good. She knows her shit."

"She's already worked out the body was in cold storage. No decay to speak of."

"Cold storage."

Nguyen could imagine the cogs or circuits or whatever they were in her brain buzzing or whirring.

"Someone's playing games with us. I don't like that," she said in a low voice.

That was more like the Forell he knew.

"Keep me up to date. I want a briefing tomorrow. What you found in the States, what your team's been up to here. Cold storage, eh?" She hung up.

60

EARLIER THAT SAME SUNDAY MORNING Pauli Desica had driven the BMW into the basement of The Belvedere.

Geronimo fidgeted, drumming his fingers on the door. "How long will it take to get to the airport?" he asked.

Desica glanced at him. "Just a mo." He fiddled with the GPS, keyed in Melbourne Airport. Essendon and Tullamarine came up. "Which one?" he muttered. He selected Tullamarine and a route came up. "About half an hour."

Geronimo checked his watch; it was 9:55am. "Our flight leaves at 2:10. Plenty of time. We can dump this, get out there by 11. Rest in the business lounge for a couple of hours."

Desica grunted, pulled the BMW up near the lifts, looked around the dim garage. The place was silent, no movement. He released the trunk and they both got out. Checking again that there was no one near, Desica pressed the lift button.

"If there's no one in the lift, we're okay."

The lift on the right pinged.

"Hang on, I've got an idea," Geronimo said. He pushed a button inside the lift, waited until its doors closed, then pressed the up button again.

"What are you doing. Shit, we need to get out of here."

"Just thought we should put it back in the same lift. Confuse the assholes."

The right lift appeared, and Geronimo did the same thing.

"Jesus, Al. We can't fuck around for your little games."

The middle lift appeared. Empty.

"Here we go."

They lifted the body and put it into a corner of the lift, slumped against the chrome bar. Geronimo pressed the top floor button.

"Hope Steenvater has a nice surprise."

Desica had jumped back into the driver's seat and started the car. Geronimo got in. There was a gentle beeping sound.

"Put on your fucking seat belt!" Desica said.

Geronimo did so, and the beeping stopped.

They drove out, and Desica followed the GPS onto the freeway.

"We'll be there in 25 minutes, according to this."

Neither spoke for a while. Then Geronimo laughed.

"What?"

"I was just imagining them getting into the lift."

"Who?"

"The Steenvaters. The lift doors open, and boom!—there's Antwerp. I'd love to see their faces."

Desica grinned. He kept to the speed limit of 80 ks, and in less than half an hour pulled into the long-term car park.

They took their bags from the back seat and, before shutting the door, Desica put the car keys behind the sun visor. He looked around: row after row of cars, stretching in all directions. He saw a sign with a huge E, and they trundled their way to the shuttle bus station.

"When I checked online it said there's a bus very few minutes," he said.

After three minutes a red bus appeared, and they put their bags into the rack and sat down, while the driver announced he was stopping at the international Terminal 4 as his final stop.

They got off and looked for the United Airlines counters, then went to the Business check in. Because they were hours early—it was before 11—there was no one lined up. And no one at the counter. They waited, and soon a young woman in a United uniform appeared and beckoned them to approach the desk.

"Passports, please," she said in an Australian accent.

Desica handed over the two passports, made out in the names Joseph Stevenson and Peter Knight.

She checked the photos, glancing at each in turn, then printed out two boarding passes.

"Mr. Stevenson, Mr. Knight," she said, smiling at each in turn and giving them their passports. "You'll need to fill out these departure cards"—she handed them one each. "You'll find the business lounge near the departure gates after passport control. Here are your invitations. Just show them at the door." She circled a small map on each card. "Here."

"Thanks, Ma'am," Geronimo said.

She attached labels to their bags, Desica watching carefully to make sure she did so.

"Have a safe flight."

They both nodded, and Desica turned to Geronimo. "Now for a little bourbon, and then, thank God this will all be over."

"Just have to remember our names for another couple of hours."

"No, you fuckwit. We gotta keep them until we get through the LA end. Remember?"

Geronimo bristled, but knew Desica was right. "Sure, sure. Don't get your knickers in a knot."

"Knickers? What the--?" Desica said.

"It's an Aussie expression, you dumb fuck." Feeling that honor was satisfied, he patted Desica on the shoulder as they wheeled their cabin bags into the customs area.

They filled out their departure cards, and lined up in the Business Class queue, where they were guided into lines before an automatic passport reader.

Desica stood where indicated, inserted his passport open at his photo into the device and waited while his face was scanned. A light blinked and an instruction appeared on the screen to remove his passport. A Home Affairs officer approached him.

"Sir—would you mind following me? This will have to be done manually."

He followed the officer, a short woman in a dark blue uniform, to a side room, where Geronimo was also waiting with another Home Affairs officer, a tall younger man, who said to them both, "This won't take long." She nodded to her colleague. "Your passports, please, and departure cards and boarding passes." She put out her hand.

Desica looked at Geronimo, who raised his eyebrows. He shrugged and they handed them over.

She perused them for a few moments. "Larry, can you get these fixed?"

He took them and left the room.

"I see you gentlemen are heading to LA. Pleasant time in Australia?" She had a bland expression on her face. Typical bureaucrat, thought Desica.

"Yes, great thanks."

"What were you doing here? I see you checked 'tourism' on the departure cards.

"Well, we saw quite a bit of Sydney and Melbourne. Caught up with some friends. Great restaurants."

"Did you get to Healesville?"

"Healesville?"

"To see the kangaroos and koalas."

"No, we didn't. Maybe next trip."

"I can recommend it. Healesville. It's about a 40-minute drive into the hills. There are also platypuses there. Or is that platypi?"

"Platypuses? Platypi? What are they?"

"Our cute Australian marsupials. They're mammals but they lay eggs. Live in rivers and streams." At their blank looks, she added, "They've got duck bills."

"Well, ma'am, we didn't see those critters either. Something to put on the list."

"The list?"

"You know, the bucket list."

The door opened and a fat Federal policeman entered. He glanced at both men, and at some papers in his hand.

"Mr. Knight? Mr. Stevenson? I'm Sergeant Gershon Ladbroke."

They both nodded.

"Is there a problem, Sergeant?" Desica asked.

"Just a couple of details we need to check. Shouldn't take long. Mr Knight? Would you please come with me? Mr. Stevenson, please stay here for the moment. Take a seat."

Geronimo followed Ladbroke out, and into a room down the corridor; the young Home Affairs officer who had taken their passports was sitting at a desk, and stood up.

"Sit down, please," Ladbroke said. "This is Mr. Aghan."

Geronimo sat, looking up at the policemen. Ladbroke had a large gut spilling over his belt, sandy hair thinning on top, a calm expression on his face. Aghan was skinny, dark haired with designer stubble.

"What's the problem, Sergeant?" Geronimo asked again.

"Your passport." He stared at Geronimo.

"My passport? Doesn't it have an electronic visa?"

"It may do, it may do. That's not the problem." He paused. "See, we have these photos of you, from the FBI. Says you're Al Geronimo. Is your passport a forgery, Mr. Knight?"

Geronimo stared straight ahead. "What are you talking about?"

"We'll have to take your prints. Won't take long. You probably know about that, anyway."

"What do you mean, know about that?"

"We just need to clarify this. Could be a simple misunderstanding. Larry, can you take the prints?"

Aghan had the equipment on a side table. He took Geronimo's prints. "Thanks, mate," he said.

"Okay, you can come back with me."

He led Geronimo back and escorted Desica to have his prints taken as well.

"Larry, can you scan them for me?" He gave Larry a slip of paper. "And email them please, to the office for checking."

Desica was taken back to the first room, and left alone with Geronimo.

"Jesus," Geromino said. "What the fuck?"

"Yes," was all Desica said. He picked up his cell.

"Is it wise to use that?"

"Just letting them know we may be delayed."

"It's still three hours before we're due to take off."

"Hello? I can't talk," Desica said, "We're having a check made. Customs. They say they think we're using fake passports."

He listened. "Okay. Okay. Yeah. Okay."

He put the phone down. "We're fucked, I'd say."

Geronimo paced around the room.

"Can we call a weasel?"

Desica picked up his cell again. Dialed, waited.

"You have someone here we can call? You know, a lawyer." He waited. "Thanks." To Geronimo he said, "They'll get in touch direct. We'll get a call from whoever."

"They work on a Sunday?"

Desica just looked at Geronimo who, looking shamefaced, said, "Sure, wasn't thinking."

"That would be right."

"WHAT'S THIS ABOUT, Gershon?" Aghan asked.

"Seems Vicpol want them. And now so do I. And so should you. They're using forged passports, complete with eVisas. The FBI says they're mafia, from Chicago. Wonder what they've been up to here. And how did Vicpol find them?" He mused for a minute. "We should have known about this."

"Lucky Vicpol wanted them. Otherwise they'd have gone straight back to the States. We'd have been none the wiser."

"We'll get the fingerprint results back soon. If they're the ones, I'll call, let's see—" he shuffled his papers, "Detective Inspector Nguyen. He may be able to put us into the loop. Meanwhile, feel like getting us a cup of coffee?"

"Sure, Sarge. How do you take it?"

"Latte, mate. Just one sugar—I'm cutting down."

"Okay." Aghan left the room, and Ladbroke picked up a newspaper and turned to the sports pages.

Aghan returned a few minutes later, and handed over Ladbroke's coffee.

"You're not having one?"

"No, I'm cool."

"Why didn't you say? Jesus, I would've gone."

"No, no probs. I needed a walk. How long before we get a response on the prints?"

Ladbroke looked at his watch. "Dunno. Could be an hour, half an hour if we're lucky. I'll give whatsisname, Nguyen, a call."

He checked the papers and dialed.

"Hello. This is Sergeant Gershon Ladbroke. AFP."

"Yes? AFP? Sergeant Graham Brothers here. What can I do you for?"

"Can I speak to Detective Inspector Nguyen?"

There was a pause.

"Look, sorry, mate, he's just dashed out. Can I take a message?"

"Can he call me back?" Ladbroke spelled out his name and mobile number. "This is pretty urgent, too."

"I'll make sure he gets back to you."

"Well, Larry" Ladbroke said. "They reckon they've got something urgent." He grunted, and winked. "Let's see what the prints show, first." He picked up the form guide.

ONCE NGUYEN WAS OFF the phone with Forell, he noticed the phone message on his desk. The AFP. Sergeant Gerson Ladbroke. He didn't know him. He dialed the number.

"Detective Inspector John Nguyen here. You rang before."

"G'day, mate. Gershon Ladbroke. Sergeant, that is. We've got a couple of likelies that I think you want to see."

"G'day, Gershon. Have we met?"

"Not as far as I know."

"Well, thanks for the call. Who have you got?"

"We've picked up two red flags—a Joseph Stevenson and a Peter Knight."

"Stevenson? Knight?" Nguyen was puzzled. He was jetlagged and though the names were familiar, he couldn't immediately place them. "Can't place them. Are you sure they're a red flag? Look, we're in the middle of something. Can I call you back a bit later?"

"You put out the red flags, Detective Inspector. It says here, John Nguyen. They're Americans. Maybe those were not their real names. They match some photos you flagged, of Al Geronimo and Pauli Desica. I'm at Tullamarine, and they were about to board a plane. We're keeping them on ice for the moment, till we find out which names are real. We expect the prints will come back shortly. Just confirmation, I expect. But as I say, the flags have a link back to you, Detective."

"Jesus. Thanks, mate. If they are who I hope they are, Gershon, we're in real luck. Al Geronimo and Pauli Desica are two Mafia, from Chicago. They could be the killers we are after."

"Killers?"

"Yes—and we've finally found the body. That's what I've just been caught up in."

"So what do you want me to do with them? I think I'll have to charge them—traveling on fake passports, you know. But you could come and have a chat, if you like."

"For God's sake don't let them get on that plane. Where are they flying to?

"They were going to LA. But they are not going anywhere."

"Listen, can I come out now? I need to interview them."

"Sure thing. I'll take them to our station here, on Service Road." Ladbroke gave the address details to Nguyen. "You can't miss it."

Nguyen beckoned Brothers over. "That was the AFP—the guy who rang earlier. I think he has our killers."

"What the —" Brothers said.

"Let's go."

61

THEY REACHED THE AIRPORT in just over half an hour. Brothers drove to the corner of Service Road and Francis Biggs Road, and parked outside the AFP station. They jumped out and walked to the entrance.

There was a reception desk, brightly lit and unstaffed, and they walked up to it. There was a buzzer, which Brothers pressed.

A tall, solid woman came through a door behind the desk. The exasperated look on her face softened when she saw Nguyen and Brothers. She looked at them quizzically.

"Is Sergeant Ladbroke in?" Nguyen asked. "I'm Detective John Nguyen and this is Sergeant Graham Brothers. From Victoria Police."

"Just a moment." She glanced at them, then disappeared through the door.

A minute or so later a large man appeared. He walked around the reception desk and approached, hand extended. "Gershon Ladbroke, gents," he said.

They shook hands, and Ladbroke said, "Killers, eh? We got confirmation. They are definitely Geronimo and Desica, all right, or my uncle's my aunty. How did you get onto them?"

"It's a long story. I'll fill you in later, if that's okay. But, boy oh boy, you are a godsend." Nguyen smiled. "We've had this—no. I'll tell you later."

They followed Ladbroke through the door, along a corridor to a holding cell. "Here they are." He pointed at the door. "Do you want them in an interview room?"

"That'd be good."

Ladbroke took them along another corridor, opened a door into a middle-sized interview room. "Wait here. I'll bring them to you."

There was a table, with four chairs, a video camera and microphone, and three more chairs along the wall.

Ladbroke reappeared with two men in handcuffs. He pointed to two of the chairs. "Take a seat."

They sat down. "Gentlemen, this is Detective Inspector John Nguyen, and Sergeant Graham Brothers, from Victoria Police. This is Mr. Al Geronimo and Mr. Pauli Desica."

"Our lawyer is on the way," Desica said.

"Excellent," said Nguyen.

"Why are you here?" asked Desica. "I thought the passport stuff was Federal."

Nguyen paused for a moment.

"Certainly the 'passport stuff' is a Federal offence. I'm sure our Federal colleague has that in hand." Ladbroke grinned.

"We'd like to ask you a few questions, if you don't mind."

"We do mind. As I said, our lawyer is on his way."

Nguyen ignored this comment.

"Do you know a Freddie Antwerp?"

Both men stiffened a little.

"Ah, you do."

"No comment," Geronimo said.

"Tell me, why did you kill him?"

"Kill him? Kill him? We didn't. We didn't kill no one."

"That's strange. We've just come from his body. Stuck in a lift at The Belvedere. That ring any bells?"

"We didn't kill him."

"Ah, so you know him, do you?"

"Who?"

"Freddie Antwerp."

"Never heard of him."

There was knock on the door, and the policewoman who they'd first seen put her head through, signaled to Ladbroke. He left the room, and returned with a wiry man with grey hair and a sneer.

"I'm Arthur Canterbury. You must be Mr. Knight and Mr. Stevenson." He looked at the two mafiosi. "I represent them," he said to Nguyen.

"You mean Mr. Al Geronimo and Mr. Pauli Desica, don't you, Mr. Canterbury?" Ladbroke said. "I'm Sergeant Gershon Ladbroke, and these two gentlemen are Detective Inspector John Nguyen and Sergeant Graham Brothers of Victoria Police."

"What has Victoria Police got to do with this?" Canterbury asked. He had a clipped English accent, and looked angry.

"That's what *I* said," Desica said.

"Shut up," Canterbury said. "Well? Certainly there's been some misunderstanding about these gentlemen's passports."

"That's right, a misunderstanding!" Geronimo interjected.

Canterbury stared at him, and he shut his mouth.

"We're not here about your passports," Nguyen said. "You're right. That is a matter for Sergeant Ladbroke. We're here about the murder."

"What murder?" Canterbury's voice rose an octave. He glared at Nguyen, then at Desica and Geronimo. "What murder?" he said in his normal voice.

"Mr. Freddie Antwerp. His murder," Brothers said with some satisfaction.

"And who the hell is Freddie Antwerp?" Canterbury wasn't sure whom to direct this question to, looking first at Brothers, then at his two clients.

"He's an IT guy. A cybersecurity expert. Works for, I should say, worked for, a Mr. Henry Steenvater at Cambridge Bank."

Both Descica and Geronimo glanced at each other at Steenvater's name.

"A good friend of your clients, I think, Mr. Canterbury." John Nguyen felt that at last all the balls were lining up.

"I demand to have some time with my clients. Otherwise, they'll say nothing."

"Yeah," said Geronimo. "We're not saying nothing."

Desica kicked Geronimo's leg under the table.

"Be our guest," Nguyen said. "Is that okay with you Sergeant?"

Ladbroke nodded, and the three police left the room.

"Constable, could you please make sure our clients don't leave the room? Oh—this is Constable Amelia Green." He introduced them.

"Would you like a coffee?" Ladbroke asked.

"Not for me, thanks," Nguyen said. Brothers shook his head.

"Yes please," said Green. "White, no sugar."

"But a glass of water?" Ladbroke asked.

"Sure," Nguyen and Brothers said simultaneously.

Ladbroke led them to a kitchen area, and poured a glass each.

"So this Antwerp. You just found him today?"

"Well," Nguyen said, sipping his water. "He first turned up a fortnight ago, dead in a lift, at an apartment building. The Belvedere."

"Actually, first in someone's bed," Brothers put in helpfully.

"Well, he disappeared, and now he's turned up this morning in the same lift. Same place."

"The Belvedere?"

"The Belvedere."

"The same body? A fortnight later?"

"The same body, a fortnight later."

"Jesus. That's something." He grinned. "Fucking amazing. And how did these two Yank jokers get involved?"

"We caught them on CCTV stuffing Antwerp into the boot of their car."

"A stolen car," Brothers said. "One we haven't found yet."

"That's where we got the photos of the two Yanks. And they were good enough for the FBI to identify them. So I put out the red flag. And thanks to the efficiency of Border Force and the AFP, Bob's your uncle."

"Well, murder trumps passport fraud."

"Can we take them back to Melbourne?"

"Be my guest. I'll just do the paperwork."

"Let's go back. The Canterbury jerk has had enough time. Oh, and Graham, can you call Constable McTeish, get her to drive out. We'll need them in separate cars."

Nguyen eyed Ladbroke. "Gershon—would you mind coming in with us. You know, two per car?"

Ladbroke thought for a moment. He looked pleased. "Well, let me check. Should be okay."

They put their glasses down on the sink. Ladbroke put them into the dishwasher, and made a coffee for Constable Green. They walked back to the interview room.

Green was standing outside the room, and Ladbroke handed her the coffee. He knocked on the door and opened it.

"Okay if we come in now?"

"Very well," Canterbury said. He seemed less aggressive. "My clients accept that their passports aren't quite in order. But they had nothing to do with the death of Antwerp. Or anyone else. And they need to be charged or released. They have a plane to catch."

"We'll be taking them back to Melbourne." Seeing Canterbury bristle, Nguyen added, "You'll be present at the interviews?"

"Where are you taking them?"

"To St Kilda Road."

"Right. Don't start without me." He stalked out.

Nguyen smiled at the others.

CAROL McTEISH WAS AT the airport in half an hour, and during that time Ladbroke organized the paperwork to release Geronimo and Desica into the custody of Victoria Police. It was agreed that she would drive with Brothers, with Geronimo in the back seat, and Ladbroke would travel with Nguyen, with Desica. Both Americans were handcuffed.

62

PROMPTLY AT 8 PM Deirdre knocked on the door of Apartment 2302.

Steenvater opened the door, still in his suit but without a tie. He craned his head and peered around the lobby, then gestured impatiently. "Come in."

She entered and followed Steenvater as he led the way into his study. As she entered, a woman appeared.

"Veronica, this is Deirdre Makepeace. Ms. Makepeace, my wife, Veronica," Steenvater said. "Ms. Makepeace works for the Bank of Ballarat."

"Hello, dear." Veronica Steenvater said.

"Hello, Mrs. Steenvater."

They shook hands.

"Would you like a cup of tea?"

"No, thank you."

"Well, Henry told me you have business to discuss, so I'll leave you to it."

"Sit down," Steenvater said, sitting down himself. Deirdre sat in a leather armchair.

"So, let's get down to tin tacks. You mentioned you had some ideas. What are they?"

"First, can we agree on an arrangement?"

"An arrangement?"

"I don't want to do anything illegal."

"Who mentioned the word illegal?"

"You did say on Friday that the mafia was involved."

"They need to be kept right out of it."

"Yes, but if this money has been siphoned off."

"Skimmed into untraceable accounts."

"Skimmed off, then. If it's been skimmed off, it's probably stolen money, isn't it?"

"Technically speaking, each customer may have lost about half a cent. Is that theft? Interesting question. Who would sue for less than half a cent? Or for a few dollars if there were multiple transactions."

"It's the principle of the thing. If all this money has been stolen, then won't the police want to get hold of it?"

"The police would need a complaint. Someone would have to report a theft. Who's going to do that?"

"Supposing that's true, and there are no complaints, what happens if I find the money for you? Will the mafia know?"

"How would they know?"

"Surely if all this money suddenly appears, people will notice. And then the mafia will notice. How did they get on to it in the first place?"

"Hmm," Steenvater said. "Good question." He fiddled with a pen on the coffee table between them.

"My idea," Deirdre began.

"Yes?"

"You make it official."

"Official?"

"If your Bank authorizes the search, then when the money appears the mafia can't touch it. Nor can the police."

"Yes, but then, what's the point? The Bank would certainly be pleased—adding millions to the bottom line. But why would *you* bother?"

"I'd get a finder's fee."

Steenvater put the pen down, and clasped his hands.

"And so would you," Deirdre said.

"Eh?"

"You'd authorize me to search for the money. And I'd get a finder's fee."

Steenvater took on a crafty smile.

"A finder's fee. Hmm."

"And as I said, you'd get one too, of course," Deirdre said. "The Bank's got nothing to lose. From the Bank's point of view, all they do, if this works out, is get extra money."

"What sort of finder's fee?"

"I was thinking twenty per cent."

"Twenty per cent? Of a billion dollars? You've got to be joking."

"The money may not exist."

Steenvater sat back in his chair.

"And you'd get a finder's fee, too, of course," Deirdre said again.

"Me? A finder's fee?" he repeated. "How?"

"From the Bank's point of view, it's your idea, isn't it? You get a finder's fee, too. At least the same as I'd get, if not more."

He thought about it.

"Everyone wins," Makepeace said. "The bank gets money, I get a finder's fee, and you get a finder's fee."

"I could never authorize twenty percent."

"Surely you'd get double what I'd get."

"Yes, yes. Of course. But the Bank has precedents, standards, protocols. Conventions."

"This is very unconventional, wouldn't you say?"

"Of course it's bloody unconventional. But ..." he trailed off, thinking. He muttered, as if to himself, "The reward, or finder's fee, can't be too big, or ... hmm. Hmm."

He sat up, beamed. "I tell you what, I can make it three percent. That could be 30 million."

"And you'd get five percent or whatever you negotiate. If I find the money."

"Hmm." He smiled. "Something like that."

"Tell you what, if you authorize me to look for this mythical money, pay me a fee while I search, and give me five percent if I find it—then you arrange to get ten percent. That way the Bank gets 850 million dollars."

Seeing he was about to continue to haggle, she said, "And you'd be a hero, wouldn't you? Think how you'd be seen. Delivering 850 million dollars to the Bank's bottom line. You'd be able to grow your department. If you wanted to keep working." She smiled at him. "After all, you'd have 100 mill."

He clasped his hands across his waist, then patted his paunch. "Hmm," he said. "Hmm. Okay. A deal."

"Really?" She laughed. "Should we shake hands, or something?"

He extended his hand and she rose to shake it.

"Of course, I'll need to document all this," Steenvater said. He frowned, then relaxed. "An exchange of letters, a MoU to start with."

"Certainly. We both need protection. And so will the Bank."

He frowned again. "What about you? Will there be a problem with the Bank of Ballarat?"

"How do you mean?"

"You working on this for me."

"Do they need to know? I mean, I could take leave."

"You'd have access to confidential Cambridge Bank business."

"They wouldn't care about that—but would Cambridge Bank?"

"Hmm. Hmm. I'm sure we can work a way around this."

"Mr. Steenvater—"

"Henry," Steenvater said. He smiled but he still sounded pompous.

"Henry," she said. "Doing it this way, it's all above board. Do you see?"

"What do you mean, above board? Of course it's above board. It was above board when Freddie Antwerp was researching for me."

"What, with the mafia?"

"The mafia, my dear, had nothing to do with me. In fact, they were threatening me. Me. Would you believe it?"

"Did you report them? I mean, to the police, or someone?"

"Of course not. Do you take me for a fool?"

"Surely it would protect you."

"Rubbish—it would have made things worse. If I'd gone to the police—" He shuddered. "Let's just say that discretion is sometimes the better part of valor."

"Well, if I'm to help you on this, I want no part of the mafia." She glared at him. "No part at all."

"Understood." He stood up and paced across his study. "They won't know you're doing this. They don't even know you exist, do they?"

"No, I suppose that's true."

"So, unlike Freddie, you'll be working completely without their knowledge."

"They don't have someone in your office, who might see what I'm doing? Even that I'm there? An inside man or woman?"

"Of course not. Certainly not. Seeing that poor Freddie is dead." Seeing her look, he added, "He was their person, you see."

"Their person? Then why did you hire him?"

"I didn't know at the time. I didn't know until they came to see me."

"The point I am trying to make." She shook her head. "It's got to be above board, legit. You'll authorize me, Cambridge will have a contract with you and me. Maybe it's best if I leave Ballarat Bank, that'll simplify things, so I'll need a salary from Cambridge. Would that be a problem?"

Steenvater shook his head straight away. "No problem. In fact, much better if you work for us."

"So when I find the money, Cambridge will be in the know, so the mafia won't be able to touch it. That's much better protection, isn't it?"

Steenvater looked at her, his eyes opened wider. "Good point. Good point," he said

Deirdre stood up. "Should I go now?"

"Yes. I'll get the paperwork organized. Can you come in on Monday?"

"Yes," Deirdre said. "First thing?"

"No, how about 1:30. Give me time to fix the authorizations and paperwork."

He opened the study door, and Deirdre followed him out. Veronica was sitting in their living room, and she stood up.

"Finished business, dear?" she said.

"Yes, yes. Most satisfactory," he said. "Ms. Makepeace is leaving now."

"Good bye," she said, taking Deirdre's hand. "Good luck."

"Good bye," Deirdre said.

63

AFTER RETURNING TO HER apartment, Deirdre called Steve, and gave him a rundown of the meeting.

"You think he's on the level?" Steve said. "I mean, he could be stringing you along."

"Let's wait and see the paperwork. If it's got the right authorizations, and he starts paying me to do the looking, then what have I got to lose?"

"You're right. I'm just worried that somehow he may have already done a deal with the mafia."

"But this will protect him, too, won't it?"

"I'm not sure the mafia takes much notice of bits of paper. If they think he's ratted on them, surely they'll come for him. Or have I been seeing too many Hollywood Godfather movies?"

"But he was right when he said they don't know about me."

"Not at the moment." Steve paused. "Should I come over? Or do you want to come here?"

Deirdre surveyed her apartment. Did it give her a queasy feeling? She peered into her bedroom. She'd slept there since the discovery. She was okay. No stress or trauma, or post trauma, or whatever it was. Or would she even know? And then that guy turning up again. In the same lift she and Fran had put him in.

"Steve, I'll come over to your place. Is that okay?"

"Sure, Dee. Of course. I think that'll be for the best."

"See you soon." She hung up. Then she had a thought, and called Fran.

"What's up?" Fran said, and laughed. "How's lover boy?"

"Fran. Fuck off," she said. She sighed loudly. "He's good, actually. Been really helpful. And I need to tell you something that's developed."

"You're not? Seriously? Are you? How can you tell so soon?"

"What? No. No. Don't be ridiculous. It's to do with Steenvater."

"Steen who?"

Deirdre explained that Henry Steenvater ran the IT at Cambridge Bank, his link to the Millennium Bug, the skimmed off money, the mafia, and the man in her bed, Antwerp.

"A billion, you say?" Fran said.

"Could be."

"And he's going to pay you to find it?"

"That's the plan."

"Well fuck me. That's great."

"It could really set me up." She laughed.

"Hang on, girl. Did you say the mafia killed the guy in your bed, this Antwerp?"

"I don't know. It seems likely, doesn't it?"

"But how did they get him into your apartment?"

Deirdre shivered. "I've no idea."

"And why put him in your bed? And, now I think of it, why kill him?"

"I don't know."

"Maybe he was double crossing them with this Steen—Steenvater guy."

"Probably. Does it matter?"

"Well, if they bumped off whatsisname, Antwerp, couldn't they bump you off just as easily?"

"They don't know I exist."

"True, true," Fran said. "Hmm."

"What?"

"Just thinking."

"About?"

"Nothing. Just another rabbit down a burrow. Forget it."

"Come on. What?" Deirdre was getting exasperated.

"Well, if this Steenvater guy is in cahoots with the mafia, he'll be in danger if he goes against them."

"That's what Steve said."

"I don't get why, if they bumped off Antwerp, why they didn't go for Steenvater, too."

"They're after the money. He's their entree into Cambridge Bank."

"Then why kill Antwerp?" Fran asked again.

"Who knows?" Deirdre said.

"It's just that …" Fran paused.

"Just what?"

"If Antwerp was the guy who was going to find the money, and he's out of the picture, won't they want someone else?"

"Someone else?"

"Another IT expert to find the money."

"But that's me."

"You know that. Steenvater knows that. Steve knows that. Even I know that—now. But do the mafia know it?"

"No, they don't."

"Exactly." Fran laughed.

Deirdre was silent. This all seemed to be going in loops. Then the penny dropped.

"Oh," she said. "They don't know I'll be searching for the money. So they'll want Steenvater to find someone else to do what Antwerp was doing."

"Exactly."

"And that means someone else will be chasing the missing money. At the same time as me." Deirdre paused as another thought occurred to her. "But they'll have to find someone they can trust. As you say, another IT guru. That'll take time to find one, won't it."

"I suppose that'll give you a head start," Fran said. "But it's already been twenty years. They can wait to find the right person. Hey—want to come up for a drink?"

"Thanks, but I'm going to Steve's."

"What—he's invited you over?"

"Already been there.'

"Deirdre, that's great. Go girl!"

"Fran, he's a good guy."

"Yeah, yeah."

"Yes. He is."

"Well, that's good. For now. See you soon? Maybe go for a walk next Sunday, and talk and catch up on everything?"

"Okay. Yeah. A walk will be good."

"Okay. And Deirdre?"

"What?"

"You're doing great."

"What?"

"Bye."

"Bye."

She hung up, then called an uber.

IN THE DRIVE OVER to Steve's she ignored the uber driver, and went over in her mind her meeting with Steenvater and her conversations with Steve and Fran. She'd have a contract with Cambridge Bank, authorized by Steenvater, to search for the money. With a finder's fee. The mafia would be trying to find another Antwerp. And again, the niggling thoughts, why did they kill him? And why in hell did they put him in her bed? And how did they do that? She shook her head in frustration. Another thought occurred to her. Should she clear it all with her boss at Ballarat Bank?

She thought about what she'd say. She'd put it up as being offered a contract, and probably pick up intel useful for Ballarat. Maybe Ballarat was affected, too. Her earlier search hadn't shown up anything, though admittedly it was pretty cursory. I'll talk it through with Steve. That will help me clarify things.

She was smiling when she got out and buzzed Steve's apartment.

He let her in and met her at his door. She filled him in, watching for his reaction. He listened quietly, and smiled from time to time.

"That's great, Dee. So Steenvater is going to employ you?"

"Yes—we agreed I'd go in on Monday afternoon to sign the papers. If they are in order, I think I'll have to resign from Ballarat Bank."

"What, and join Cambridge?"

"Yes. If they take me on."

"Good. That puts the whole thing on the level."

Deirdre frowned. "Of course it's on the level."

"I'm just thinking of you. Can I have a look at the papers?"

"Sure, if you want to."

"I mean before you resign from Ballarat Bank. You have to be careful."

"Of course I'll be careful. Real careful. I'll get a lawyer to look at it, too."

"Okay. That's good." He put his arms around her. "I just don't want you getting hurt."

She shrugged out of his embrace and looked him in the eye. He smiled back warmly.

"Okay." She kissed him. "It's just—it's been a while since I've been in a relationship." She paused. "I have to get used to trusting again."

"Of course." He kissed her back. "This is sudden for me, too." He stood back, his hands on her shoulders, looking at her. "You're —" he broke off. He mumbled something.

"What?"

He took a deep breath and repeated the words, "I want this to work."

She smiled, danced out of his arms, twirled around, then hugged him.

"So do I!"

64

NGUYEN PUT DESICA IN hand cuffs in the back seat with Ladbroke beside him. As they drove, Nguyen said, "Tell me, Mr. Desica, what brought you to Australia in the first place?"

At first it seemed that Desica wasn't going to answer, then he said, "Tourism. As I told the Sergeant."

"First time here?"

"Yeah."

"Where do you live back home?"

There was a pause. "Chicago."

"Never been there—just LA and New York. What's it like? How does Chicago compare to Melbourne?"

"Well, it's summer here, winter back home."

"And are you in the IT business too, like Mr. Steenvater?"

"Not really." He laughed with a sense of bitterness. "I'm an accountant."

"How did you two meet? You and Antwerp? In the States?"

Desica thought for a while. "No comment."

"What, you knew him back home?"

"Met him here. That's all I'm saying."

BACK AT THE OFFICE, the two Americans were put in separate interview rooms.

"We may have to front the magistrate tomorrow," Nguyen said to Brothers. "Hopefully get them into remand. We don't want them put on bail. So we can talk to them now, then work out what we charge them with. But you'll need Canterbury to be present."

"Canterbury should be on his way. He knows they're here," Brothers said.

"Well, let's go in. You never know what they might say before he arrives. They're in two separate rooms, aren't they?"

"Yeah. On the third floor."

They took the lift, and Brothers unlocked the door to one of the rooms. Desica was sitting at a table, drinking coffee.

"We meet again," Nguyen said. They sat down at the table. Desica glanced up and nodded. Nguyen switched on the tape recorder.

"Where's, uh, Canterbury? I've got to wait for him."

"Sure. He's on his way, I understand. I need to tell you that you have the right to remain silent, and anything you say may be used as evidence."

Desica stared at him and said nothing.

"While we're waiting, can you help us with a few details?" Nguyen said.

"I told you, I'm not saying anything." Desica scowled.

"Just while we're waiting for Mr. Canterbury. Maybe we can clear this all up, and you'll just have to deal with the passports."

"Clear what up?" Desica said.

"The Antwerp business."

"I said before. We didn't kill him. That's all you need to know." He sat back in his chair.

"What brought you to Australia?"

"Tourism. I told you that in the car. But I can't wait to get back home."

"Do you mind telling me when you flew out here?"

He remained silent.

"Come on. We've put a request in to the airline. They'll let us know."

"Isn't there a date stamp in the passport? Look at that."

"Sergeant Ladbroke has them. We will certainly ask him, while he's here."

"Well, about four weeks ago," Desica said.

"And what were you doing as a tourist?"

"Looking around."

There was a knock on the door, and Arthur Canterbury came in, his face livid.

"What's going on? This is an outrage, questioning my clients without me."

"Calm down, mate," Brothers said. Canterbury looked pained at the word 'mate'.

"We were just exchanging pleasantries," Nguyen said. "We haven't got started properly yet. We were waiting for you. Just asking what tourist type things they were doing."

"What tourist things?"

"We don't know, yet." He looked at Desica. "Well?"

"No comment," Desica said.

Canterbury smiled.

"Take a seat, Mr. Canterbury." Canterbury did so with ill grace.

"Let's start. First of all, how do you know Henry Steenvater?"

"Henry who?"

"Steenvater. He lives at The Belvedere, top floor."

He stayed silent, but looked at Canterbury.

"Come on. Come on. We have him meeting you at the lifts on the security TV. And he told us you visited him last Sunday week."

"Banking business," Desica said.

"We can check with Mr. Steenvater later, if you like. What sort of banking business?"

"Confidential. You'll have to check with Mr. Steenvater."

"I'm asking you. You flew all the way from the States, saying you came as tourists. Now you are talking banking business. Which is it? Tourism or banking? And what banking business? And how was Freddie Antwerp involved?"

"We had nothing to do with Freddie," he said, then shut his mouth.

"Oh, so you know him?"

He stayed silent, and Canterbury drummed his fingers on the table.

"Met him in New York, did you?" Brothers asked.

Again, he was silent.

"I can understand you might have followed him out here. But why kill him? Was that why you were sent?"

"You're off your fucking tree. We didn't kill anyone."

"That's not what the FBI say about you and your friend, Mr. Geronimo."

"The FBI says lots of things."

"Officers, is this getting you anywhere?" Canterbury asked. "Or are you wasting all of our time?"

"Do you want to stop us questioning these men?"

"You're not getting anywhere, so yes. I want you to stop."

"Well, Mr. Canterbury, be patient." Nguyen said. "Mr. Desica. You say you didn't kill Mr. Antwerp."

"That's what I've been saying all along."

"Well, never mind that. I'm just trying to understand what happened. If you didn't kill him, did Mr. Geronimo?"

"No way. How many times do I have to say it? We didn't kill him."

"Do you know who did?"

"No, for crying out loud."

"If neither of you had anything to do with Mr. Antwerp's death, then why don't you tell me what did happen. That way we can clear this up. Right here."

"And we can go?" Desica said.

"Well, let's just say that if you had nothing to do with Antwerp's death, then we won't need you for that. But there are other matters."

"What matters?" Canterbury said.

"The fake passports. Our Federal colleagues will want to have chat to you about that. And the billion that's gone missing."

"What billion?" Canterbury stared, incredulous. "What's gone missing? Why haven't I been told about this?"

Desica smirked. "Yeah, what billion?"

Brothers smacked the table in frustration. "You know, the Millennium Bug billion."

Desica kept his mouth shut, and smiled.

"What are you on about?" Canterbury said. "First, it's killing Antwerp, now it's a billion missing dollars. Anything else?"

"Calm down, calm down, Mr. Canterbury. Don't burst a blood vessel." Nguyen shook his head. "Mr. Desica, if you and your pal didn't kill Mr. Antwerp, then why did you put his body in your car?"

"Wasn't my car."

Brothers sat up. "That's something else," he said. "Car theft. One BMW, still missing. Where is it?"

"Just tell us why you stuck Antwerp in the boot—in the trunk," Nguyen said, interrupting.

Desica glanced at Canterbury, who looked at Nguyen.

"Detective. Can I have a moment alone with my client, please?"

Nguyen nodded, and he and Brothers stood up and left the room.

Outside in the corridor, Brothers said, "Do you think we'll get anywhere with this, Boss?"

Nguyen shrugged.

Less than five minutes later Canterbury opened the door. "My client is prepared to make a statement. I trust you will let the Federal agencies know he has been co-operative."

"I can't promise anything. It depends on what he says,"

"It seemed a good idea at the time," Desica said.

"A good idea?"

"We found Antwerp in the lift on Sunday morning. Dead. Already dead. Not by us. It was shock. We'd just come out of Steenvater's apartment, called for the lift—and there he was! Last thing we expected. Nearly made me blaspheme." Desica stared at both of them. "Put yourself in my shoes."

"I'd rather not," Brothers said.

"We'd just been to see Steenvater to get a ... progress report, and see if he knew where Freddie was hiding out. And there he was. Right in front of us. We checked him, of course. But dead. Stone, cold dead. We thought it would be better to get rid of him."

"But if you didn't kill him, then why would it be better to get rid of him?"

"Failure to report a death," Brothers said. "Another crime."

Nguyen frowned at Brothers. "Let's just focus on the issue. Why get rid of Antwerp?"

"He was in the same building as his boss, Steenvater. Finding him would mean questions would be asked, wouldn't it? The whole thing would have blown up in our faces. Seriously, Detective. What would you have said to us if we'd rung and said, excuse me officer, we found a stiff in the lift!"

Brothers tried not to grin.

"Exactly. So, we took him away until we could work out what to do with him."

"And where did you take him? While you decided."

"Put him in a cool room. You could say, kept him on ice." Desica laughed.

"Where was this cool room?"

"I can't remember. But there's plenty of food cold storage places in this town. How can I remember which one?"

Brothers made a note.

"Continue," Nguyen said.

"It was Al's idea. To keep him for a while, and then put him back in the lift." Desica paused, took a sip of water. "It was after Steenvater had fucked us around. We decided, why not make things hot for him? So just before our flight, we collected Antwerp, put him in the lift, then drove to the airport. That's when we got picked up, and you found us."

Nguyen and Brothers stared at him. Canterbury had a tight smile on his face.

"So you see, officers," Canterbury said. "My clients had nothing to do with Antwerp's death. Nothing at all."

"Illegally moving a corpse," said Brothers. "And illegally storing it." Catching Nguyen's impatient glance, he said, "Just keeping tabs on the crimes, sir."

Nguyen cleared his throat. "Are you saying," he said to Desica. "That it was Steenvater who killed him?"

"I'm not saying nothing. You asked what happened. That's what happened. We didn't kill him. You'll have to ask Steenvater about that, or anything else. But, you know, it does make you wonder."

"What?"

"Why Steenvater would kill him, and why put him in the lift? Fucking amateur!"

"We'll pause the questions for the moment." Nguyen nodded at Brothers and stood up. "You'll stay here for a while, Mr. Desica. Mr. Canterbury, do you want to stay with your client?"

Canterbury nodded.

"We'll speak with Mr. Geronimo."

"In that case, I'll have to be present." He stood up and left with them.

The three entered the room where Al Geronimo was sitting, staring into space. He looked up as they entered.

"Mr. Canterbury," he said. "Can I go now?"

"You cannot," Brothers said.

They sat down, and Brothers switched on the recording gear.

"Your colleague has told us what happened, Mr. Geronimo. Can you confirm it for us?"

Canterbury gestured. "You can tell them about what you did with Antwerp."

"You sure?" Geronimo said. Canterbury nodded.

"Well, we didn't kill the fucker." He shut his mouth.

"Who did?"

"I don't know. Steenvater, maybe? We just found him in the lift."

Geronimo told them a similar story to what they'd just heard.

"And why did you put his body back in the lift?"

Geronimo grinned. "Didn't Desica say?"

"He said it was your idea."

Geronimo laughed. "Sure was. Sure was. I bet you was puzzled when you saw him."

Once he'd stopped laughing, Geronimo explained about Steenvater backing out from their deal. "Why not have it blow up in his face, eh?"

"What deal is that, Mr. Geronimo?"

"Don't answer that," Canterbury said.

Geronimo smirked. Nguyen looked down at his notes.

"So where's the car?" Brothers asked.

"What?"

"The BMW."

"Oh, that? At the airport. In the car park."

"Which one?"

"What is it? Long term, I think."

Brothers made a note.

"Thank you, Mr. Geronimo. That's all for the moment. You'll stay the night locked up. And see the Magistrate tomorrow."

"Can I have a few words with my client?" Canterbury said.

Nguyen stood up and he and Brothers left the room.

"I think we need to have another chat with Henry. Don't you?" Nguyen said.

"Definitely."

"What's the time now?" Nguyen looked at his watch. Hmm, 9:30. Not too late to give him a call—we'll see him tomorrow morning. Tell you what, get young McTeish to set it up. Is she around?"

"On it, Winner," Brothers said.

"And get someone to look for the BMW."

Brothers nodded, grinned.

65

BROTHERS FOUND MCTEISH IN the common room.

"Not gone home yet?"

"How could I go before hearing what happened with the Yanks?"

Brothers filled her in about the Americans confirming Sue Gossiter's original diagnosis about Antwerp being held in cold storage. "And we've found the stolen car, the BMW. Or that's what we've been told. It's in the long-term car park at Tullamarine airport! And we need to speak to Steenvater again. Nguyen wants you to set the meeting up for tomorrow morning," he said.

McTeish grinned. "Shall we bring him in?"

"What do you reckon?" Brothers asked.

"It would sure upset him. *Senior bank executive down at the cop shop.* Do you really want to know what I think?"

"That's what I said."

"Well, I reckon it might be better to give him a false sense of security. Talk to him on his home turf, I mean. Either at his office or at his home."

"Sounds good to me. Give him a call."

McTeish checked her phone. "I've got his number." She shut her eyes for a moment, then dialed. The call was answered almost immediately.

"Hello? What's happening?" Steenvater's voice was a whisper.

"Mr. Steenvater?"

"What? Who is this?" The voice resumed its normal level.

"This is Constable Carol McTeish, Mr. Steenvater. From Victoria Police. I work with Detective Nguyen and Sergeant Brothers."

"Yes?" he snapped. Then, in a calmer voice, "How can I help? Who is it again?"

"Carol McTeish. Detective Nguyen would like to speak to you tomorrow morning. Would you prefer to come here to the station, or we can come to your office or your home?"

There was a silence. Then Steenvater spoke, "That's out of the question. I have commitments all week."

"Mr. Steenvater, may I remind you, this is a murder investigation. You don't want to be seen as impeding an investigation, do you?"

"Damn difficult," he muttered. "What time tomorrow?"

"As early as you like. How about 8am?"

Again, Steenvater paused before replying. "Just checking my commitments. Can you come here to my home? I can make it at 8."

McTeish gave a thumbs up sign to Brothers, and whispered, "His apartment, 8am."

Monday

66

At 7:30 Monday morning, Nguyen spoke to Brothers and McTeish. "I want Carol to come, too."

Was she trying not to preen? Brothers thought. She seemed to be holding herself back from pumping her fist.

"You seem to get under his skin," Nguyen said. "And we will have to keep Mrs. Steenvater separate, too. You can help. And for the time being, let's not mention Antwerp turning up."

They piled into Brothers' car and drove the short distance to The Belvedere.

After buzzing the intercom, Steenvater came down to let them ride up in the lift. He was dressed in a dark grey suit, and greeted them frostily. When they reached the top floor, he beckoned them to come in, and led them to his study, gesturing for them to be seated.

Veronica Steenvater bustled in from the kitchen and asked if they would like coffee. She took their requests and left.

Nguyen nodded at McTeish, who stood up and followed Mrs. Steenvater.

Henry Steenvater stared at Nguyen and Brothers. "You wanted to see me? Well, here I am."

"Henry, we've been talking to your friends."

"My friends?"

"The Americans. Mr. Desica and Mr. Geronimo. The ones you claimed you didn't know."

Steenvater paled, then set his jaw. "Who?"

"Desica and Geronimo. Or perhaps you know them as Mr. Stevenson and Mr. Knight?"

264

"What about them?"

"We've been talking to them, and they've been talking to us."

"So?"

"So, we'd like the truth from you. Don't forget, we saw you on the tapes meeting them in the basement garage on Sunday morning. Why did Freddie Antwerp come to see you on Saturday night?"

Steenvater let out a sigh. "Stevenson and Knight were pressuring him. He wanted my help."

"Why—what did they want from him? And you helped them by bumping him off?" Brothers put in.

"Good God. What sort of person do you think I am?" Steenvater looked at both of them. "Better not answer that," he muttered. "I certainly did not kill Freddie Antwerp. He was alive when he left here."

"And what time was that?"

"About 11, 11:30 Saturday night. It was late."

"And how was he?"

"Fine, fine." Steenvater paused. He seemed to come to a decision. "Well, maybe not so fine. He was actually a bit dazed."

"Dazed? What do you mean?"

"He stumbled and fell in the kitchen here. His head was bleeding a little, onto his shirt, so I suggested he take it off. I took it to our laundry sink to rinse the bit of blood out of it. When I finished, and went to give it back to him, he'd gone."

"Gone?"

"Yes. He'd left. He wasn't there. That's the last I saw of him. So you see, I didn't kill him. Anything else I can help you with, Officers?"

"Why didn't you tell us this earlier?"

"I just didn't think it was all that important. I didn't know he was dead. I didn't even know you were interested in him, till later." Steenvater shrugged.

"What did Desica and Geronimo—Stevenson and Knight—have to do with Antwerp?"

"They followed him here. I think he was doing a job for them, or for their bosses back in the States."

"But you hired him. Why was that?"

"Actually, Niki Grainger hired him."

"On your instructions."

"Well …" Steenvater rubbed his hands together, tightened his lips. He blew out his cheeks. "Yes, I suppose, on my instructions."

"And why was that?"

"He was the expert. You know, cyber security. He approached me first."

"From the States?"

"Yes, from LA. He got me thinking about the Millennium Bug."

"What, on a phone call?"

"Initially, a phone call. Then we communicated… . Officers, I was trying to protect the Bank. If Freddie could help us find the billion dollars, that would have been something. Given the stock options a bit of a goose."

And you weren't going to pocket your share of the billion, were you, Nguyen thought.

"So you hired him to trace the money?"

"Exactly!" Steenvater smiled. He seemed relieved.

"And this was six months ago?"

"Yes, six months at the end of this month."

"Did he find anything?"

"Ah, well. There is the difficulty."

Nguyen signaled to Brothers to say nothing. They waited. Eventually Steenvater said, "It takes time. It's very complicated. He had to chase down stuff from 20 years ago."

"So why were your American friends here?"

"Ah … hum. It appears that they started Freddie on this search. And then when my bank was mentioned he contacted me, through our website. They were keen on the outcome, too."

"So why did they kill Antwerp?"

"Kill Antwerp? I've no idea. Did they?"

"Well, someone did. Have you got any other suggestions?"

Steenvater regained some of his arrogance. "He left here alive and kicking. Er, bleeding, and alive." As if realizing what he'd just said he shut his mouth.

"So, Freddie visits you, leaves without his shirt — by the way, where is his shirt?"

"I don't know. Veronica gave it a proper wash. She'll have put it somewhere. Shall I —"

"All in good time, Henry. We'll ask her later. I'm just a little perplexed. You say Freddie left you without his shirt. You didn't try to find him, or wonder what had happened to him?"

"It was pretty late. I've got no idea what these Yanks get up to. For all I knew, Freddie had another shirt in his car?"

"What car?"

"I just assumed he came in a car. Didn't he?"

Nguyen glanced at Brothers, who discreetly shook his head.

"So," he resumed, "Freddie left, then the next morning your mafia friends turned up. Did you tell them about Freddie?"

"Well, of course I did. They were very insistent."

"Thank you, Henry. We'll have a quick chat with Veronica, and pick up the shirt."

They stood up, and Brothers opened the door, to see McTeish approaching with Veronica Steenvater, a white paper parcel in her hands.

"Mr. Antwerp's shirt," she said, thrusting it forward like an offering.

67

"WELL, THAT SORT OF CONFIRMS Steenvater's story," Brothers said, referring to the shirt, when they were back at the station.

"It certainly confirms that the Steenvaters washed a shirt—we can presume it belonged to Antwerp," Nguyen said, rubbing his jaw. "Let's assume Antwerp did leave Steenvater's apartment. Why would he do so without his shirt? And how did he end up in Makepeace's apartment, in her bed, dead? Was he in a rush? I mean to leave without his shirt? Did Steenvater threaten him? Was there a fight, which is how the blood got on his shirt?"

"However he hurt his head—that caused his death, didn't it?" McTeish said. "According to Forensics."

Both Nguyen and Brothers looked at her, Nguyen with eyebrows raised.

"So," she continued, "Antwerp left Steenvater's apartment hurt, bleeding from the head." She was musing half to herself, then saw them looking at her. "So he would have been dazed, concussed. Would he have known what he was doing? Maybe he got into the lift to leave the building. And maybe it stopped at Makepeace's floor. If she came home pissed, what if she was in the lift? Maybe she'd just got in when he summoned it, and it went to the top before she pushed the button. Then she'd got out—and maybe he did too—and followed her in?

"That's a lot of maybes," Brothers said.

"Could work, though, couldn't it?" Nguyen said. "I mean, she was out of it, he was dazed, probably confused. She doesn't really notice he'd followed her in, staggers into bed. And he flops down next to her—and the brain injury kills him during the night."

"So you're saying nobody murdered him? He just fell and hit his head? An accident?" Brothers said.

"Fell or was pushed. That we don't know," Nguyen said. "I do think our American friends are off the hook—for the murder, at least, maybe even for manslaughter. Shit."

"But they are still up for moving and hiding the body, plus the passport stuff," McTeish said.

"And stealing the car. Don't forget stealing the car," Brothers said.

"And the missing billion dollars—if there is a missing billion," Nguyen said. He slumped in his chair. "Why don't I feel happy? We've just about worked out what happened, but who would believe it?"

"The boss will be happy, won't she?" Brothers asked.

At the thought of having to explain it all to Superintendent Forell, he slumped even further. Then sat up.

"Actually, she may not like it at first, but at least she has a dead body explained without a murderer on the loose. Plus she'll have the two mafia idiots locked up. The media will like that. And, therefore, so will she."

68

Nguyen knocked on Superintendent Forell's door.

"Come in." The voice was measured.

He opened the door, walked in.

"Ah, Detective Inspector," Forell said. "Sit down." She came around from her desk and sat opposite him at the coffee table. "Looking at your face, do we have some news?"

"We do—and we don't."

Forell's eyes took on their customary steely expression. "What do you mean, do and don't," she said in her calm, low voice.

"Well, we've caught the two mafiosi."

"What, Antwerp's killers?"

"Not exactly."

"John," Forell said. She used first names when she was annoyed. "What do you mean, 'not exactly'?"

"They may not be the killers. In fact, it's likely they aren't."

"But—" she gave an exasperated sigh. "John. John. John. You caught them on CCTV. That's why I went out on a limb to send you to the States. If they're not the killers, why have you arrested them?"

"Well, they certainly took the body away. And put it back." Seeing Forell's expression, he added, sheepishly, "In the same lift they took it from. We've charged them with a range of offences."

"So they took the body, and hey presto, brought it back, but they're not the killers?" Nguyen noticed that she actually raised her voice this time.

"It looks like no one killed him," he finally said.

Forell just glared at him.

"He fell over. Hit his head."

"Then how the fuck did he end up in whatshername's bed?"

Nguyen grimaced. "That we're not too sure of. That's what I mean by we do have news, and we don't."

Forell stared at him. She slumped, then smiled. Nguyen paled in anticipation. "Well, well. Let's see." She held up the index finger of her right hand. "One. We've caught two mafiosi. The media will love that. And the Commissioner. Justifies your trip."

"Two." She held up a second finger—almost, Nguyen thought, like she's giving me a 'fuck you' sign. "Antwerp wasn't killed—therefore no murder problem. However." She paused, rubbed her cheek. "We have two more problems."

"Yes, boss?"

"Yes." She held up the index finger of her left hand. "One. How did Antwerp get into that girl's bed. Without a shirt, wasn't it? And—" She held up a second finger. "Two. The missing billion—what happened to that?"

"Maybe there isn't a missing billion," Nguyen said half to himself.

"What?" Forell's voice was quiet, almost a whisper. She glared.

"Nothing. Just wondering—maybe the whole thing was a wild goose chase. The mafia got Antwerp to try to find it, got him to pressure Steenvater. But they didn't find it. Maybe it was just a rumor. An urban myth."

"Hmm."

"And we'll find out about Deirdre Makepeace and her bed."

"No one else knows about the billion, do they? Or about Makepeace?"

"Well her girlfriend does. And her boyfriend."

"What—she's got a threesome going?"

"No. But her girlfriend Fran, er, Fran Callas, helped her put the body in the lift. Makepeace has hooked up with that ex footballer, Steve Dalmatico. So he knows, too." Nguyen recalled something else. "And the Steenvaters."

"And the Steenvaters? Do they know about Deirdre Makepeace?"

Nguyen thought. "Actually, I don't think they do. But Steenvater certainly knows that Antwerp left his apartment with a knock on his head and without a shirt."

"Go on. Get out," Forell said. She stood up and went and sat back behind her desk. She flicked her fingers at him, her face suddenly weary. "Get on with it."

Nguyen got out.

NGUYEN SAT DOWN AT his desk, with mixed feelings about Superintendent Forell. He was annoyed that she was unhappy with him, yet couldn't help admire the way she handled herself. "Get on with it", she had said.

He called Brothers and McTeish into his office.

"The Boss wants us to get on with it," he said.

"What does that mean?" McTeish asked.

"It means we find out how Antwerp ended up in the girl's bed. And we check more carefully with Steenvater about the billion dollars. Check how sure he is it actually ever existed. And she holds a presser to announce we've caught a couple of mafia."

"Er, sir," McTeish said. "If she holds a press conference, what will she say they're charged with?"

"Well, there's passport fraud," Brothers said.

"Yes, that'll do for a start," Nguyen said.

"And," Brothers said, as if ticking off a list, "we can mention stealing the Beemer, stealing the body, storing it—and replacing it." He smiled. "That should shake up the reptiles."

"But—" McTeish shut her mouth, slumped.

"But what, Constable? Spit it out." Nguyen said.

"Well—if any of that is said, then won't the—er—media have a field day? They'll make us a laughing stock."

"What do you mean?"

McTeish reddened, swallowed. "It'll open a can of worms, won't it? I mean, if you think the Supe should hold the conference, then of course we'll do it. I just don't trust the media. They'll ask why the mafia stole the body. Then the billion dollars will come out. And the journos will say we've caught two low life pranksters who played musical chairs with a dead man, just to give us the finger."

Nguyen recalled Superintendent Forell's ambiguous fingers. He frowned, cleared his throat. "Hmm. There is something in what you say."

"But boss, Forell has to tell them something," Brothers said.

He punched the desk. "Of course she'll tell the media something. We'll just have to talk to her about what to tell them." He stood up, paced. "McTeish is right. At this stage, the less we say the better. You won't want to be near Superintendent Forell when she's steamed up."

"It'll have to be done before the media pick it up when it gets to court. There's always press at court. Particularly if they cotton on to the mafia being involved."

"Yes. That's true. So we have to be careful with what we charge them with. Certainly the Feds can do the passport stuff."

"What about the Beemer, the body, the storage, the sticking it back?" Brothers said.

"Think about it, Graham. Do you want to explain all that catastrophe? McTeish is right. I certainly don't."

"What, so it all gets hushed up?"

"They'll get charged, deported, straight into the hands of our American friends. They'll take good care of them. And we can go check the Millennium Bug with Mr. Steenvater." Then he added, "Unless."

"Unless what?" Brothers said.

"Unless we can get them for the murder of Antwerp."

"But they didn't do it," McTeish said. She looked shocked.

"Are you sure? It's too unbelievable—'a murder wot no one done'."

"But it wasn't a murder."

"Wasn't it? It could have been. Think about it. How did he hit his head? Or better yet, who hit his head? How did the body get into the bed? A dead man doesn't walk in and take a lie down."

"I've been thinking about that, Boss," McTeish said.

"What? What have you been thinking about?" Nguyen was exasperated.

"Well we may never know exactly what happened, but ... Sue Gossiter told us he hit his head, or was hit in the head, didn't she?"

"Yes. We know that."

"So say Steenvater wasn't lying, and Antwerp did walk out of Steenvater's apartment while his shirt was being washed. He was in a daze. He called the lift. And that's when something just occurred to me."

"What?" Nguyen and Brothers exclaimed simultaneously.

"Sarge, remember when we searched Antwerp's flat? Remember what floor it was on?"

Brothers rolled his eyes up in concentration. "The 17th," he said.

"And what floor does Deirdre Makepeace live on?" Before they could say anything, she said, "Also the 17th!"

"So, they both lived on the 17th floor. So what? It's just a coincidence," Brothers said.

"But don't you see—Antwerp was in a daze, so once he left Steenvater's apartment, in his confused state he may have just pushed the button for 17 in the lift, thinking he was in his own building and gets out at level 17. Makepeace's apartment door's open, because she was drunk and didn't shut it. He staggers into Makepeace's apartment. And collapses on the bed. She was already in it, completely out to it all." McTeish smiled in triumph.

"Assuming he did push the button for 17, how did he get into Makepeace's apartment?" Brothers said.

"As I said." She looked at him. "She came home drunk. She left the door open."

Nguyen looked at McTeish, thought for a while, then said, "That's as good an explanation as any, I suppose."

"So no murder," Brothers said, disgusted.

"Sarge," she said. "Do you think Steenvater killed him?"

Brothers shook his head. "No, damn it."

"Did the mafia guys kill him? That's possible, but then, if they killed him, how would they have got him into Makepeace's apartment?"

Brothers shook his head.

Nguyen said, "There's no way we could establish that bit in court." He rubbed his chin. "Certainly carrying out the body, then storing it, then putting it back—that looks pretty incriminating."

"But if we charge them with murder, everything will come out, including Antwerp reappearing. We'll still be a laughing stock," McTeish said.

"Okay, Carol. I hear what you're saying. I'm not suggesting we simply charge them, and that's that and we take whatever comes our way. But we still might get something useful from Steenvater, and until we speak to him, I'm simply saying that we should keep this very much a live option. And we can always let the mafia boys think we're going to charge them with murder, so we can squeeze more out of them."

"Yes, sir."

"If it suits the Supe to go quietly, then quietly we'll go. If it suits her to go the whole hog, then we'll throw the book at them. It's up to us to get the evidence, one way or another. I'll have to talk to her again."

"What about Geronimo and Desica?" McTeish asked. "Do we go to the Magistrate this afternoon?"

"We'll hold them over for the moment. We can keep them till tomorrow without an order, and then we'll have a better idea about what to charge them with. Can you call the Magistrate's office, Carol, and ask to postpone it. And we'll have to let that fucking Canterbury know, too. We need to talk to Steenvater again, then make a decision."

69

Nguyen rang Steenvater. "Henry, can we see you again?"

"But we already spoke this morning."

"Yes, I know, but we need to clarify a couple of things. It won't take long."

"Is this really necessary?"

"I'm afraid so. It's essential. Would you rather come to us here, or we come to you?"

"Well, you better come to my office. Around 2—2:30?"

"Thanks. See you at 2:15."

Nguyen asked Brothers and McTeish to join him on the trip to Cambridge Bank. As they got out of the car, he said, "Carol, can you sniff around, talk to other people in his office, while we're talking to him?"

McTeish beamed. "Of course."

Brothers led the way as they headed into the lobby and he got security to phone up. Steenvater's assistant, Carmen, stepped out of the lifts about five minutes later.

"Sergeant Brothers? Constable McTeish?" she said with a small smile, shaking their hands.

"This is Detective Inspector Nguyen," Brothers said, and Nguyen shook her hand, too.

"She seems a tad friendlier than last time," Brothers whispered in Nguyen's ear as they entered the lift.

They rode in silence until they reached Level 31, and Carmen led the way out.

"Just wait here a moment, please," she said as she put her head into Steenvater's office.

A moment later Deirdre Makepeace emerged. She saw the police and stopped, nodded and waved at them, then pressed a button for the lifts.

Before Nguyen could say anything, Henry Steenvater emerged and beckoned them in.

Nguyen turned to McTeish. "Carol—speak to Makepeace. Find out why she's here."

She nodded, and hustled to the lift, just managing to get in after Makepeace as the doors were closing.

"Detective Nguyen. Good to see you," Steenvater said, extending his hand. "Sergeant Brothers." He was all forced smiles.

"Could I ask what Ms Makepeace is doing here?" Nguyen said.

"Ah, that would be telling, wouldn't it?" Steenvater chuckled. Seeing the expression on Nguyen's face he indicated they sit down, and said, "Don't worry. I'll explain."

They sat down and Nguyen eyed Steenvater, impatient to get on with it. Carmen came in. "Would you like tea or coffee?" she said.

Brothers was about to speak but saw Nguyen shake his head.

"No thank you."

She withdrew, with a flounce of her head.

Nguyen looked at Steenvater, who sat smiling. Finally, he said, "Well?"

"Well what?"

"Ms Makepeace. Why was she here?'

"Ah yes. She's doing a job of work for me."

"I thought she worked for the Bank of Ballarat?"

"She did."

"How come you know her? You never mentioned her before," Brothers said, clearly annoyed.

"I just met her last week."

"Last week?" Nguyen realized he had shouted, and with an effort spoke more quietly. "Very interesting. How did you meet her?" Nguyen said.

"She rang me, last Friday." Steenvater was relaxed. What a smug bastard, Nguyen thought.

"And what work is she doing for you?"

"Well, Detective. Can I speak confidentially?"

"What do you mean?"

"This is confidential Bank business. It can't get out."

Nguyen waited, just looked at him.

"Very well. I've hired her to try to find the stolen money."

"You what?" Brothers said.

"You heard me. Ms Makepeace is a very good IT professional. Seeing that poor Freddie can't do it now, she's stepping up." Steenvater sat back, unsuccessfully trying to keep a smile off his face.

"Is this search official?" Brothers asked.

"Of course it is. We've given her a contract. If the money's there, she'll find it."

"And what about Geronimo and Desica? Are they part of this arrangement?"

"Of course not. That's another reason to keep this confidential. We don't want any, um, accidents happening to Ms. Makepeace."

Nguyen wiped his hand over his brow. "I don't think they'll be hassling Ms Makepeace," he said.

"If they find out about it, they may well try. That's why it's so important to keep this confidential."

"We've just arrested them," Brothers said.

"What?" Steenvater sat up straight. "Where did you find them?"

"At the airport. Just before trying to fly home to the States. And just after replacing Mr. Antwerp at The Belvedere."

"Freddie? He's alive?" Steenvater gasped. "Why didn't you tell me earlier. I wouldn't have needed Ms. Makepeace."

"Alas, no," Nguyen said. "They put him back in the lift he was in before. Dead. Stone cold dead."

"I don't understand."

"Nor do we, Henry. Nor do we. That's why we've come to see you. You say that Ms Makepeace just happened to call you last week, out of the blue."

"That's right. And I don't like your tone, Detective. *She* rang *me*. I'd never heard of her. And she told me that she found Freddie dead in her bed."

"Bit of a coincidence, don't you think?"

"Absolutely. Turns out she lives in The Belvedere, too!"

"How did she know about you, if you had never met her?"

"Ah, that's from you lot. She told me that she'd learned that the dead man was Freddie Antwerp. From one of you. And that he worked for me."

Nguyen glanced at Brothers, who was staring straight ahead.

"And how did she approach you?"

"She rang me at work. We met. At a cafe near here. She was with an ex-footballer, Steve Dalmatico. Played for St Kilda. You know him?"

"And you hired her on the spot?"

"No, not at all. I left them. In a bit of a huff, actually."

"Then how did you get back in touch?"

"She rang me, and we met again last night. That's when I discovered she also lives in The Belvedere. We met at my penthouse."

"And?"

"And, she offered to try to find the money. All above board, Detective, I assure you. Cambridge Bank has approved the arrangement."

"When was that?"

"A couple of hours ago. But—" he leaned forward. "As you would appreciate, if this got out before any money was found, it would be very damaging. Very damaging. Hence the confidentiality. If she finds it, then we can announce it. If she doesn't—well." He sat back, hands across his stomach. And smiled. "You do understand?" He eyed both of them.

"I understand that you've hired her, yes." Nguyen blinked, rubbed his chin. "And the need to keep things quiet."

"We'll keep schtum," Brothers said.

"But in return, I want your undertaking that if you hear anything further from our friends Geronimo and Desica, or rather their friends—then you'll let us know straight away. Clear?"

"Of course."

"We don't want Ms. Makepeace to end up like Mr. Antwerp," Brothers said, helpfully.

"And we don't want criminals working into our banking system, either," Nguyen said. "Thank you, Henry. We'll see ourselves out." He stood up, and Brothers followed suit.

As they waited for the lift, Brothers said, "Would you believe it?"

"What?" Nguyen was impatient.

"That Steenvater has double crossed the mafia."

Nguyen looked at him, then shook his head. "Fuck. Fuck. Fuck."

70

McTEISH WALKED INTO THE LIFT as the doors were closing, and looked at Deirdre Makepeace.

"Hello, again."

"Hello."

"Strange meeting here, isn't it?"

Deirdre thought a moment, then smiled. "Yes, I suppose it is."

She looked at Constable McTeish, and saw a young woman not unlike herself ten years earlier—intelligent, eyes shining with determination, making her way in a world shaped by an earlier masculine hierarchy that was trying not always successfully to accommodate women, and in fact anyone regardless of their diversity.

"How did you come to be with Henry Steenvater?" McTeish asked.

"It's Carol, isn't it?" Deirdre said.

McTeish nodded.

"He's just employed me, Carol. I'm resigning from the Bank of Ballarat, and joining Cambridge."

"Bit sudden, isn't it?"

"Yes, it certainly is." She smiled.

The lift reached the ground floor, and they walked out.

"Could we have a quick chat?" McTeish said.

"Sure." Deirdre smiled again. "How about over there." She pointed to the Ambrosia Cafe. "This is where I first met Mr. Steenvater."

"Oh? When was that?"

"Um, a couple of days ago. Last Friday, in fact, yes, that's right. Friday."

They sat down and a waitress with a large white apron down to her ankles took their order.

"How did you come to meet him?"

"I rang him."

Deirdre explained how she'd rung Steenvater, they'd met, and she'd seen him again yesterday evening. "That's when he offered me the job. I just signed the papers. Start next week." She grinned.

"Oh," McTeish said. "Does that mean you've left the Bank of Ballarat?"

"I'm resigning today."

"But how did you know Steenvater was looking to employ someone?"

"I suggested it."

"What, you knew him?"

"No, not at all. I mean, I'd seen him at a conference or two, but I'd never met him. The first time was on Friday afternoon. Today's the third time."

McTeish appeared to be digesting this information. Then she said, "Is he your sort of person? I mean, you do know the dead man was working for Steenvater?"

"Oh, yes. Of course. I'll be doing what he was trying to do."

"You're what?" McTeish exclaimed, then calmed down. "What's that?"

"Find a lot of stolen money." Seeing McTeish's expression, Deirdre said, "It's all legit. Cambridge Bank has authorized it. But, you know, it's confidential. You can't speak of this. Please?"

"I can imagine that the mafia would want to know."

"Exactly! That's the main reason it has to be under wraps. But also, there may not be any money. The whole thing could be a hoax. A wild goose chase."

"There's one thing I don't understand," McTeish said. "Assuming it did happen, why didn't whoever set the system up just run off with the money themselves?"

"That's possible, of course. Maybe it's gone. But the software could still be operating, which means money is still being syphoned off. Anyhow, Henry, Mr. Steenvater, doesn't think the money has been accessed. He thinks whoever did it, back then, is no longer around."

"How do you mean?"

"He thinks they were pressured back then in an attempt to reveal the account details, and the pressure went too far."

"But why wouldn't this search have started back then. Why did the mafia only get on to it now?"

"I don't know. They must have heard the rumor."

"Rumor?"

"It's one of those urban myths in IT circles."

"Yes, I get that," McTeish said. "But why investigate it now?"

"I think a relative of the scammer must have spoken up. That's my assumption."

"That is I suppose a possibility."

They sipped their drinks.

"How are you finding police work?" Deirdre said.

"I'm enjoying it." McTeish sat up, her eyes shining. "This case particularly. It's so weird."

"I can't get over that man being in my bed," Deirdre shuddered. "That was certainly weird. More than weird. Awful."

McTeish leaned across the table. "But did you know his body turned up again yesterday?"

"Yes. Ugh. It was awful. Detective Nguyen called me down to identify him. Confirm he was the same man who was in my bed. And in the same lift." Deirdre tried to stifle a giggle. "Sorry. I know it's not funny."

"Not funny, but certainly weird, eh?" McTeish smiled, at which Deirdre laughed again, then sipped her coffee, choked and swallowed.

They sat looking at each other. After a time Deirdre said, "Do you get the run around?"

"How do you mean?"

"You're a woman. They're guys. Do you just get the dirty work?"

"Actually, Detective Nguyen is pretty good." McTeish paused. "And, you know, so is Brothers. Nothing 'metro' about them. Can't say the same for some others I've worked with. But they give me a go—I do get opportunities." She smiled at Deirdre. "How about you? Isn't IT a nerd-fest? Lots of anti-female stuff you read about."

"There is the odd creep every now and then, but actually my boss is a woman too, and the Bank is pretty strong on diversity. They had a few scandals a couple of years ago, and they want to make sure that doesn't happen again."

"Your boss? But aren't you resigning?"

"Yeah. I should say, my soon to be former boss."

"That's what I don't understand, Deirdre."

"What's that?"

"You, now, will be working for Steenvater. He hardly seems the model of enlightenment."

Deirdre looked at McTeish. "It's a real opportunity. I can deal with him."

"Hmm."

Across Collins Place the lifts pinged, and Nguyen and Brothers emerged.

"I have to go," McTeish said. "I'll get this. It's been good talking to you." She went to the bar to pay.

Nguyen and Brothers entered Ambrosia, saw Makepeace, and sat down at her table.

"Well, Ms Makepeace," Nguyen said.

"Detective Nguyen," Makepeace said.

McTeish returned. "I've paid," she said.

Nguyen looked at her. "Sit down, Constable. Anything else? Did she tell you she's now working for Steenvater?"

"Yes."

"And resigning from the Bank of Ballarat," Deirdre interrupted.

"Ah, I see," Nguyen said. "All problems solved."

"I think so," Deirdre said, and stood up. "I have to go."

As she left, McTeish said, "Well, sir, the problems are solved, aren't they, when you think about it. Poor Mr. Antwerp fell and accidentally died. We'll be putting the two mafia guys away, either here or in the States. And Cambridge Bank has authorized Deirdre here to find the stolen money."

"A nice summary, Constable," Nguyen said. "All's well that ends well. Eh?"

"I just wish," Brothers muttered, "that we can still get them for stealing the fucking car and moving the body."

71

Nguyen called Brothers and McTeish into his office.

"You know, fuck it all. I'm starting to think we just cut our losses, and let the Feds deal with Geronimo and Desica." He scratched his knee, yawned. "The money stuff—out of bounds, I'd reckon. In the unlikely event they find it, then we get involved. And charge whoever set it up."

"If they're alive," McTeish said.

"What do you mean?"

"Well, Deirdre Makepeace seems to think whoever did it back in 2000 was knocked off then."

"Jesus Christ! How would she know?"

"She said Steenvater suggested it."

"Steenvater." Nguyen shook his head. "Anyway, that's a side issue. Suggestions about the mafia guys, anyone?" He eyed at the two of them. "No? Okay, I'll brief Forell, and make sure she's on board."

He waited, but neither Brothers nor McTeish said anything.

He stood up, and Brothers said, "You know, boss. You're right. There's nothing to gain from pursuing every rabbit down every hole."

McTeish looked like she wanted to say something, too.

"Come on, out with it, Constable."

"Well, boss. I just wanted to say thanks."

"Thanks?"

"Thanks for including me in the team. I've learned a lot. And even though it's been a weird one, that's kind of good, isn't it? I mean, it's been difficult and frustrating, sure. But wow—what stories we'll be able to tell when things settle down." She blushed. "Sorry."

"Don't be sorry. You know, I've found that the worse things are during a case, the funnier they can be much later, over a beer." He grinned at the two of them. "And now we can get back to regular policing, with no FBI, no donuts, no disappearing and reappearing stiffs, and, best of all, no arrogant heads of IT departments."

Epilogue

LATER THAT DAY, Nguyen again called Brothers and McTeish into his office again. They sat facing him, smiles of satisfaction on their faces.

"Well, guys. A great job. Well done." He said. "I've spoken to Forell. She asked me to pass on her thanks. And that's pretty unusual. We've saved the force from embarrassment, locked up a couple of the mafia, and cemented relations with our US mates. But we still have a few loose ends to tie up."

"Loose ends?" Brothers said.

"Yes, Graham. I'll need you to get in touch with that—what did you call him?—the donut in Sydney, and let him know his dad is alive and lives in LA. I suppose you should check the protocols—is it okay to let him know who his dad is? Maybe we have to get the dad's permission first? Carol, can you check that out?

"And, Graham, please let Wainright know that his car is at Tullamarine. I presume someone has found it there?"

"Haven't heard about the Beemer yet—but I'll get onto it, Boss. I'll ring Wainright myself. It will be my pleasure to let him know it's in one piece and wasn't burnt out. He should be happy about that. And I'll let him know we'll be in touch again when we've confirmed where it is at the airport."

"Maybe he'd prefer it was written off," McTeish said.

"Why do you say that?"

"Then he'd get a brand-new car from his insurance."

"Well, too bad."

Nguyen continued. "I'll let Nat Turner and April Martinez know— the US mates I worked with in LA and New York—so they can tell both

Antwerp's sisters and his ex-wife, that Freddie wasn't murdered after all."

"Just a sad, tragic accident," McTeish said with a straight face.

"Exactly. And maybe Nat can let the Antwerp sisters' dad know he has a son in Sydney. He could find out whether he wants his son to know, assuming there's no problem with the artificial insemination laws here."

"What about Deirdre Makepeace, Boss?" McTeish asked.

"Would you like to tell her we reckon the whole thing was just a bizarre set of coincidences, and that she's not in danger, and can get on with her life," Nguyen said.

"Sure. But what about her working for Steenvater? And the missing billion?"

"That was her decision. She'll have to live with it, working for that man. And if she finds the missing billion, I reckon she'll suddenly become a philanthropist, or whatever the rich do to help the community and minimize their taxes."

They were all silent for a time; each looked like they were pondering some aspect of the case.

"You know, when you think about it, everything was inevitable," Nguyen said. He flexed his shoulders back and stretched his arms, smiled at the other two.

"How do you mean?" Brothers said.

Nguyen saw McTeish's reaction.

"Carol's got it," he said.

She smiled.

"Come on. Come on," Brothers said. "How inevitable?"

"Just think about it. From the moment we got the phone call, to the moment we wrapped it all up, everything happened—inevitably."

DESICA AND GERONIMO SHARED the same cell in the Remand Centre. Their case was being heard in six weeks, and the prosecutor had negotiated with Canterbury. As a result, they just faced charges of passport fraud, which had a maximum penalty of ten years jail, both in

Australia and in the US. The Antwerp stuff had not been proceeded with, and Canterbury had negotiated a settlement with the BMW's owner, Richard Wainright, and he seemed happy with his new car.

"The police don't want to be embarrassed," Canterbury had said to them at his last visit. "And besides, you didn't do anything serious. Cambridge Bank hasn't laid a complaint about the missing money, if indeed it is missing. If they tried to go you for moving the body, everything would get into the media. They were happy to forget it, particularly as they knew the Federal charges were afoot."

"Afoot?" Geronimo had said.

"Active."

"Well why didn't you say that?"

"What will we get?" Desica said.

"It's your first offence here. And you are lucky you're not illegal immigrants. That wouldn't have gone down well. You're lucky the Antwerp business isn't public—that would certainly have made it worse."

"Worse? Worse than what?"

"Than the ten years you could get. I think you'll maybe get two to three years here in Australia. But as I said, it could be worse."

"Jesus. There couldn't be just a fine?"

Canterbury's thin lips moved to half-form a smile. "It's possible, but unlikely."

"Why won't they just deport us?"

"They will—once you're sentenced, and once you've served whatever time you get, and maybe it might be shorter for good behavior. Then they'll deport you. And then, of course, you will have to deal with whatever awaits you in America. Or it might be possible to waive your stuff over here and send you directly home."

Both Desica and Geronimo slumped.

"Which would you rather?" Canterbury said. "Serve jail here, in Australia, or in Chicago?"

"Here," they both said at the same time.

DEIRDRE TURNED TO STEVE as they lay in bed. "Did you check the paperwork Steenvater gave me this morning?"

"Yep. I had a quick read. It looks okay. The Bank takes all the risk. By the way, not a bad salary he's offering."

"They have to match what I'm currently getting. It's actually a bit higher."

"Better than a marketing manager at a footy club."

She smiled, kissed him. "One of the perks of being with me."

"One of them? There are others?"

She grabbed her pillow and hit him with it.

"Oof. Just joking."

"How do you feel about The Belvedere now, with all that history."

Deirdre sobered up, thought about her apartment. "You know, maybe I should find another place. I don't want to keep thinking of that … guy in my bed."

"Like to move in here?"

Deirdre froze.

"Here?"

"Why not. Plenty of space."

"But we've just met."

"And?"

Deirdre thought.

"We've got to know each other through a pretty unusual thing, haven't we?" Steve said.

"We sure have."

"If we've survived that, we should be able to survive anything, don't you reckon?"

Steve …" she kissed him. "That's very sweet."

"But?"

"Just very sweet." She made a decision. "We have to be open with each other."

"Yep."

"I mean, I didn't think I wanted a relationship." He tensed, lifted his head to look directly at her. She hastily added, "But, it's great being with you."

He relaxed. "It's great being with you, too. I didn't think I wanted another one, either."

"So—do we want to risk it? I mean, what if we get on each other's wick? What if I can't stand your friends? In fact, I haven't met any of your friends. And you've only met Fran."

"She seemed okay."

"Just okay? What are your friends like?"

"It's you I want to be with. But, I'll introduce you to them." He rolled over onto his elbows and looked at her, smiled. "And that will happen whether or not we live together. Won't it?"

She thought about it. "I suppose."

"Anyhow, it's just a suggestion. I don't want you having flashbacks or whatever if you stay where you are. And I love having you around. In fact," he nuzzled her neck, "I can't get enough of you."

Sometime later she said, "Maybe we just give it a trial. See how we go."

Acknowledgements

THANKS TO MY WRITING GROUP colleagues Claire Gaskin, Richard Bell, Tania Cossich, Leo Jahn, Prue Mercer, Kim Smith, Lucy Wilks and Ilse Zipfel, to my daughter Vivian Gerrand and to Tallulah Brown and Jeremy Gerrand for their encouragement, my mate Jack Dann for suggestions, Tony Howard, AM, QC, for advice on legal issues, Bob Sessions for general support and encouragement, and the astute Cherry Weiner who helped enormously. Thanks too to Maggie, who didn't just tolerate my many, many hours on this, but actually supported me in doing so.